BOOKS BY JEREMY HODGSON

HISTORICAL ROMANCE
Dance on the Terrace (2021)

ADVENTURES IN RESEARCH
Curing Emily (2022)
Secret in the Seas (2022)

ROMANTIC AFRICAN ADVENTURES
Leap of a Lifetime (2023)

I0593305

TAKE ME INSTEAD

A LEGENDARY ROMANTIC ADVENTURE

JEREMY HODGSON

ISBN: 978-0-7961-1719-9
e-ISBN: 978-0-7961-1720-5

Jeremy William Hodgson
Villa 99, Tamarina Golf Estate
Black River, Mauritius
90922
jwhodgson42@gmail.com

Beta reading by Priscilla Bancy
Edited by Tracey Hawthorne

For my wife Michele

EARLIEST ANCIENT EGYPTIAN GODS AND GODDESSES

Nut: goddess of the cosmos.

Geb: god of the earth.

Hathor: goddess of love.

Ra: god of the Sun.

Shai: god of fate and destiny who decides a person's lifespan.

Anubis: god of funerary rites and protector of graves.

THE CHILDREN OF NUT AND GEB

Osiris: god of the underworld.

Horus: god of protection and kingship.

Seth: god of deserts and violence.

Isis: goddess of health and healing.

Nephthys: goddess of the air.

PROLOGUE

IN EGYPT, LEGENDS ABOUND due to the great age of the civilisations that developed and grew there. The origins of the myths may have been forgotten in the mists of time, but if someone recounts a story to a visitor, it may not have changed for four thousand years.

Visitors may hear about how the gods Nut and Geb created our world. We have proof that this legend is old, for it appears in hieroglyphic panels.

– In the beginning, Nut, the goddess of the sky, created Geb, the god of earth who lies below her, and they coupled and produced children: Osiris, Horus, Seth, Isis and Nephthys. Isis loved Osiris and coupled with him, but Seth was jealous and killed Osiris, and to stop his resurrection, he scattered parts of his body throughout the kingdom. Isis, whose love was all-consuming, collected the body parts and reassembled them after working magic on a plant she could use to protect Osiris from another attack. Then she breathed life back into him.

But if a visitor listens to a herb seller in one of the many souqs in Egypt, they might hear the same legend with a different ending. It's the story of a wadi that belongs to Isis.

– Isis called on her mother Nut to implore her child Geb to give her a small wadi where the people could grow her plant to protect all, and this Nut did. Isis worked her magic to ensure Seth would not find the wadi, making it invisible and allowing no one in, and only one man to take the plant to the people when she sent a sign.

And if a visitor who knows the legend visits a herb seller and he meets a young traveller wearing worn desert clothing, trading with the herb seller, then, with luck, the traveller might tell him more.

– And when the great drought came and lasted for eight thousand years, the wadi began to die until the people in the wadi begged the goddess Isis to help them to continue serving her. When Isis heard their plea, she sent them Pharaoh Ka'vn, with his woman, and Hathor anointed them with love and made her his Queen Kah'teh.

– The Pharaoh and his Queen listened to the people of the wadi and left to speak with other gods. Then Isis spread her wings and carried them back to the wadi. There, Pharaoh Ka'vn called on Geb to release waters from his body so that the people might live and Isis could continue healing all.

– Isis gave Pharaoh Ka'vn a mighty rod. With this, he struck the earth, plunging it deep into the body of Geb, and Geb released waters that flowed into the wadi, and the people rejoiced.

Don't try to find the wadi. Geb promised Isis he would keep its location a secret

1

SEATED IN THEIR PATROL CAR on the Manhattan side of the East River, Gary Somers and his partner Ed Kowalski were eating their sandwiches. They were on the afternoon shift, and four o'clock was lunchtime.

Among many other hidden places, tree-shaded Honey Locust Park beside the lower lane entry of the Queensboro Bridge was one of their favourites for a short break for food. The late-afternoon sunshine dappled the leaves of the trees, the evening crowd walking dogs or exercising children had yet to come, and the park vegetation reduced the continuous hum and occasional bark of traffic or the blart of a braking truck.

Only minutes before, they had heard a call on the radio.

'Queensboro bridge lower Manhattan exit. Traffic officers needed to clear an exit jam. Queens traffic officers to delay traffic entering lower bridge entrance.'

'Fucked if I want to be a traffic cop,' Gary said. 'Let those guys manage it. If it's still a screw-up when we've eaten, we'll go look.'

They were not an unusual pair of New York cops. Ed had grown up in Greenpoint, Brooklyn, affectionately called Little Poland, and Gary had grown up in Harlem, where a visitor from Africa would feel at home. The difference was enough to render competition futile, and the similarities between the two men, not only in size and build, but in their motivation to join the police force, had made them a formidable pair who trusted each other completely. Each knew the other would protect him in dire circumstances.

Gary, munching on his sandwich, was watching a rat that appeared from the blackness below the bridge where the sunlight failed to reach; it sniffed, looked up and down the road, and then crossed in a quick scamper into the park. 'Smart buggers, those rats – it must be looking for leftovers from the midday crowd.'

A ship's horn on the river gave out two blasts, and Ed, taking another bite, said, 'That's another captain pissed off with weekend fishermen.'

The radio crackled to life again. 'Calling all cars, calling all cars. Multiple vehicle collisions on the Queensboro Bridge, westbound lane. Officers to block entrances lower level on both sides.'

'Shit.' Gary tossed his sandwich and lunchbox onto the back seat, started the engine, switched on the siren and the flashing beacon, and, with a screech of rubber, reversed rapidly down the slip road. Thrown forward, Ed braced himself against the dashboard; he didn't try to engage his seatbelt.

An arriving truck braked to let the police car into the stream of traffic. Gary stopped his vehicle immediately, blocking the entry to the bridge's lower level. He popped the trunk, and the two men jumped out. Half a minute later, they had blocked the entrance to traffic with a row of red traffic cones.

The two officers threw themselves back into the patrol car, and Gary spun the wheels to catch up with the last of the eastbound traffic already on the bridge, a hundred metres ahead. The siren screamed at the motorists, electrifying the vehicles ahead to pull into the right lane to let them through. As they neared the middle of the bridge, they saw stationary cars on the opposite roadway, parked sideways and behind them, some on top of others.

'There's the pileup,' Ed said to his partner, then spoke into the radio microphone. 'Kowalski and Somers. We cordoned off the eastbound lower entrance. Traffic police will be needed there.

We're on the bridge, and vehicles about halfway along the westbound lane have piled up.'

As Gary drove past the first vehicles involved in the mass collision, they could see it had been a chain reaction. Ed counted fifteen, the last cars lying in a haphazard pile; some had ridden onto those in front. Finally, they saw an eighteen-wheeler. It was apparent it had run into a stationary car and that the trailer had jack-knifed across the roadway, smashing a car in the slow lane before its swing ended in the lattice bridge steelwork.

Gary stopped opposite the articulated truck as Ed reported on the radio what they were seeing. 'Fifteen cars piled up, possibly many injured. There's a wrecked eighteen-wheeler – we'll need a crane for that. We'll also need a fire crew – fuel leaks are certain.'

Gary got out of the patrol car and climbed over the barrier to the truck. A saloon was half under its front wheels; the impact had smashed it forward, into and under the car ahead.

Poor bastards are probably dead.

The truck door had popped open, and the unmoving driver lay flopped over the steering wheel. Gary mounted the step, reached forward and checked for a pulse. There was nothing, and the driver's chest wasn't moving. 'The truck driver's dead,' he called out to Ed. 'He must have died before the accident, and the truck ran on without braking. I'll look at the car it ran into.'

The car had its bonnet under the car ahead, the rear scrunched up and partly under the truck. The driver's door was jammed, with a broken window. Knocking out the remnants of the driver's window with the butt of his pistol, Gary reached in and felt for a pulse.

'Ed, bring the oxygen. There's a guy here with a weak pulse.'

He glanced into the rear. It was empty.

Twenty-eight-year-old Kelvin Shareef knew he was dead.

When the juggernaut rammed into the rear of his rental car, time slowed, and everything seemed to pass in slow motion. Lying back, relaxing on his fully reclined seat at the tail end of the waiting queue of vehicles, he felt and heard the impact, the rear of the car and the boot crunching with a screech of tortured metal as first the rear crash absorbers gave way, and then the crumple zone absorbed the impact. The car jerked forwards, and Kelvin slid backwards. In a reflex action, he drew in his legs to try to secure himself on the seat. Then he heard the impact where his car hit the one ahead, and the front screamed as the crash absorbers and then the forward crumple zone folded under pressure from the slowing juggernaut behind him. As if in slow motion, he watched in horror as the steering wheel shot towards him, then rose towards the roof as the crumple zone did its job, but then it reversed its movement as the car ahead rode onto his. It came down like the sword of Damocles, and he felt the excruciating pain of the lower wheel rim hitting his rib cage and heard the multiple cracks of the bones fracturing. The collapsing dashboard smashed into his lower leg, breaking the bone, but that was a pain he didn't feel – yet. He didn't hear the passenger door pop open and slam forward as the car's passenger cell, strained to its limit, let it go with a bang, microseconds before the truck cab stopped as its trailer swung wildly across the other lane.

Then the blood-freezing smashing, screeching and crunching din died, and Kelvin could hear screams, groans and cries for help.

Kelvin himself couldn't scream. He couldn't breathe. He tried, but the pain was unbearable, and no air entered his lungs. His heartbeat slowed as the muscles received less oxygen as the minutes passed. His blood oxygen level dropped, and oxygen starvation brought hallucinations. He heard a voice say, 'Throw him back.' Then darkness came.

He wasn't aware of the life-giving oxygen that forced its way into his tortured lungs, reaching his bloodstream and enabling his heart muscles to begin recovering. His pulse rate rose.

'I can feel a pulse, Ed, and his chest moved. The door on the passenger side has popped open. Can you climb over the car and enter from that side?'

Ed climbed over and crawled into the diminished passenger space.

'Gary, we can't touch this guy. His chest looks like the steering wheel caved it in, but he's lucky – the seat back folded right back, else he would have the steering column through his heart. The rescue crew must cut the car off him; he's stuck under the dash.' Getting the oxygen going, Ed told his partner, 'His chest rises when I open the valve, but he's not breathing. It goes down when I close the valve.'

'Okay, Ed, stay there and switch the oxygen on and off, like breathing. I'll call for medics.'

'Gary, his dick is outside his pants.'

'Shit! The poor bastard was probably jacking off while in the traffic jam. Put his dick back in his pants; it'll give him some dignity if he doesn't make it.'

Within ten minutes, twenty ambulances, three fire engines and crews equipped with the jaws of life were at work up and down the length of the collision scene.

Kelvin Shareef was still unconscious, breathing with the help of a mechanical pump, when an ambulance took him to the emergency entrance of the nearby Hospital for Special Surgery.

No one noticed the young woman with curly black hair who first ran, then walked, down the bridge's pedestrian path into Manhattan. At the bridge exit, she paused, straightened her clothes, patted her hair, and then continued towards Central Park.

Forty minutes later, X-rayed and heavily medicated, Kelvin was wheeled into an operating theatre, where two green-garbed surgeons opened his chest.

'Gordon, this is unusual,' one of the doctors said to his colleague. 'The report says a steering wheel did this, but it has smashed the ribs up, not in. And his lung is untouched.'

'It does say he was under the steering wheel.'

'Then he's luckier than all the others I've seen. It's an easy job. Just move the ribs into place and plate them. I'll do his leg while you do the ribs.'

Nearly an hour later, Gordon said, 'I've closed his chest. Do we leave him on the artificial lung or use a ventilator?'

'He's covered by travel insurance. The police gave the hospital admin the card in his wallet. Let's intubate him and keep him in a coma. He can't breathe normally. His chest muscles have taken a hammering, and the pain will be excessive. I'll leave the leg in an open cast while he's unconscious.'

Ten days later, Kelvin opened his eyes and saw a nurse with golden curly hair. He closed them.

I'm dead, and this is the angel who will take me to heaven.

The blonde nurse stepped back, and a doctor took her place. Leaning forward, he shone a light into Kelvin's eyes, first one, then the other.

'The pupil reacts. He's waking.'

Kelvin closed his eyes. *Shit. There's someone from hell as well. Which one will take me?*

'Mr Shareef, can you hear me? Open your eyes.'

Better to know. I'll ask. Kelvin opened his eyes and mouth, but only a croak emerged.

'Don't try to talk. You're in hospital after a car accident. You've been in a medically induced coma for ten days. Blink once if you understand, twice if you don't.'

So I'm not dead? Or did Shai throw me back?

Kelvin blinked once.

'You have three broken ribs, two others cracked, and a broken left leg. We've set and plated everything. When you can eat normally, in a few days, an ambulance will take you to a convalescent home for physiotherapy. Do you understand?'

Kelvin blinked again, once.

I heard him say, 'Throw him back.'

Then he went to sleep.

The nurse with curly hair came to tell him where he was going for his recovery. That she should come and not some dour admin secretary didn't surprise him; it had happened to him many times. He knew he was attractive at a metre ninety, with regular features, grey eyes, a strong jaw, skin that never lost its tan, and dark, almost black hair to his ears.

When he thanked her, she said with a warm smile, 'That's my

job, Mr Shareef. Now, when you have fully recovered, come back and see us. I'll be glad to see you in good health.'

When the hospital discharged him to the convalescent home in Whitestone, Long Island, they returned his belongings to him – collected by the police from his hotel room, the address traced by the contact details he'd given on the rental car-hire form – along with his wallet and mobile phone. He called his parents in Ashdown, England, only to learn from James, the butler, that they were still away on their adventure in the Amazon. He decided to relax and enjoy his rest in this city, almost six thousand kilometres from his home.

Three days after he arrived at the home, an aide brought him a copy of the *Herald Tribune*, two weeks old.

'Mr Shareef, you may not have seen a report in this paper. It's about the accident you were in.'

Reading the report, Kelvin realised how lucky he'd been: twenty-two people had suffered severe injuries, and four, including the truck driver, had died. *Maybe Shai did throw me back.*

Two months from the day of the accident, Kelvin was finally ready to go home. Six kilograms lighter, he felt almost back to normal.

He called home again.

'Shareef residence, good afternoon.'

'Hello, James, Kelvin here. Are my parents at home?'

'No, sir. I understand they are still travelling in the Amazon.'

'Okay, James. Can you send Muammar to fetch me from Gatwick tomorrow? I'll message you later with the flight details.'

'My pleasure, sir. Your suite is always ready.'

A taxi took him to Kennedy Airport.

2

THE *SERVEUR DE TROTTOIR* leaning casually against the wall of the Deux Magots brasserie on the Place St Germain de Pres on the left bank of the Seine had unobtrusively watched the beautiful young woman sitting alone at a typically French pavement bistro table.

He had watched the woman arrive. She was wearing heels, and he thought her walk was sexy, and her figure merited the gallic gesture of appreciation, kissing the joined tips of the fingers and waving them at her. He guessed her age at around twenty-seven.

He had served her coffee and tart while confirming she had no ring on her ring finger, but she had paid him scant attention, barely looking up from her phone.

Fifteen minutes later, another young woman arrived. The *garcon* saw her come but only looked closely at her when she joined the beautiful woman. *An unruly bouffant hairstyle, no makeup, loose dress, flat shoes.* Then, smoothing her skirt down over her bottom, she sat down. *Nice derriere. Athletic and about the same age as the other woman, but not a patch on her.*

He approached their table to take her order and heard the newcomer say, 'Sorry I'm late Em. You're looking great!'

Kate had known Marylyn since they were children. Her nickname for her oldest friend, 'Em', was simply the first letter of Marylyn's name.

'I never thought I'd meet my best friend again in Paris,' Kate continued.

'Kate, nice to see you again,' Marylyn said, reaching across the small table and giving her friend's hand a warm squeeze. Glancing at the *garcon*, she asked Kate, 'Do you want coffee and a croissant?'

When he left with the order, Marylyn said, 'I'm auditing the French branch of one of our clients. Why are you here?'

'A meeting with a French distributor whose sales have dropped.' Kate's job involved marketing fashion accessories and perfumes for many global brands. She was good at it, and had risen to marketing director for Europe for her company.

'You must have been busy – you look tired,' Marylyn observed.

Kate shook her head and smiled. 'Well, I've dressed down today,' she explained. 'I have a couple of days off. I'm flying to Edinburgh this evening, returning to London on Monday morning.'

The garcon interrupted as he brought her coffee and croissant, and Kate took a bite as Marylyn asked, 'Do you have a boyfriend waiting in Edinburgh?'

'No, I'm meeting my sister and her family there. Her husband is taking her two boys trout fishing, and I'll keep my sister company. Maybe I'll have a chance to peek up a kilt.'

Marylyn laughed. 'No eligible male company in sight? You said you were hoping to find the right man.'

'Since my disastrous one-month marriage to Gavin, three men have asked me to come to bed, and I've refused them all. And of those, I've had only one invite in the last two years. Nine months ago, a man invited me, but I decided I wasn't interested and refused. You know my predominant contacts are women, both at work and with clients, so I don't have the opportunities you have to meet men. I don't see a ring on your hand, so I assume you still have the three possibles lined up?'

'Yes, but not the same guys as when we last met, and I think I'll change one this weekend.'

'Em, I don't know how you do it!'

10

'I'm doing audits, so I visit one or more companies each week.' Marylyn, a chartered accountant, had worked her way up through the ranks of an international auditing group to a senior position. 'I must dress well, just as you do, and there's always a new man out there if I keep my eyes open.'

'And you still have that rule about sex?'

'Yes: only one at a time, and not until he fulfils all the requirements – which usually means never. And when I decide he's out, he's out for good. Since a guy two years ago, I've become far more critical.'

'Who was he?'

'I now believe I did love him, although I was too busy working to push for marriage. He never asked – a lovely, amusing character.' Marylyn sighed, then continued, 'You must try to look elsewhere, Kate. I've been on short cruises with a boyfriend and given my number to other men who've called me after the cruise.'

'Em, you're shameless.'

'Until I find the right man, Kate, I will be. He must be something special to allow me to work until I become a partner and can consider taking time out to raise kids. Are you still in the same job?'

'No, I'm now the marketing director for Europe. I won't become a vice president for several years, but marketing directors travel less often than I have for years. It gives me more flexibility, and I will get more time off.'

'Then, Kate, you should try a cruise.'

'I don't like the idea of those massive ships with thousands of passengers. They're too much like being in an office block with thousands of workers. And taking bus rides with sixty passengers while a loudspeaker tells you what you're seeing isn't my idea of a holiday. I prefer a desert island.'

'I've been on three small cruises with a boyfriend – one in the

Amazon, another in the Norwegian fjords, and one on a gulet cruising the Turkish coast, hoping to develop a close relationship. I'm still waiting for a man to invite me to cruise the Nile or the Danube. If I were short of candidates, I would book one with many more passengers. You won't have much chance of meeting a man when wandering around Scotland with your sister.'

Kate replied with a shrug. 'I suppose not. Maybe Gavin put me off sex for life.'

'Have you got over the feeling that every man you meet has a whip in his hand?'

'Gavin only threatened to tie me up and torture me – he didn't actually do it. Still, it was a horrible enough experience to give me that feeling, and, yes, I do still have it. And I still haven't had an orgasm.'

Concerned, Marylyn asked, 'Maybe a therapist would help?'

'I've seen one. A woman who talked too much; cost a packet of money and in the end said she couldn't do anything for me without many more sessions, which was impossible because I was always travelling. She did say it would come right when I met a man who needed me as much as I needed him.'

Marylyn had an idea and asked, 'Do you attend management seminars and other meetings?'

'Yes, but most of the men at those are married, and the rest don't interest me. Many are gay, and the others talk about football.'

'Then go cruising in places where the men are different. I cruised the Greek Isles for a fortnight on a private boat with two other couples. You need to relax.'

'Okay, I'll look at it. I must go, to check out of my hotel and leave for the airport. Keep in touch, and if we are in the same town at the same time again, we can meet for dinner.'

Kate was back at work in London by Monday midday, and although she did think about Marylyn's advice once or twice during the following week, she did nothing about it. Then she met Harry.

She'd gone to view a new TV ad for one of her company's products, and discussed it with the ad agency representative. 'The visuals are great, but the soundtrack is terrible. It sounds like screeching cats. Who did it?'

'Some guy the director dug up. It's supposed to be modern, like the visuals.'

'I said the visuals had to be modern, not the sound. Tell him to find someone else.'

Two days later, she received a request to meet the replacement sound engineer – who turned out to be Harry, a very slim, mild-mannered individual, two or three years older than herself and taller. And, she decided, with amused brown eyes.

'Are you a musician?' Kate asked.

'No. My father's a professional musician, so I grew up listening to music. I'm a mixer – I take bits of different song and film soundtracks, and cut and mix them into a soundtrack that suits a video. Are you a music lover?'

Kate shook her head. 'Ten years ago I was crazy about rock and techno, but today I prefer the blues.'

'Not symphonies or opera?'

'I've never been to a symphony or attended an opera. They just don't appeal to me.'

Harry nodded. 'So what's the mood you want to feel when you watch the ad?'

'We're promoting femininity, so the viewer must feel the

product will make her super-feminine. Watch the video several times, break it into pieces, see what each piece is pushing, and find music that matches that objective.'

'Okay. I'll synchronise a new soundtrack to the video and show it to you on Friday.'

She thought the new soundtrack superb and said so, and Harry invited her to the opera with him the following evening.

Over the next month, she learnt a lot about operas and symphonies. Harry took her each Friday to a concert and each Saturday to an opera. They had an early dinner before each performance.

She enjoyed Harry's wide musical knowledge, and it interested her to learn from him the structure of the symphonies. He told her about the parts he liked the most in each performance, and why, and about the history of the most famous opera singers.

But, although Kate enjoyed the evenings, and it seemed Harry did too, he remained in some ways an enigma. He never talked about himself, so she knew almost nothing about him, even after several dates. He held her hand when they went into the theatre to find their seats, but she had a curious feeling that it was only out of politeness, rather than an urge to be intimate. He would put his arm around her in the taxi home, but although he had the opportunity, had not kissed her. She wondered several times if he was gay.

After the last opera performance, as they were heading back to Harry's place in a taxi – where, as usual over the last month, Harry would get out, and Kate would continue the trip to her own home – Harry said, 'Kate, we've enjoyed every evening out together. How about coming home with me to find out if we can make beautiful music together?'

That's different – Harry's gentle, not like Gavin. Maybe we can. She was still thinking about his invitation as the taxi drew up in front of his apartment building. *I haven't once thought about going to bed with him, and now I'm thinking about sex with him when he hasn't kissed me once!* She remembered the psychologist's words. *He doesn't need me, and I don't need him; I don't love him. It will be another fiasco, and I don't need any more of those.*

She firmly said, 'Harry, I enjoy going out with you but I don't love you, and I don't want sex without love. The taxi can take me home. Good night.'

Harry opened his door and said, coldly, 'Kate, I'm sorry you feel that way.' She knew he was holding back anger when he said abruptly, 'Good night.'

3

MUAMMAR COLLECTED KELVIN at Gatwick, and during the ten-kilometre drive to the family home, the two men chatted in Arabic.

'Is my grandfather well?'

'Yes, sir. I see him sitting on the terrace in his wheelchair when the weather is fine, looking through his photo albums. He has no problems recognising me and tells me of his childhood in Cairo.'

After the Second World War, Kelvin's grandfather, Lateef Shareef, had emigrated from Egypt with his young wife, Heba. After a successful career importing Egyptian cotton to England, he'd retired as the cotton industry in Britain shrank in the face of foreign competition. He'd bought the family home, located idyllically in a forest clearing within walking distance of the Ashdown Park Country Club, for his retirement because his passion was golf and because the mansion was big enough for an extended family in the Egyptian tradition. There was no conflict between the family members living in the sprawling house, for Kelvin's parents spent most of each year elsewhere.

'Does he tell you the same stories each time?' Lateef, now ninety-three years old and widowed for fifteen years, was beginning to show signs of his long life.

'No, sir, although he sometimes forgets what he has told me. I don't mind, as he likes telling me, and he remembers something different each time.'

'I expect he'll live to be a hundred,' Kelvin said. 'Is there any news of my parents' return?'

'I heard they'll be returning in two weeks, but Mr James can tell you more, sir.'

At the house, Muammar took Kelvin's bag to his suite, and James welcomed him home and gave him the same sparse information about his parents' expected return, also in Arabic. One of England's many oddities, the butler had been born in Egypt to an English soldier who had stayed in Egypt after the war and married an Egyptian girl. He had come to England when his wife died and brought his young son with him.

James offered to bring a cup of coffee to the terrace. Kelvin knew it would be an Egyptian coffee and accepted with delight.

As Kelvin made himself comfortable on the terrace, he looked happily out over the impeccable grounds – kept that way, like the house, by a trusted staff. He thought about his parents – his father, Darius, a renowned geologist turned explorer who had since discovered several deposits of minerals and gemstones, and his mother, Layla, a GP, who had insisted on accompanying her husband on his international forays for two reasons: she refused to sit moping alone in a house while he gallivanted around a world filled with sex-mad women, and she wanted to be on hand to nurse her husband back to good health should he become ill.

Kelvin, their only son, had withstood the pressure to follow in his father's footsteps. However, his younger sister, Shani, had done so: a tomboy when young, doing what their father did suited her to perfection. Kelvin had instead followed in his mother's footsteps and had studied medicine for three years, when – to his mother's disgust – his father's genes took over. 'Kelvin, you're halfway to becoming a GP in England,' she'd pointed out. 'Although many countries will accept you as a doctor, I think you will have wasted three years if you stop now.'

Despite Layla's misgivings, he had switched to pharmaceutical medicine, before becoming an explorer of a different kind. Kelvin had successfully identified plant molecules for medical treatments in various parts of the world and licensed the information to pharmaceutical companies.

His current project had been born from an idea he'd had when reading about ancient herbs. He'd decided to find the plants the ancient Egyptians had used to make embalming fluids for mummification, and then search for plants growing in modern Egypt with similar elements. Just before the car accident, he'd been visiting Brown University in Rhode Island, and when his car had been crushed on the bridge, he'd had in his bag chemical analyses of fluids taken by the university's scientists from mummies in several museums. The analyses had survived the crash, and the police had returned the bag to him along with his other belongings.

Setting the coffee on the table, James asked solicitously, 'Sir, you appear to have lost weight. Have you been ill?'

'About five kilograms, James. I was involved in a car accident in New York and spent two months in hospital.'

'Have you recovered completely, sir?'

'Yes, but I need to spend lots of time exercising to return to my fitness level. I hope you can feed me a protein-rich diet.'

'You can count on it, sir. Will you go to the club gym and play golf? I'll tell Muammar to service the golf buggy.'

'No, don't worry about it; I won't be playing golf. I'll use the practice tee for my swing. I'll do my cross-country runs, and run to the club for the gym and swimming. When will my grandfather be down?'

'Eleven on the dot, sir, regular as clockwork. He's had breakfast, and his caregiver is giving him his morning massage.'

'Still the same caregiver?'

'Yes, sir. Abayomi is your grandfather's favourite.'

'Then I'll wait here for him. Bring me another coffee, please.'

When the old man joined his grandson on the terrace, Kelvin listened to stories about the merits of girls in Egypt, brought on by his answer to his grandfather's oft-asked question, 'When are you getting married?'

And Kelvin's standard answer: 'When I find the right woman, Grandad.' The old man had been delighted when Kelvin had added, 'I'm going to Egypt soon. Maybe I'll find one there.'

Over the next three weeks, with careful attention to his diet by James and the family's cook, Kelvin gained over three kilograms and lost the pinkish hospital pallor, replacing it with a light tan earned on the cross-country runs and the sun bed in the club massage room.

He took the news of the further delay in his parents' return in his stride – it wasn't unusual – and began spending time on the golf course, slowly building up his strength and fitness. It seemed to be working, too: no matter how hard he hit the ball now, his ribs no longer twinged when he swung a club on the driving range.

One morning, as he lined up another ball on the tee, he heard a voice behind him.

'That's an impressive swing. You consistently hit two fifty yards. Are you a pro?'

Kelvin turned to look at the speaker. *Solid-looking young woman, shorter than me, brunette, brown eyes, friendly face, kissable lips.*

'No, and I haven't played a game for nine months. I'm not practising. I'm exercising after an accident. What distance do you manage?'

'On a warm day, two hundred, but most of my drives are one-eighty or less.' The young woman gave Kelvin a considered look. 'I haven't seen you at the club before today.'

Kelvin extended a hand. 'I'm not here that often, so that's not surprising. I'm Kelvin Shareef.'

She took his hand, shook it firmly, and said, 'Matilda Malone. Pleased to meet you. What was the accident? What happened to you?'

'Car crash in New York. Four broken ribs on the left and a fractured lower leg. But I'm fine now. Swinging my driver has eliminated my stiffness, and swimming and running have rebuilt my strength.' Giving Matilda a cheeky smile, he continued, 'I'll risk sounding stupid: do you come here often?'

She grinned. 'That *is* a classic pick-up line. I live in Horsted Keynes, so I can drive here to practise or play on Saturdays or Sundays. During the week, I commute into London from Hayward Heath on the Gatwick Express. If you've recovered, how about a game of golf? I don't have a regular partner.' She cocked her head to one side, smiling, and Kelvin saw her eyes twinkle as she added, 'Golf or otherwise.'

'When?'

It surprised him when she said, 'How about tomorrow, if we can book a tee-off time and you're free?'

'Then let's go and find out.'

They played the next day, and she beat him. When they booked for the following Saturday, Kelvin said, 'Matilda, if we finish our game around four, could we do an early dinner and a show in London?'

Matilda thought about it. It would mean golf clothing and a drive to the club in the morning, then a return drive to her home to shower and change for an evening out. It seemed a bit much, so she asked, 'Could you rather fetch me from home for golf in the morning? I can bring my evening wear, if I can shower and change at your house. Then you can take me home after the show.'

'Of course, my pleasure.'

They chose a show, and everything went smoothly, except Kelvin lost the game again.

He learnt that Matilda was a doctor's secretary, and that she had chosen Horsted Keynes as a place to live because her parents ran a plant nursery near Brighton, only twenty kilometres further south.

Stopping in front of Matilda's apartment block after the show, Kelvin lifted her bags from the bonnet storage of his Porsche and set them on the pavement. He closed the bonnet, and when he turned back to her, he saw her standing with a bag in each hand, her handbag over a shoulder, looking curiously pissed off.

'Matilda, let me carry those,' he said.

'I can manage them. Thank you for the evening and good night.'

Driving home, he wondered about the abrupt ending to the date. *Perhaps I should have kissed Matilda before taking the bags out of the car*, he thought.

They repeated the golf and show the following Saturday. Kelvin won the match – but only by one stroke – and they enjoyed the performance, a comedy.

This time, when Kelvin drew up in front of Matilda's apartment block, he remembered the cool ending of their date the week before, and leaned across the seat to kiss her. He was surprised at the warmth of her response: she pressed herself to him and kissed him back, passionately.

'Next week Saturday?' she asked, looking up at him with a small, knowing smile.

'I'd love to, but I must cry off. My parents are due back on Thursday, and I haven't seen them for nearly a year, so I must keep them company next weekend. I'll give you a call when I know I'm free.'

'Okay, Kelvin. Don't forget me.'

'I won't.' Kelvin kissed her again.

This time, on the drive home, Kelvin had a new concern. The passionate kiss with Matilda had done nothing to physically arouse him, which wasn't normal for him. *I wonder if there's something still wrong with me. I must see my doc.*

He called the family doctor in Harley Street on Monday morning for an appointment. The secretary told him to come in at eleven on Thursday.

4

A WEEK LATER, Kate went to her parents' home in north London for the weekend. Her father, Amin Mansoumi, had left Iran when he qualified as a doctor for further study to specialise in paediatric surgery. After meeting his wife, Yara, another paediatrician, he remained in England and became a recognised specialist in child deformities.

Yara, had been born in Egypt to parents who'd left Iran with the Shah in 1979 and, after their death, had moved to England to continue her education.

Kate was their second child. Her sister, Ava, older by four years, had become a dentist and married a doctor. They lived outside Welwyn with their two young children.

Kate had rebelled against a doctor's life with its long and irregular hours. She had decided marketing and London nightlife were far more interesting.

Amin and Yara's house hid in tall trees on the north side of Totteridge Common Road, less than two kilometres from the Barnet Hospital, where both had worked since their marriage.

'Hello, Mother,' Kate said as Yara opened the door. Kate's mother-tongue was a mix of Egyptian and Persian Arabic, which her parents spoke at home, although her English accent was that of an upper-class Londoner.

'Hello, Kate,' said Yara with a pleased smile. She and Kate

looked alike, with smooth olive skin, although, seen side by side, Yara had a more matronly figure. 'We haven't seen you in ages. Where have you been?'

'Scooting around Europe, but I'm back for a week or two.'

'When will the company promote you to VP so you can stay home?'

'Not before the current VP retires in five years, unless she dies or a competitor poaches her.'

'Put your bag in your room, and come to the kitchen. You can help me with lunch. Your dad will be back at one. He had an emergency to deal with – a car accident where the kid wasn't wearing a safety belt.'

Half an hour later, Kate was in the kitchen, watching while Yara prepared the meal.

Her mother said, 'The chicken is in the oven, and I'll do the mixed salad. You can do the tart. The apples and pastry are on the counter.'

'Okay, but I was hoping for sholezard.'

'Rice pudding is too heavy at midday, but I've made some for tonight. It's in the fridge.'

'I could eat sholezard any time.'

'I know,' Yara laughed. 'I've seen you eat half of what I've made in a sitting. You don't look undernourished, though. Are you getting enough exercise?'

'Gym and swim, Mother, and a run in Millwall Park.'

'Alone?'

'There's always a hundred or more runners, and I take the docklands railway to the park – it's door to door, and there are always people in the carriage.'

'I didn't mean that. I meant with a friend.'

'I know you did, but no. I don't have a boyfriend, and although I've met a few men of the right age, none stirs my feelings.'

'It's been, what, six years since Gavin? Are you over it now?'

'I thought so until last weekend, but maybe I'm not.'

'Tell me.'

While preparing the tart, Kate told her mother about Harry.

'Kate, unless you can solve your problem soon, you'll spend five years working to become a VP and then wake up to find you have no one with whom to live the rest of your life and no children.'

'I know, Mother. I met Marylyn in Paris. She's in the same boat, so we talked about it, but at least she has several prospects. She told me to take a cruise holiday. She said she'd done three and met interesting men each time.'

'We've got about half an hour while the tart bakes,' Yara said, watching Kate put the apple tart in the oven. 'Fetch two glasses and some white wine, and let's sit in the solarium. I've something to say.'

Dreading a lecture, Kate did what her mother asked.

'Kate, I won't argue with what Marylyn suggested,' Yara began as the two women sat drinking in the sun, glasses in hand. 'You might meet some eligible men on cruise ships, but I think I should give you a doctor's opinion. Your unsuccessful marriage was with an English man. While I don't think that nationality should be a handicap to eligibility, I can imagine that when you meet a man like Harry, the similarity of language and gesture recalls your ex-husband to your subconscious. You're more likely to relax and forget if the man speaks Arabic. I recommend that you take a holiday in a place where you're likely to meet men of different nationalities. I don't recommend going to Iran, though – that might be dangerous. But many countries speak Arabic.'

'Mother, I refuse to go to any country that forces women to wear the veil and where families arrange marriages, and I won't convert to Islam.'

'I agree with you. I'm not suggesting you do. Just think about it.

If you're taking a holiday, bear it in mind. But don't go to a place like Charm El Sheikh in Egypt – it'll be full of European tourists, and the only Arabic speakers will be the hotel staff.'

'I wouldn't go there anyway. I don't want to go from a giant office building with a thousand staff to a place with three or four thousand tourists.'

'Hello, Kate, you're looking well,' Amin said, striding into the kitchen and setting his doctor's bag on the table.

'A typical doctor's welcome, Dad,' Kate laughed. 'Try using "lovely" instead of "well". How are you, and how's the child?'

'I'm as fit as usual, and the child will live, although I'm angry again at careless parents who don't strap their kids into the car. The boy hit his head on the window-switch when the accident threw him across the car – a local skull fracture but no serious spinal injuries.' Her father stopped and looked around in comic exaggeration. 'I was hoping to meet a boyfriend.'

Kate sighed. 'Mother can tell you about my boyfriend problem, Dad.'

Yara, seeing her daughter's exasperation, interjected. 'Come, let's eat. Kate, help me carry the food.'

Once seated, Amin said, 'Kate, I told you about my project to educate parents about kids' accidents some months ago. I persuaded the Health and Safety Department to fund a TV ad campaign. The ad agency is presenting the proposed six adverts on Tuesday afternoon at three at their offices. I'd appreciate it if you could come too, view them, as you do for your marketing, and then let me know what you think.'

'What if I think they're terrible?'

'If you say why, and I agree, I'll tell them the same thing.'

Kate nodded. 'Okay. I might need to shift an appointment, but I'll be there if possible.'

'Thanks, Kate.' Her father smiled warmly at her. 'Now, did you bring an evening dress?'

'Yes. Mother warned me. She said you had guests tonight. Who are they?'

'George Tomlinson, a cardiologist, his wife Constance, a gynaecologist, and their son Grayson, who's specialising in ophthalmology.'

Kate looked accusingly from one parent to the other. 'Are you two trying to set me up again?'

Her father pretended to be shocked. 'Not at all! We know you say you will never marry a doctor. But he's a nice young man, and your mother likes him.'

Kate's father was right on the button: Kate knew what a doctor's life was like and had no desire to sit at home waiting for her husband to return from treating an urgent case. So when she was introduced to Grayson that evening, she gave him a small smile that didn't reach her eyes.

Grayson got the message: the attention he gave her was, at best, lacklustre. For most of the evening, he discussed medical issues with her father, while Kate suffered a veiled investigation from Constance, evidently as set on finding a spouse for her offspring as Kate's parents were for her.

'Are you going to remain in marketing?' Constance asked finally, and Kate gave her a prepared reply.

'Absolutely. I'm now the director for Europe, and in six or seven years, I'll be vice president of marketing, covering the world. It means lots of travelling to different countries, and that's what I love doing.'

'You accept that you'll miss out on having a family?'

'I made that choice years ago.'

5

KELVIN WELCOMED HIS PARENTS back home, standing on the sweeping front staircase of the mansion with James. As Muammar extracted their luggage from the car, the three embraced and looked each other up and down. Darius and Layla both looked fit and healthy, with deep suntans.

'Kelvin, you're looking pale.'

'Yes, mother. I had an accident in New York. I'll tell you about it, but I've recovered, and I'm getting my tan back while running.' Then he asked his father, 'Did you have a successful trip?'

'We found nothing in the basin but several deposits when we moved into the western hills. I'll tell you more later. Are you going to stay for a while?'

'Several more weeks, I think, then I might go to Egypt. Come, James is going to serve lunch in the solarium.'

Half an hour later, seated around a veritable banquet, Kelvin told his parents about his New York accident and recovery.

Layla, her medical training vying with her maternal instincts, looked concerned. 'No twinges left?'

'None. I'm swinging a golf club better than before and have played eighteen holes several times. But to be sure, I have a medical booked for Thursday.'

'Who do you play with?'

'A woman I met at the practice range. She beats me on handicap.'

Darius, a keen golfer himself, gave a low whistle of approval. He then changed the subject. 'Okay, how did you do in the eastern Amazon?'

'I found two plants with an interesting active molecule,' Kelvin replied, his face showing enthusiasm. 'One might be helpful in a specific disease, and the other exhibits a pharmacological action the lab defines as an accelerator – it binds to other molecules and rapidly carries them into the body. I've patented them and licensed them to a pharma company.'

'With an escape clause, I hope.'

'Yes, three years to generate royalties, or I offer the patents to a competitor. And you, Dad, what did you find?'

'A cobalt and copper indication near the Bolivia-Peru border, and a lithium reef at a much higher altitude on the Bolivian border. I've sold the data to two US mining companies with a royalty clause. They must do diamond core drilling within three years.'

'Your turn, Kelvin,' Layla said. 'Why are you going to Egypt?'

'It's only a hunch, but Egyptian medical practices lasted four thousand years, and there are thousands of references in the papyri to medicines, of which less than a third are identified. As they were all natural ingredients – plants, minerals, and animal parts or excretions, including human sources – I feel it's highly probable that a plant with medicinal properties used in antiquity disappeared from the pharmacopoeia but may still exist.'

Her maternal instincts coming into play once more, Kelvin's mother eased the conversation back to the woman her son had mentioned. 'So, who's the woman you play golf with? Have you finally found a girlfriend?'

'My golfing partner is a nice girl my age, nothing more. I don't have anyone else right now, and I don't want a serious relationship; it would put a crimp in my travels. Sorry, Mother, you'll have to wait a bit longer for a grandchild.' Seeing an opportunity to shift the focus, Kelvin added, 'How is Shani doing?'

'I've given up on your sister,' Layla said in evident exasperation. 'Every time we see her, she has a different love-struck young man following her. They're all idiots, and Shani probably thinks the same, but they take her where she wants to go until they give up.'

'Kelvin, a pleasure to see you!' boomed Doctor Rouhani, who had been the family GP for thirty years. 'You look fit and healthy. Why have you come to see me?'

'Looks can be deceiving, doctor,' Kelvin said, then launched into the story of his accident, time in the convalescent facility, and recovery at home. He'd brought the various medical reports and discharge forms, X-rays and scans, which the doctor carefully looked through as Kelvin spoke.

'Well, it appears to me that your recovery has gone as well as can be expected,' Doctor Rouhani said, as Kelvin finished. 'So what can I do for you now?'

'I met a woman a few weeks ago, and things went well, but when it came down to it ...' Kelvin looked at the doctor and squirmed uncomfortably in his seat.

'Ah,' said the experienced GP. 'Erectile dysfunction?'

'Well, I don't know if it's that serious,' Kelvin said quickly. 'We didn't get that far. But we did have a passionate kissing session, and that's when I realised something wasn't right with me. Before the accident, I would have had an erection, or at least most of one. This time, nothing. I'm glad she didn't invite me in; I think I would have failed.'

'You didn't mention any damage to that area. Was there any?'

Dr Rouhani said, his businesslike manner helping Kelvin to regain his composure.

Kelvin shook his head. 'Not as far as I know.'

'I shall schedule an MRI scan for you, just to be sure, and we'll also arrange for a complete blood and urine analysis to check no blood imbalance is behind the problem. Meanwhile, I've got something for you to do.'

The doctor moved to a cupboard in a corner and took out a small packet. 'We call this a stamp test because these strips resemble a strip of postal stamps with perforations. The pack has several paper strips, and one side on one end has adhesive. When you go to bed, glue two strips tightly around your flaccid penis, below the glans, separated by a short distance. In the morning, check to see if they have broken.'

Fascinated, Kelvin took the package from the doctor as he explained.

'Your sleep has cycles of rapid eye movement, or REM, sleep, and non-REM sleep. During REM sleep, you experience dreams, and physical changes occur. One of these is an erection. Men your age usually have one or more erections during the night. If the erectile tissue fills as it should, the paper strips will break. If the paper breaks, the blood tests are normal, and the MRI shows nothing, the problem may be psychological.'

Kelvin recognised Dr Oliver Kromhout's treatment room as soon as he entered it: he had seen it in numerous films in which characters required psychological help. There was a large oak desk stationed solidly in front of a wall of bookshelves packed with heavy-looking leather-bound tomes. In the small space opposite the desk, grouped next to a glass-topped coffee table, was a wingback chair upholstered in a rich paisley and a dark leather couch on which, Kelvin presumed, patients would recline while having their heads shrunk.

'I have the report here from Dr Rouhani,' Dr Kromhout said, giving Kelvin an encouraging smile and indicating a sheaf of papers on his desk. 'Apparently, you've no medical condition that would prevent you from achieving an erection, and the report says your experiences of the morning wood are normal. I see that you had a vehicle accident in New York and that the issue you're experiencing now did not exist before that. How long after the accident did you notice the problem?'

'Well, I was in the hospital for two weeks, then in a convalescent home for two months, and then back home for a month before I noticed, so about three and a half months.'

'So the cause must be something that happened during this period. Let's start at the beginning. Lie back on the couch, relax, and tell me everything you remember about the accident.'

Feeling increasingly like a character in a movie, Kelvin did as the doctor asked. Behind him, out of his line of sight and presumably sitting in the wingback chair, the psychologist took notes – Kelvin could hear a pen scratching on paper.

Half an hour later, Kelvin had completed the story in as much detail as he could remember.

'Good,' Dr Kromhout said. 'Now, I want you to think back to the morning before the accident. Tell me what you did and why you were on the bridge.'

'That's very hazy, Doctor. I can remember the moment of impact when the truck smashed into the back of the car, but not much else.'

'Then let's go back to the day before. Do you remember that?'

'Yes, I was at Brown University in Providence, Rhode Island. I had been there for three days. I packed my bag in the afternoon, then took the train to my hotel in Queens. With the change at Penn Station, it took nearly four hours. I arrived at the hotel in time for dinner and went to bed.'

'In the morning, did you have breakfast?'

'I'm sure I did. My usual American breakfast is bacon, eggs over-easy and hash browns.

'And after breakfast?'

'That's where it blanks out.'

The doctor thought about what Kelvin had said. 'I think we must stop for today. We'll take this up at the next session.'

When Kelvin had left, Kromhout completed his patient notes, then reread the police report about the accident and the various medical reports he'd received. Finally, he went back to the police report, noting the part that listed the contents of Kelvin's pockets after the accident: credit cards in his name, a travel insurer's card, two tickets to a Broadway show on the night of the accident, and an Executive Escort Agency business card.

Later that afternoon, after his last patient for the day had left, Kromhout called the escort agency. It was morning in New York, confirmed by the sultry greeting of the person who answered the phone: 'Executive Escorts, good morning.'

'Can I speak to the manager, please? I'm Dr Oliver Kromhout. I'm calling from London, England.'

A short wait later, another sultry voice came on line. 'Good morning, Dr Kromhout. I'm the manager here.'

Quickly providing his credentials, the psychologist explained that he was treating a patient with some memory loss following a car crash. 'When the accident occurred, the patient had two tickets for a Broadway show in his pocket and a card from your agency. I don't want to know anything about the escort, but I need to know if my patient had an appointment with one of your escorts that afternoon. The police report shows he's unmarried, so my query has nothing to do with marital infidelity.'

'Give me your name again.'

'Dr Oliver Kromhout.'

'Send that police report to the email on the card, and call back in an hour.'

'Thank you.'

One hour later, the doctor called back. 'Yes, your patient did indeed have a date with one of our escorts that day,' the manager told him. 'She was actually in the car when the accident happened but was unhurt. She says she hopes your patient gets better.'

Armed with this knowledge, Dr Kromhout scheduled regular follow-up appointments with Kelvin. It took three weeks, with sessions twice a week and careful prompting by the doctor, for Kelvin to remember piece by piece the events that had occurred before the crash.

Alone and with nothing to do before his pre-booked return flight to London the following day, Kelvin had decided to see a Broadway show and, at short notice, had called the escort agency whose card he'd obtained from the concierge.

He couldn't remember clearly what the young woman had looked like, other than that she'd had a head of dark, curly hair. He recollected her hand opening his fly and her words when they stopped in the traffic jam: 'Move your seat back.' She'd lowered her head to his crotch as he slid back and dropped the seat until he was almost horizontal and invisible to those in the car ahead.

'What did you think when the truck hit your car?'

'That I was going to lose my penis. Then dying seemed reasonable.'

At their final appointment, Dr Kromhout told his patient, 'Kelvin, there's nothing physically wrong with you. You know what happened, and you've learnt the woman was unhurt. She was lying on the seat, and the police report says the door popped open, so she just slid out of the car and ran. There's no logical reason for your mind to block an erection during usual sexual activity. I can only recommend you find a woman who, after you tell her your issues, will sympathise with your problem, be patient, and help you overcome it.'

'How long will it take, Doctor?'

'I've no idea. Weeks, months or years. It's up to you and you alone.'

An unbidden thought that popped into his head made Kelvin grimace. *The girls will probably call me Zero Kelvin.*

6

KATE ENJOYED THE REST of the weekend with her parents, particularly the Sunday afternoon. The three of them had gone to the Dunstable Downs to have lunch at the Old Hunters restaurant at Whipsnade, and now they were standing at the top of a slope, watching paragliders and hang gliders taking off. Her father had recently treated a couple of youngsters with spinal injuries from paragliding, and the local paragliding club had asked him for advice on whether they should insist on waist support.

A young man walked over and said to her father, 'You're Doctor Mansoumi, unless I'm mistaken?'

'I am.'

'I'm Brad Roper, a member of the paragliding club committee and an instructor. I'm pleased to welcome you here.'

After introductions and handshakes all round – with Brad holding Kate's hand just a little longer than necessary and looking deeply into her eyes as he did – Amin said, 'I came to see a few landings, but it seems we came to the wrong place. We should be down at the bottom. The back injuries your committee mentioned happened on landing.'

Brad nodded. 'We can hike down from here. Follow me, and I'll tell you a few things as we walk.'

He took them to a path and led them down, speaking as they walked. 'Bad landings are usually because the pilot touches down on the slope while flying along it. We can fly only when the wind blows towards the slope to generate the uplift, so judging how far it will blow us towards the slope in the last landing phase is difficult. Another problem occurs when a chute yanks the pilot backwards because he hasn't kept the chute trimmed on takeoff, and he ends up landing on his backside when his chute pulls him backwards. Those injuries, though, are most often just a sore bum.'

Reaching the bottom of the slope, they watched several paragliders land, and then Brad pointed and said, 'There. That guy is too close to the slope. If there's a gust, he'll have a problem.'

They watched the pilot touch down clumsily, though he managed to avoid falling.

'Why didn't he turn into the wind?' Amin asked.

'You lose height when turning and swing outwards, so trying to turn into the wind would have actually made the situation even worse. Watch the guys up there.' Brad pointed into the sky above them. 'When they turn, it's like riding one of those funfair roundabouts: the body swings way outside the turn, and you go faster, and you can hit the ground at the wrong angle if you're going too fast. Look at that guy with the blue chute. He's an instructor, and it's a tandem jump. He has a passenger strapped to him. He'll turn into the wind, slow the chute much earlier, then land almost vertically, taking just a pace or two.'

The four of them watched the professional make a perfect landing and the elation of his passenger, who was punching the air and whooping in delight.

Amin remarked, 'Okay, I can see what's required. I think waist support will help. The only thing is, will it make it more difficult to do a takeoff run wearing a belt?'

'We must try one, and then adjust the design if necessary.'
Amin nodded.

Brad turned to Kate. 'If you'd like to try a tandem jump, I'll take you.'

'I would, but I don't think a skirt is the right kind of clothing.'

'That's not a problem. I'll give you an overall.'

'Okay.'

Twenty minutes later, Brad and a helper had laid out the chute and lines; he'd strapped on a harness and had a helper do the same for Kate, who'd changed into the overalls. They strapped on their helmets, which were fitted with tech to enable them to communicate while in the air. Then Brad snaplinked Kate in front of him, pulled the fastenings tight, and said, 'When I say run, run, keeping your legs as close together as you can. I'll run with my legs outside yours. When we land, lift both legs until we're down and stationary. You have a mike in the helmet to talk to me, and I can talk to you.'

Her heart beating hard with excitement, Kate ran a dozen steps before she felt herself lifted into the air. She felt her stomach drop as they rose from the earth, and the glider carried them silently away from the ground; the ground noises receded until she could hear nothing but an occasional car horn. Then Brad talked continuously, explaining what he was doing as they ascended on the rising airflow, and flew along the ridge. They did a wide U-turn, flying back along the slope to where they had taken off. Brad then turned away from the hill, and they descended, making towards the flat field.

Kate could sense the chute slowing as Brad said, 'Now I'm braking. Lift your legs. Touchdown!' He took a single, surefooted step forward as the parachute collapsed.

Kate felt elated, now understanding the delight of the tandem passenger she'd seen land earlier.

'That was marvellous! Thank you so much,' she said to Brad as he disconnected from her harness.

Walking back up to the top of the hill carrying the chute and harnesses, Brad said, 'I enjoyed that flight too. I'd like to know you better. Will you come to dinner with me next Saturday?'

'I'd like that,' Kate said, surprising herself. 'I live in Canary Wharf. We can meet in town, or I can go to my parents' house near Elstree.'

'Give me your number, and I'll message you once I've made a reservation.'

They met in Soho for dinner. Kate initially found Brad charming, but as the evening wore on, she wondered if he was just a bit too smooth. He told her he was a salesperson for a tool company, covering areas south of London, so he spent his week away from his apartment near Dunstable.

During that first dinner, he told her about the different paragliding sites he had flown. He said he took his paragliding gear in his car with him on his sales rounds, and when an opportunity to try a different venue arose, he took it.

He didn't ask to go home with her or suggest extending the dinner date into something more. But he did invite her to go paragliding with him that Sunday.

They did three tandem flights, during which Brad instructed her on how to control the wing in flight. She loved the feeling of being suspended in the air, and on the last flight, Brad made a spiral descent, and Kate felt the thrill of the whirling drop.

'A few more lessons and you'll fly solo,' Brad told her as they walked back up the hill. 'Can you join me again next Friday?'

'I'm sorry I can't, Brad. I'm going to Germany on business. I won't be back until the week after next. Call me then if you're in London.'

Kate had a successful trip to Germany, Austria and Switzerland. Back in her office in London, she was working on her monthly report when Brad called.

'How about dinner Thursday? Same place,' he suggested.

Kate's misgivings about Brad made her inclined to say no but she had fallen in love with paragliding, and worried that if she declined a date with him, he would refuse to take her on another flight.

'Eight o'clock?' she said.

'Great, see you then.'

Although Brad was pleasant, and Kate was interested when he talked about the development of paragliding and paramotoring, and the improvement in parachute technology spurred on by the sport and the paragliding association, she found herself increasingly turned off by Brad's unfortunate habit of bragging, and by how little interest he seemed to have in her life. By the end of the evening, she was wondering why he had invited her.

Brad's parting words at the end of the evening seemed to confirm her suspicion that he wasn't really that into her: 'I won't be here next weekend; I must go north. I'll call you the week after next.'

The following Saturday morning, Kate drove to her sister's house in Welwyn. She'd agreed to babysit Ava and William's two sons, aged seven and nine, for the weekend while their parents attended a conference in Brighton.

Ava met her at the door with an effusive welcome. 'You're a godsend!' she said, hugging Kate hard. Ava, the shorter of the two, had a close-cropped haircut that Kate thought made her look like her father, yet was likely more practical when peering into mouths. 'William will be down soon. We're ready to leave. Bobby and Richie are in the garden, probably squashing insects. They seem to be in the bloodthirsty stage.'

'What's the conference about?' Kate asked, dumping her overnight bag at the guest room doorway.

'New anaesthetics,' Ava said, then motioned to the kitchen. 'There's food in the fridge. The kids shouldn't give you any problems. When they finish destroying the insect life of Britain, they'll want to read or watch TV.'

The boys came into the house long enough to greet Auntie Kate and wave goodbye to their mom and dad, then rushed back into the garden. Watching them through the kitchen window, Kate rooted through the fridge and began preparing lunch.

After the boys had wolfed down the sandwiches she made, they opted to watch TV. She selected a book from her sister's collection and tried to read for a while, but found her concentration wandering. Weirdly, she felt lonelier in Ava's house with the two boys watching cartoons across the room than in her own flat, where she could look out the window and see boats on the Thames River and people in the square below strolling around or sitting at the tables in front of a restaurant or coffee shop.

Checking her sister's pantry, Kate found cake ingredients and spent a couple of hours mixing and baking two dozen chocolate cupcakes. When they came out of the oven, she mixed up three bowls of different-coloured icing, found a small jar of sprinkles, and persuaded the boys to join her.

'What are you doing, Bobby?' she asked, as the eldest boy, his tongue poking from a corner of his mouth in concentration, began work on a cupcake. 'Is that a picture you're painting on the cupcake?'

'Yes, Auntie Kate. I saw it on television. The green is the grass, the blue is the sky, and the yellow is the sun.'

'That's marvellous. What else will you do?'

'I'm gonna use the sprinkles to draw animals on the other cupcakes.'

'Rabbits and cats?'

'No, elephants and lions.'

'Did you see them at Whipsnade?'

'Yes, a long time ago.'

'Did you see seals?'

'They were funny. One of them played with a ball.'

'If you put some blue icing in the green, it would be a pool; then you could put a seal next to it.'

'Cool.'

Kate had an idea. 'How would you guys like to visit Whipsnade tomorrow?'

The suggestion loosed an immediate and noisy chorus of agreement.

'That would be great!'

'Yay! Can we see a lion eating something?'

'I don't know. We'll go tomorrow morning after breakfast and see.'

The morning walking around the animal pens kept Kate well and truly occupied: the two boys kept asking questions, and she kept having to answer. By lunchtime, they were tired, so they went to a burger-and-fries kiosk and ate at a table in the sunshine.

Watching the younger boy nodding off over his food, Kate decided to leave. In the car, the boys fell asleep immediately in the back seat. Kate remembered the child her father had talked about, injured when not strapped in; she looked at the boys and thought, *I'm in no hurry; I'll have a snooze, too, until they wake.*

Her forty winks produced a dream in which, suspended from a parachute wing, she glided along the Dunstable Downs. As she spiralled down in a whirling circle, she woke with Bobby shaking her arm.

'Auntie Kate, I need the toilet.'

The two boys, fully awake after digesting their burgers, recharging their batteries and visiting the public toilets, wanted to return to the animals, but Kate had another idea.

Dunstable is only two or three kilometres away. 'I'll take you to see flying people. Would you like that?'

'Really flying? Up in the sky, not in an aeroplane?'

'Yes, Bobby.'

'Then I want to see them.'

Fifteen minutes after leaving Whipsnade, on the top of the Dunstable Downs, Kate told the children, 'We'll sit here on the grass and watch.'

Five minutes later, a young woman wearing flight overalls walking past them stopped and said, 'Nice kids you have there.'

'They're not mine. They're my sister's.'

'Oh, that explains it.'

'Explains what?'

The woman looked momentarily embarrassed, then admitted, 'I saw you with Brad last Sunday. He never dates women with children.'

'Really?' Kate said. 'Why not?'

'You seem like a normal woman, taking care of kids, so I'll tell you. If you're the kind that likes what I mention, ignore me. Brad's a wild guy and doesn't like attachments. Has he proposed airborne sex yet?'

'What's that? Is it possible?'

The woman laughed. 'Oh, yes! He gives them a pair of overalls with a slit between the legs, tells them to wear no panties, and spears her just after takeoff. It gives a girl a huge orgasm. I loved that, but I hated what happened afterwards.'

Kate didn't want to hear any more. 'Well, I'll believe it when he suggests it.'

'He took off ten minutes ago with a blonde,' the woman said, clearly slightly miffed. 'She's probably having an orgasm right now.'

'Brad's here?'

'Yes, he came with her at midday. It's his second flight.'

The bastard told me he was away this weekend. Maybe I do want to hear more. 'Okay, tell me. What happens afterwards?'

'An invitation to continue the sex in his flat. After such a great orgasm, most girls would accept. And that's when the bad part happens.'

Kate had a sinking feeling. *Is Brad another Gavin?* 'Bondage and torture?'

The woman shook her head. 'He gave me a glass of water, which must have had a drug in it. A few minutes later, I discovered he shared the flat with another guy, who took Brad's place with me in the bed. I was so zonked out I could barely move, never mind express an opinion about what was happening.'

'So you were forced to have sex with the other guy?'

'Basically, yes. I couldn't resist because of the drug. And his mate was keen on anal sex. I hurt for weeks afterwards. I tell any of the girls I see with Brad, but he changes his hunting ground to other sites for months, so I don't know how many others he and his mate have hurt.'

'Thanks for telling me,' Kate said, feeling her face heat up with anger. She turned to the boys. 'Come on, Bobby, Richie. We must go. Mummy and Daddy will be home soon.'

When Brad called her a few days later, inviting her to dinner and paragliding, her answer was sharp. 'No, Brad, and don't call me again. I'm an ordinary woman not attracted to aerial orgasms, and I don't share a bed with more than one man at a time.'

7

KELVIN HADN'T BEEN IN CONTACT with Matilda during the time he'd spent with the psychologist, and he'd thought for a while before calling her now. In the end, he decided to do so because he wanted to play golf again, and remembered how much he'd enjoyed playing with her.

'Hello stranger,' she said coolly.

Kelvin cleared his throat and said, 'Yes, I'm sorry I haven't been in touch. My parents came back, and I've had lots to do. But I'm free this weekend. How about a game of golf?'

'Kelvin, you dropped me like a hot potato!' Matilda protested. 'You never called, so I looked around for someone else to play with. I'm sorry, because I enjoyed being with you. I have a new partner, so if I play, I play with him. I need someone I can rely on.'

'I understand, Matilda. I'm probably going to Egypt soon, so I'm pleased to hear you have someone to play with. If I see you at the club, I'll say hello.'

'Likewise, Kelvin. Thanks for calling. Bye.'

During the three years Kelvin had studied medicine, he had formed a firm friendship with a fellow student, Ahmed Badawi, who had come from Egypt for the same courses in London.

It had proved to be an enduring friendship too. Although Kelvin had changed his focus to pharmaceutical medicine and had earned a doctorate before becoming a wanderer in remote parts of the planet, he maintained contact with Ahmed, who had become a registered GP in England and practised in Guildford. Ahmed maintained close ties with his parents in Cairo and spent two summer months in Egypt each year.

Kelvin called him on his mobile phone that evening. The conversation began, as it always did, between two friends who knew that the whereabouts of the other were in doubt.

'Hello, Kelvin. Where are you?'

'At home with my parents. And you?'

'In Guildford, although I'm leaving in two weeks for Cairo.'

A little disappointed, Kelvin said. 'Then we must meet soon. I must talk to you. I'm free to meet any time. When can you make it?'

'How about Saturday, for dinner? Seven-thirty, at the Jeita?'

'I was going to ask if you would like to come to the club on Saturday afternoon, then have dinner with my parents and me, and spend the night.'

Ahmed sensed the urgency in Kelvin's voice, so replied, 'Can do. I close the surgery at twelve on Saturdays. I can meet you at the club at three.'

'Then that's a date, Ahmed.'

Kelvin spent the next three days in the British Museum. He was a registered researcher member and had access to the upper floors, where the museum stored the artefacts from ancient Egypt, and had visited frequently over the years.

Each morning, he drove his Porsche to Gatwick Airport, parked in the covered parking close to the station, took the Gatwick Express train to Victoria Station in London, and then hopped on the Tube to the museum.

His first task was to list all the known hieroglyphic symbols that referred to plants. Kelvin believed plants and minerals were ancient sources of the fluids used in mummification.

He was strolling around, viewing the artefacts, when a young woman came over and asked if she could help. Tall and slim, she looked unmistakably Egyptian; her face reminded him of a stone bust of Nefertiti.

Kelvin switched to Arabic. 'Possibly you can. I'm Kelvin Shareef. I want to learn what hieroglyphs could represent a plant or ingredient in medical treatment.'

The woman smiled, pleased. 'I'm Zahra Hamdy,' she said, offering her hand in greeting. As Kelvin shook it, she continued, 'A starting point might be one of the hieroglyph dictionaries. I'm not sure you will find many referring to plants or medicines – most of the hieroglyphs listed will be ones that describe historical events. Several dictionaries in the next room, compiled by different researchers, cover a long period.'

'Then that's where I'll start, thank you.' After a pause, Kelvin said, 'From your accent, I guess you are from Luxor. Why are you here and not in the Luxor museum?'

'I'm a part-time museum guide,' she explained. 'I was at the Luxor museum, but there were missing pieces in the history of the period I'm studying, so I came here to see if I could find them. The British Museum has the most extensive Egyptian artefact collection outside Cairo' She gave Kelvin an assessing look. 'You are Egyptian, but your accent reminds me of Cairo English,' she observed.

I thought it was better than that, thought Kelvin, and said, 'I was born here. My mother was born in Cairo, and so was my paternal grandfather. Can you show me where those dictionaries are?'

'Of course. Follow me.'

He did, admiring her walk as she led the way. *Maybe I can't get it up, but I still know what's worth looking at.*

Zahra left him at a table with an old leather-bound volume. Kelvin spent two hours working through the book, then broke for a quick lunch at the on-site pizzeria, after which he continued his studies until the museum closed. During that time, he found three relevant hieroglyphs. The first said, 'Unidentified plant, this glyph occurs in a list of products produced on a farm in the Saqqara region.' The second was similar, except the words 'in a garden' replaced 'on a farm'.

The third was the most exciting: 'Possible herb included in medical treatment for animal or man. It appears on a tablet discovered near Luxor.'

Kelvin scanned all three symbols into his laptop and added the notations and references.

Leaving the museum, he met Zahra at the door.

'Hello again, Kelvin. Have you had any success?'

'I have three references to look up and the other books to study. Are you here tomorrow?'

'Yes. I'll come at eleven when the museum opens.'

'Then can you show me the second book?'

'Of course.'

As they walked out together, Kelvin asked, 'Has anyone told you that you resemble a statue of Nefertiti?'

Zahra laughed. 'No. The usual pick-up line is Cleopatra.'

'It wasn't a pick-up line. I'll bring you a photo of the statue I've in mind tomorrow. You can tell me if you see a resemblance in the shape and bone structure.'

'Are you an expert in bone structure?'

Kelvin smiled. 'As much as any Batchelor of Medicine. I'm taking a taxi to Victoria. Can I offer you a lift if you're going that way?'

'I'm walking to Tottenham Court Station. I take the northern line, so thanks, but no.'

'Then I'll see you tomorrow. Bye, Zahra.'

'Bye, Kelvin.'

He didn't take a taxi; instead, wanting to stretch his legs, he walked to Holborn station and took the Underground. He had to change lines, but he knew it was faster in the rush hour, and he liked to catch the same train every evening if he had nothing else to do.

The following day Kelvin showed Zahra the photo of the Nefertiti bust, and she said, 'I can see a resemblance, so if it was a pick-up line, it's the first time any man has offered backup proof. But she's known as a beautiful woman, and I'm not.'

Kelvin chuckled. 'As beauty is in the eye of the beholder, I'm entitled to my opinion. Don't knock it.'

'I won't. I'll classify you as one more misguided man.'

Kelvin found two more references at the museum that day and two more on the third day. Satisfied with what he'd discovered so far, he closed the book he was working on and sought out Zahra.

'Would you like to join me for lunch at the Great Court restaurant?'

'I'd be glad for the break and the company,' she replied with a smile.

Once they'd found seats and ordered food, Kelvin remarked, 'Zahra, you're not wearing a ring, so I assume you aren't married?'

'No, I'm not – and, please, Kelvin, don't ask why not.'

'Okay, I won't. I know what it's like in Egypt, with parents arranging marriages. I'm surprised, that's all – a single girl from Luxor in London is unusual. Do you have a boyfriend here?'

51

'No, I live in a flat with another woman. She's younger than me, and I only met her three months ago,' Zahra said, making it clear to Kelvin that her flatmate wasn't a chaperone. 'And you? Are you married?'

Kelvin immediately joined the dots. *She's lesbian and left Luxor because there's little tolerance for gay people in Egypt outside Cairo.* 'No,' he said, with a wry smile. 'I've spent the last three years in remote places, like the Amazon jungle, so there hasn't been much chance of meeting the right girl. Anyway, I'd have to decide to settle before I can seriously think of a long-term relationship.'

'Hence the skilled pick-up line?'

'Not at all,' Kelvin said. 'A short-term relationship is too much of a handicap to my research project. If I felt desperate for sex, I'd pay for it. But I don't.'

'You're an interesting man, Kelvin. Are you coming to the museum next week?'

'I'll probably be here regularly for at least the next two to three weeks.'

'Then perhaps we can learn more about each other. I've only met one man I can share confidences with, and he's gay.'

Her words made Kelvin think she was lonely. 'Zahra, that alone makes me want to learn more about you.'

8

'HI KATE, I'M IN LONDON for three days from tomorrow.' It was Marylyn, calling from Coventry. 'If you don't have a LIL, can I stay with you?'

'What's a LIL?'

'A live-in lover.'

Kate heard Marylyn chuckle down the phone. 'I don't have a lover, live-in or not. It will be great to see you again.'

Marylyn arrived the next day carrying a thick folder. 'I have a present for you,' she said, handing it to her friend.

'What's in here?'

'Brochures on all the cruises found on the web, big, small, long and short, in dozens of countries, grouped by country. Instead of visiting pubs, we'll sort through them and discover what you might like. If the same brochure has activities in more than one country, there's a copy in each group.'

'Did you print all these out?'

Marylyn looked shocked. 'Where would I find the time? I asked a woman in the office who's making a real effort to find a partner to lend it to me. I must return the file to her once we're done.'

'Okay,' Kate said. 'I have our dinner ready to put in the oven. I'll do that, and you put your things in the guest room. Then, after we've eaten, we'll list those countries where at least half the population speaks Arabic.'

'Why only those?'

'My mother suggested that men of different nationalities won't remind me of Gavin, and I speak Arabic.'

'Your mother's smart, Kate. I agree.'

The two friends caught up while they ate the saffron chicken Kate had prepared.

'This is delicious, Kate. Is it one of your mother's recipes?'

'My grandmother's. My dad loves it like this.'

'I can understand why.' Taking a sip of wine, Marylyn changed the subject. 'Have you had no success in your man search?'

'No. Since we last met, I've met two guys. Harry was a soundtrack mixer, but it didn't work out.'

'Why? Was he gay?'

Kate looked surprised. 'No, I don't think so, although I did wonder. Why would you ask that?'

'Most of the older arty single guys are gay, Kate, haven't you noticed? I was playing the percentages.'

'Well, it wasn't that, or at least I don't think so,' Kate said. 'He was interesting and took me to several symphonies and operas. He talked knowledgeably about them, and we had a pleasant dinner each time. After a stressful week, spending a relaxing evening or two with him was pleasant. He was always polite, and I liked him. I now realise it was a comfortable relationship that suited me when I was tired. When he asked me to go home with him after one of those evenings, I thought I could have sex with him, but then, before the taxi even stopped, I realised he hadn't kissed me to that point. I didn't want sex with him that would be disappointing, so I said no. It pissed him off, so he never called again.'

'His loss, Kate,' Marylyn said, loyally. 'And the second?'

'A nasty piece of work. A real predator. After a couple of dates, I discovered he drugs women and then does a switcheroo on them, letting his flatmate have anal sex with them while they cannot react.'

'Somebody should report him to the police!' Marylyn said, her anger evident.

Kate nodded. 'Needless to say, those two recent experiences haven't helped me overcome my negative feelings about English men.'

'I don't blame you! Now, let's do something more cheerful and look at the cruise brochures.'

Compiling the lists took less time than they'd thought it would.

'That was easy,' Marylyn said. 'Only three countries in the file speak Arabic and have cruises. There may be others, but they don't advertise. Most of the Arabic-speaking countries are deserts. There's Azerbaijan with a cruise on the Caspian, Turkey with the coastal cruises on a gulet, and Egypt on the Nile. Which appeals to you the most?'

'What about the cruise duration? Isn't that important?'

Marylyn looked thoughtful. 'I reckon it takes a minimum of five to eight romantic meetings before I'm comfortable with a man. For a cruise, that would mean ten or more days. I say goodbye if I'm not happy enough to move him to the top slot after ten or twelve days. So it would help if you had a cruise between ten and twenty days. Let's see what's available in those three countries.' Running her finger down one of the lists, Marylyn continued, 'Azerbaijan only has three- to five-day cruises, so that's out, Kate.'

'The gulets are the same, Em, although they offer to include the return trip, so six to ten days.'

'That's not an option,' Marylyn pointed out: 'If you meet a man and he gets off after five days, it's a wasted trip. Scratch Turkey. Let's look at Egypt.'

'Most cruises are between Luxor and Aswan,' Kate observed. 'I suppose most tourists can't afford more time or money.'

'There's one here from Cairo to Aswan. It's fifteen days, with an option for an extra trip at the end to Abu Simbel. There may be other cruises, but they're infrequent.'

'What about the size of the ship?'

'Well, it can't be small,' Marylyn declared. 'Four cabins will mean you and a max of six others, making the chance of finding a reasonable single man near zero.'

Kate answered, 'Okay, how many passengers must there be for an over fifty per cent chance that one of them is a single man of the right age?'

'I haven't a clue, Kate, but I know someone who might.' Marylyn took her phone from her bag and looked through her contacts. 'Darryl ... Darryl ... Yes, there he is.'

'Who's he, Em?'

'The guy I told you about that I was crazy about two years ago. He's a mathematician and untiring in bed.'

'Why didn't you? Marry him, I mean.'

'Because he never asked, and I became tired of waiting. He always calculated the percentage chance of success before doing anything. When I told him he didn't need to wear a condom because I have a coil, he replied, "Maybe, but there's a twelve per cent chance that I'll catch an STD and a one per cent chance of a fallopian pregnancy."'

Kate laughed, and Marylyn laughed with her.

Kate asked, 'So did he wear a condom?'

'No. I guess the probability of enhanced pleasure was a hundred per cent!'

Marylyn tapped the call button and, within a few seconds, said, 'Darryl, it's Marylyn.' Then she tapped the 'speaker' button so Kate could hear the conversation too.

'It's long since I felt you, my love.'

Marylyn grinned. 'Darryl, my best friend Kate is with me, and

I've got you on speaker, so try to behave. You're letting our secrets out of the bag. You could have said "saw".'

'Well, it's a hundred per cent certain I saw you the last time I felt you. So "I felt you" conveys more information. Are you calling for a date?'

Kate grinned too as Marylyn said, 'Well, no, Darryl, something else, but if you want to invite me out again, I won't say no if you're ready to start where we left off.'

'You left off, my darling, not me. Where are you?'

'In London, I'll be in Newmarket for a week from Thursday evening if you want to call.'

'You can count on it. So, what's this call about?'

'We need an answer to a question. A boat has two-person cabins; how many cabins must the boat have for a more than fifty per cent chance that one of the passengers is a single male between twenty-seven and thirty-five?'

'How many boats?'

'Two sailing at intervals every two weeks.'

'At a rough guess, between forty and seventy cabins. I need to look up some data to give you a closer number. I'll call you back later. Are you going cruising to find another man?'

'No, not me. I don't need to go, as you're going to marry me. It's for Kate.'

'I said call, not marry, dear heart.'

'Means the same thing to me, darling. I'll be waiting for you to call with that number. Bye.'

Once Marylyn had disconnected the call, Kate laughed and said, 'You are shocking, you know.'

Marylyn shrugged. 'Well, he never asked before. Now he knows I want to marry him, and either he asks me or I throw him out again. I hope he asks. He's a lovely character.'

Getting back to the business at hand, Kate said, 'Well, we have a number – say, around fifty to sixty double cabins. That's two busloads if everyone goes on a land tour.'

'And that's if the cruises are full. I expect that in the hot months, they won't be. When do you want to go?'

'I don't mind the heat, and it will be easier between June and September – that's a slack season for advertising our products. The way I feel, the sooner, the better.'

Nodding, Marylyn said, 'Okay, let's send an email request to every tour agency mentioned in the Egypt file. Many will take the lazy way out and email back a brochure, but at least one will try to meet your exact requirements.'

While the women were jotting down those requirements, Marylyn's phone rang. It was Darryl. She answered and put it on speakerphone again, so Kate could hear.

'Hi, my darling. This will cost you.'

'How much, sweetheart?'

'Thursday evening, can you come directly to my apartment? I have a booking at our favourite restaurant. I mentioned your name and Carlos gave me a table.'

'It's a deal. So what's the answer?'

'Over fifty per cent if there are over one hundred and one passengers.'

'Thanks, darling.'

'Anything for you, love. I've missed you.'

Marylyn said goodbye and disconnected the call, and she and Kate beamed at each other.

Grinning, Kate said, 'I want to be a bridesmaid!'

'No counting chickens before they've hatched,' Marylyn said, laughing. 'Getting Darryl to sign and seal the contract might be difficult, no matter how often he says "darling" or "love".'

9

THAT WEEKEND, AHMED ARRIVED on schedule at the club. The two men embraced like brothers.

'Ahmed, you're looking good! Very fit.'

'You too, Kelvin; I haven't seen you look as fit for some time.'

'I had an accident in New York, so I've been exercising recently to get back into tiptop shape.'

'Then stay that way. It makes you look younger. What happened?'

'I'll tell you later. Why are you going to Cairo so early? I expected you to go in two months, like you do every year.'

'My parents have written to me and enclosed a photo, saying they have arranged a potential marriage with a young woman, and I must go and meet her. I shall say no to the arrangement, but refusing to go at all would put my mother in a difficult situation.' Ahmed frowned. 'I must admit that I failed to tell my parents I don't intend to marry for another three to five years.'

Kelvin shook his head. 'I thank the gods that my parents won't subject me to the trials and tribulations of an arranged marriage. So how do you intend to wriggle out of it?'

'I'm not sure, but first, I shall insist on talking to the chosen one without a chaperone. If she has any modern ideas, she might reveal that her parents are coercing her, and then it will be easy to say she's incompatible. She's twenty, so I can also say she's too young. Or, if her English is poor, I can claim she won't be happy in England.'

'Well, better you than me. I'm too soft-hearted, although I have an iron-clad solution if it happened to me.'

'Tell me, please! Maybe I can use it.'

'I'll tell you later. We must go and meet my parents. They're expecting us for tea.'

Layla's hamam mahshi, a dish of stuffed roast pigeons, was delicious – Ahmed and Kelvin ate with pleasure while Layla questioned Kelvin about what he'd been doing at the British Museum.

'Trying to find the plants the Egyptian doctors used for mummification.'

'I thought they used various oils.'

'They did, but the oils had to be plant-based, like dates or palms, and they must have used other herbs. I received the analyses of some mummification liquids from Brown University.'

'Show them to me,' Darius broke in. 'I might be able to tell you where the plants would have grown from the elements in the liquids.'

Then it was Ahmed's turn – Layla quizzed him about his practice before moving on to a familiar theme. 'Well, Ahmed, you're now old enough with an established practice – it's about time you found a wife.'

Kelvin glanced at his mother – was that a sideways shot at him? – and then grinned at Ahmed's deft reply.

'Not quite yet, Layla. If I could find a woman who can cook hamam mahshi like you, I would propose immediately, but I think another three years as a bachelor will allow me to buy a nice house and a second car, so any woman I bring home will not be disappointed. I plan to have four bedrooms because I want at least two children.'

'Then I'll call your mother and tell her that the only hope she has of grandchildren is if she finds a girl who can cook hamam mahshi,' Layla declared.

'Please don't!' Ahmed said, holding out his hands beseechingly. 'I would have to eat hamam mahshi cooked by a different girl every night until I developed a complex and ran away screaming because the girls looked like they had two roast pigeons instead of breasts!'

It brought hilarious laughter from all of them.

After dinner, Kelvin and Ahmed sat companionably in the solarium, sipping coffee.

'I have something personal to tell you,' Kelvin said. Ahmed looked at him, concerned, and he continued, 'I have some sort of psychological problem.'

'Have you seen a shrink?' Ahmed asked.

'Yes, and he was helpful to an extent, but now it's up to me to deal with it.'

'Tell me about it.'

Kelvin told Ahmed about the escort and the accident, then said, 'I thought I was dying and that I would go to hell without a dick.'

'Yeah, I can imagine that – super traumatic. So are you okay physically?'

'I am, but I have erectile dysfunction, and unless you can suggest something different, the shrink said I must find a woman to help me overcome the fear of losing my dick.'

'That's a tough one. Such a woman might exist, but finding one is nigh impossible. Won't the problem wear off?'

'He said it might. But it might take years.'

Ahmed put his coffee on the glass table and clapped both hands on his knees, a decisive gesture. 'Kelvin, you need a change of scenery!' he declared. 'English speakers must remind you of America, where your accident happened. I'm going to Cairo in two weeks. Why don't you come with me? I'll find you a job as a doctor on a cruise ship, just as I do. A four- or five-day cruise on the Nile, all expenses paid, where you can screw every tourist chick who asks, will do you a world of good. Many speak other languages.'

'I don't think I could work up an erection in four or five days,' Kelvin said miserably.

'There are longer cruises – Cairo to Aswan and back takes a month. You would also visit all the ancient sites along the Nile, and you could check out the hieroglyphics. You could photograph every patch of glyphs and then study them in your cabin at leisure. The passengers rarely get more than a headache or diarrhoea, and the boat will carry medicine for those.'

'Then why do they need a doctor?'

'Many of the passengers are older and retired. There are cabins for seniors and the mobility challenged, although we are more direct in Egypt and say "physically handicapped". Having a doctor on board provides a carrot for the wealthy passengers the cruise line would like to attract, because it means the insurance premiums they have to pay for travel cover are a bit lower.'

'Okay, Ahmed, when you reach Cairo, go ahead and investigate, and mail me if there's a trip I could do. In the meantime, I'll finish my research here.'

Kelvin was back in the museum on Monday, and by the end of the week, he had eighteen glyph pictures filed on his computer and decided to refer to the references.

His relationship with Zahra had also progressed. Each day at lunch or tea, they revealed more about their pasts to each other.

For Zahra, Kelvin's stories about travels in the eastern Amazon were fascinating. Meanwhile, Kelvin absorbed an intimate peek into how little some Egyptian families had changed in the last century. Women went into the world outside their house twice in a lifetime, the first time when they got married and moved to their husband's house – it was the occasion for a long, winding tour of their home city, could take several hours – and the second time in a coffin.

Finally, on Friday, he found the courage to ask a personal question. 'Zahra, are you lesbian?'

'I wondered when you would ask that, Kelvin. The answer is no. I like men, and I don't like women in that way. I suppose it's because I told you I share an apartment with a woman?'

'Well, certainly, that seemed suggestive. But what do you mean "in that way" do you mean sex?'

'No, I meant in the sense of wanting to be with someone all the time. Call it love if you want, although I didn't mean something that profound. I've never had a sexual experience with a woman, and I don't dare to with a man – it frightens me.'

Kelvin felt it only fair to reveal something about himself in return for Zahra's honesty. 'Zahra, replace man with woman and woman with man in what you've just said, and you have what I would say.'

Zahra replied, 'I want to know why, but if you tell me, I must tell you, and I don't know if I can.'

'I have the same thoughts,' Kelvin said, then decided to leave the troubling subject. 'I'll see you again on Monday. I want to find out where I can see my listed references. Here, Cairo, or other museums in the world. How would I do that?'

'There is a catalogue of references in the library. You can search for them.'

'Thanks, I'll do that next week.'

That evening, a few minutes before James announced that dinner was ready for him and his grandfather – Layla and Darius had gone out – Kelvin's phone rang. Looking at the caller's name, he answered, 'Hello, Matilda! This is a surprise.'

'I know, Kelvin. It's taken me all afternoon to build up the courage to call. Are you free to play golf with me this weekend?'

'What happened to the guy you were playing with?'

Kelvin heard Matilda sigh. 'He got what he wanted and has struck me off his list.'

'The guy's an idiot,' Kelvin told her. 'I'll call the club in the morning and make a booking. Is any time okay for you?'

'Yes.'

'And Matilda, I just want to mention that I'll be going to Cairo in a few weeks and staying there for about two months, so please don't accuse me of dropping you when I go.'

Matilda chuckled. 'Okay, I promise I won't.'

'Do you want to do a show tomorrow night, like the last time?'

'That's a great idea.'

'How about *Matilda the Musical*?'

'Isn't that for kids?'

'I suggested it because it has your name, but if you'd prefer *Pretty Woman* or *Moulin Rouge*, I'm happy with them too.'

'Go for *Pretty Woman*, Kelvin. The Matilda in the book is nothing like me.'

Kelvin stopped in front of Matilda's apartment at eleven-thirty that night. They were both in a good mood – although Matilda had beaten Kelvin on the course by one stroke ('You have to practise more, Kelvin,' she'd teased him), they'd both enjoyed the dinner they'd eaten together and the show afterwards.

Matilda's kiss this time was as passionate as the last time. When they broke apart, she said, 'I won't invite you in. I don't know how long it will be before I invite a man in again.'

'I understand,' Kelvin said. 'Don't let it worry you. I don't think I would be much good, anyway. Since my accident, I've not been to bed with a woman.'

'Not once?'

'Not once.'

'Is it a physical problem?'

'The doctor says not,' Kelvin said, then briefly outlined what the psychologist had told him. 'So, you see, I feel sure that if I did go to bed with you, and it didn't work, you'd be disappointed and think I didn't find you attractive, which isn't the case. And I'd prefer our relationship to continue instead of you breaking it off.'

Matilda nodded her understanding. 'As long as I know where I stand, Kelvin. I'll see you next Saturday.'

On Monday, Kelvin confessed his problem once again, telling Zahra at lunch about his erectile dysfunction. *My doctor said I must find a woman to help.*

'Thanks for telling me, Kelvin. I appreciate it. Now it's my turn to confess. My parents arranged a marriage with a young man.

I didn't know him, and when I met him for the first time in my parents' home, I felt something was wrong with him. For a young woman with no experience of men, I had no idea what it was. When he came again, I declined when he proposed marriage. My parents were furious, but I didn't want him, although I couldn't say why.

'Three days later, the usual taxi I took from the Luxor Museum to my home was not waiting for me, but another cab was. The driver told me that my regular driver was sick. I suspected nothing, but when I got into the vehicle, he locked all the doors and drove me to a strange house, where he entered a garage. The roller doors closed behind us. I was terrified.

'Then a man came into the garage, and I realised what was going on: it was the man whose marriage proposal I had declined. He opened the car door, pulled me out and dragged me into a room, and although I fought, he hit and raped me.'

Kelvin covered his mouth in horror. 'That's terrible, Zahra! How did you get away? Did you go to the police?'

'Afterwards, he just threw me out of the house onto the street. I stopped a passing taxi and asked the driver to take me to the police, and I laid a complaint. The police did nothing, and my parents wouldn't speak to me, as they now had a despoiled daughter. Nothing happened to the man who raped me. The only thing left for me was to leave Egypt, so I came to England.'

'I know that kind of thing happens, Zahra, but I never expected to meet a woman who had experienced it. I'm not surprised you fear men! Probably, that young man believed women should obey a man's every request, and refusing marriage was justification for punishing you. He would have done it to re-establish his self-esteem after rejection.'

Kelvin reached across the table and gently laid his hand on Zahra's. 'Not all men are like that,' he said. 'If you can find a man who respects a woman's rights and will love you, I'm sure you will eventually lose the fear, if not of all men, then at least of the ones you learn are gentle and respectful, and you will eventually come to love someone.'

'Thanks for understanding, Kelvin. Now, may I ask you a favour? I've thought about it all weekend.' When he nodded, she continued, 'Although I'm technically not a virgin, I've never kissed a man. I want to know what it's like. My flatmate has night school on Mondays, Thursdays and Fridays. Come home with me on one of those nights.'

'Zahra, being a virgin doesn't matter in most of the world, but if the favour you want from me is a kiss, I'd be only too happy to grant it.'

10

WITHIN A WEEK, Kate had received fourteen replies. Nine had appended brochures; five said they would investigate and asked if they should include airfares to and from Egypt. She replied yes, and added, 'Business class, and all land tours on offer with a private guide.'

She chose a cruise, then booked and paid for it. Her flight to Egypt was in three weeks.

That Thursday, after work, Kelvin accompanied Zahra back to her home, the pair taking the northern line to Woodside Park in North Finchley.

Zahra had an apartment in Beecholme Court. Kelvin looked around curiously at the sparsely furnished living area, he felt it told him nothing about the woman who lived there: none of the furniture or decorations gave a clue as to who she really was.

He put his bag on the floor as Zahra put hers down and turned to him.

'How do we start?' she asked.

Surprised, Kelvin hesitated, then said, 'Come here and let me hold you.'

She stepped forward, and he put his arms around her. She felt rigid, so he gently rubbed her back. After a minute or two, he felt her relax and he said, 'Now, look up at me.'

She did, and he looked deeply back into her eyes, and smiled.

When she smiled back, he bent forward and placed his lips gently on hers. She remained unresponsive for a few moments, then Kelvin felt her stiffness begin to melt away. Her lips softened as he parted them with a slight tease of his tongue, and he felt her press against him.

The kiss lasted for about a minute before Zahra broke away, saying, 'Kelvin, you're too tall for me. I'll get a crick in the neck. Come.'

She led him to her bedroom. Whether it was the dark red drapes with patterns he recognised as Egyptian, the decorations – a small sphinx, a blue scarab and a photo of the temple of Karnak in Luxor – or the scent of frankincense from an incense burner, he didn't know, but Kelvin felt immediately at home.

Zahra sat on the bed and patted the duvet next to her. Kelvin sat beside her.

'You're still too tall,' she said. 'Lie down.'

Kicking off his shoes, he lay back. She did the same and lay beside him, facing him. This time, the kiss lasted longer, and Zahra responded immediately. Kelvin gently caressed her neck, shoulders and back while their lips explored each other.

Breaking away and staring into Kelvin's eyes, Zahra said, 'It feels marvellous when you caress me.'

'It would feel better if we were undressed,' Kelvin said. Quickly, they undressed each other, and then Kelvin kissed Zahra's naked neck and shoulders. She arched her back, then kissed him similarly. A few minutes later, his tongue circled a nipple, and when he took it between his lips, she squealed, 'Oh god, it's too much.'

Kelvin's caresses grew more and more intimate, until Zahra let out a guttural groan and fell away from his searching fingers.

Lying quietly, the two waited for Zahra's heartbeat to return to normal.

Smiling at Kelvin, Zahra said, 'I had an orgasm, but I don't think you even had an erection?'

Kelvin shook his head. 'But you know it's not because of you. You are beautiful and warm,' he reassured her. Then he kissed her again, and she kissed back.

Kelvin slowly made his way down the length of her torso, kissing and teasing her skin with his tongue, and then buried his head in her groin.

She tried to push his head away, but the immense pleasure running through her body swamped her shyness, and she lay back and let herself go. 'Oh God, yes, yes!'

Later, quiet again, Zahra gently caressed Kelvin's flaccid penis and said, 'I think it did grow a bit, Kelvin.'

'I think so too, Zahra. We're helping each other.'

On Monday evening, Kelvin went home with Zahra after work again. An hour after they reached her apartment, she was lying relaxed in his arms, and Kelvin felt he should encourage her to look for a man who could do more to help her than he could. *I feel inadequate, and it will worsen when I sense I can't give her what she needs. And she needs a man who will stay beside her, not a planetary wanderer.*

'Zahra, now you know what making love is like, you should look for another man. I'm not the man for you.'

'Why not, Kelvin?'

'Unless I recover, I can't have sex, and during my medical studies, I've learnt that when young people marry, the thing that keeps their marriage working is mutual satisfaction in bed. It may be unnecessary years later, when a couple knows each other intimately, but until then, sex is the release that demonstrates they can overcome differences. If we stay together, and we cannot forgive those differences, we will first begin to dislike each other and then must separate, so we must stop now.'

Zahra nodded her understanding sadly. 'Will you come on Thursday then, for a last time?'

'Of course,' Kelvin said. 'In the meantime, Zahra, I've been thinking: before your mother brought that man home to propose marriage, did you and girlfriends talk much about men and marriage?'

'Of course, Kelvin, but they had no more experience of men than I had. We knew nothing about men. We had never even talked to men outside our immediate families.'

'Perhaps half your problem is not knowing those things. You could try to make friends with a young woman who can tell you all about dating in England.'

'Can't you tell me?'

'I'm a man. I don't know how a woman chooses a date. The best I could do is tell you of my experiences before my accident.'

'Then please do. I'm sure it will help.'

'Okay, then, I'll tell you what: I'll take you to dinner on Thursday, and we can chat. Then we can keep each other's numbers, and if you are in the dumps one day, you can phone me for a shoulder to lean on, and I can do the same with you.'

'Thanks, Kelvin. You know, you're a genuinely nice guy.'

Kelvin booked at the Ali Baba restaurant; he was sure Zahra would like it. He had been there several times and was friends with the Egyptian family who ran it. The decorations reminded him of small Cairo restaurants.

Zahra arrived looking elegant; she had changed at the museum and left her day clothes in a locker.

'You're looking beautiful, Zahra.'

Zahra adored the restaurant, as Kelvin had thought she would, and they both ordered typical Egyptian dishes.

While they waited for their food to arrive, Zahra said, 'Tell me about your experiences, Kelvin.'

'I don't know what might help, Zahra. Many times I've asked a woman for her phone number or invited her to a show or dinner, then found that she wasn't interested in me.'

'So, tell me what they said.'

'Different things, like, "I'm getting married in ten days," or "I can't, I'm married and have a husband and four kids to look after." I even had one who said, "I don't go out with men; I'm HIV positive."'

Zahra laughed, 'I can believe those would be a turnoff.'

Their order arrived, and they tucked in. After they'd cleared their plates, Kelvin said, 'Then try this one, Zahra; it happened to me once. The woman said, "I'd like to because you're interesting, but it's a waste of time; I only feel passionate when a man has a beard!"' Zahra giggled and Kelvin continued, 'I'll try and remember ones that might help. Some women I met were shy, but others were quite open. One early one was during the tea break at a pharmaceutical conference. I had spotted a young woman talking to two men, and although I wanted to, I didn't butt in, but I did keep looking at her for an opportunity. It was a surprise when she broke away from them and came directly to me and said, "I can tell you want to talk to me. I'm Martha Kevenny. Who are you, and why are you here?"'

Zahra exclaimed, 'My god! I could never do that.'

'Perhaps not, Zahra, but I asked her why she did later in the evening.'

72

'And what did she say? That she thought you were sexy?'

'No, she said, "It's a professional conference, so I assumed you were intelligent and educated. You looked at me several times, so I knew you were interested, and then I checked the items on my list." I asked, "What list?" and she said, "You're clean-shaven, with neat hair, so you look after yourself; your suntan shows that you exercise outdoors, and your clothes look new and clean. No piercings or earrings show self-confidence. Your socks are not garishly coloured, so you're not a hidden exhibitionist, and your watch looks expensive. And when I asked for your card, you gave it to me without hesitation."'

'Why was giving you the card without hesitation important?'

'I asked her that very question, and she said, "You didn't hunt around in your wallet for the card that would impress me the most." Then I asked her to dinner, and she refused. She said, "I shall look you up on LinkedIn and the professional associations, and if you've told me the truth and I'm interested, I'll call you."'

'That's incredible.'

Kelvin nodded and continued, 'And she said, "But I'll be fair: you can check me out if you wish. Here's my card." It didn't have her home address, but I'm a researcher and did my homework. She phoned a few days later, and we went to dinner. The first time she asked, "Did you check me out?" I told her everything I knew and asked, "Is that important?" She replied, "If you hadn't, this would have been our only dinner."'

'So you had a long relationship?'

'Well, it only lasted three months because I had exploring to do.'

'And what was it like in the bedroom?'

'It was two months before she asked me to go home with her. She said, "Kelvin, if you had asked me to sleep with you, our relationship would have ended, but I'm ready to find out if we fit."

So, Zahra, you don't have to accept an invitation for sex; you can wait until you're sure and take the lead.'

As Kelvin left her on her doorstep, with a friendly kiss on the cheek, Zahra said, 'Kelvin, I'll never be able to thank you enough. I'll never call unless I need help, but I'll accept your call any time.'

The next day, Kelvin beat Matilda at their golf game, then took her to dinner and a show, during which he told her his Egypt plans had firmed up.

When he dropped her at home, she said, 'Kelvin, I know you can't get hard, but I enjoy kissing you. Come inside and spend the night, and we'll cuddle. Then you can remember a girl who doesn't mind.'

Kelvin, who was genuinely fond of Matilda, was happy to acquiesce. Matilda knew what she wanted, and he did his best to make her happy. She caressed him as much as he did her, and when they fell asleep in each other's arms two hours later, he began to think that perhaps going to Egypt was unnecessary. He would have stayed if he didn't have to visit the Cairo Museum.

When he left her in the morning, Matilda said, 'Kelvin, last night was fantastic, even without the cherry on top. If you overcome your problem, you will be a fantastic lover. I won't wait for you, but when you return, call me. If I'm unattached, you have a place in my bed, erectile dysfunction or not.'

'Thanks, Matilda.'

It made Kelvin feel much better. *I'll go to Egypt immediately; if nothing pans out, I have a reason to return.*

Back at his home, he called Ahmed.

'Hi Kelvin, what's up?'

'I'll go to Egypt the first opportunity I have.'

'I'll ask the cruise agent if he's found a place for you. I'm leaving for Cairo tomorrow.'

11

AHMED CALLED FROM CAIRO two days later and gave him all the details. Kelvin wasted no time contacting Pharaoh Tours, the agent.

'Good morning, Doctor Shareef here. My colleague, Dr Ahmed Badawi, has told me you have a vacancy for a doctor on a Cairo to Aswan Cruise?'

'Indeed we do, Doctor. I'm pleased you've called,' was the response. 'Can you come to our offices in Cairo two or three days before the cruise? I have two departure dates vacant. I'll message you our address and the cruise dates. The vacancy is for both the outward and return legs. Please let me know the one that suits you.'

Arriving in the Egyptian capital two days later, Kelvin took the Ramses Hilton hotel bus. The following morning, after breakfast, he took a taxi to the cruise agent's office. They were expecting him, and an hour later, he learnt the boat would arrive from Aswan in three days at a pier beside the Nile corniche at the Sixth of October Bridge.

The office manager asked him to board the vessel at midday to meet the captain after the arriving passengers had departed and before the new passengers boarded that evening. He gave Kelvin an itinerary, the passenger list with their detailed booking forms, which included medical requirements, and a deck and cabin plan.

Kelvin signed on for one return trip, with a requirement to give two weeks' notice if he wanted to do another.

After returning to his hotel, Kelvin looked eagerly at the passenger list. He found three bookings that interested him – two for women passengers travelling together and one for a single woman.

He checked their booking forms. One couple – fifty-eight and sixty years old – with different surnames had both ticked 'Miss', so he thought they were a pair of maiden aunts. He concluded the other two, where both surnames were the same, were mother and daughter, as the age difference was twenty-three years.

The single woman was his age. The form revealed her English nationality and occupation as a marketing director, but her name intrigued Kelvin: 'Kathleen' was decidedly English, but 'Mansoumi' was not. He looked up the surname and found it was likely Iranian. He wondered if Kathleen could be a nickname. Her passport-size photo showed an attractive face framed by dark hair.

Kelvin called Ahmed.

'Hello, Kelvin. Have you arrived?'

'Yes, Ahmed. I've little to do for the five days before the boat leaves except meet the passengers and crew three days from now. But I must tell you that I'm disappointed.'

'Why?'

'I've been through the passenger list. There are only two single women, one ten years older than me and travelling with her mother. The other is my age, but she's English; you promised me someone exotic.'

'The luck of the draw, Kelvin. After you see her, if you're interested, buy an Egyptian evening dress and accessories in her size. She may be shy, and you have limited time; it might get you started. I know how the cruise works: the passengers will spend three days visiting the pyramids and the sights of Cairo, so you'll have the time to buy the dress on the first day. Leave the clothes on her bed. If you need help, the attendant assigned to her cabin will be able to tell you the right size and recommend a shop.'

'Isn't that like taking the bull by the horns?'

'Of course. You have only two weeks to cement a relationship. Start moving.'

'Okay,' Kelvin said, then swapped the focus to his friend's love life. 'How's your bride?'

'Not a bad choice, Kelvin. Her name's Ameena. I've only met her once formally, so I know little about her other than what my mother has told me, but from what I've seen, she's worth investigating. Mother tells me she's a qualified nurse.'

'Sounds promising, Ahmed.'

'And how's work going?'

'Coming along,' Kelvin said. 'I need to go to the Cairo museum to compare our itinerary with ruins where there are hiero-glyphics.'

Bidding his friend goodbye and ending the call, Kelvin examined the ship's deck plan. It showed fifty-two cabins across four decks. Kelvin located his accommodation: he had one of the large forward cabins on the reception deck, which also served as a doctor's surgery. And fate had intervened: Kathleen had a cabin two doors aft of his.

On the assumption that if he called as a researcher from the British Museum, it would ensure his status, Kelvin had twice phoned the Cairo Museum the previous week, telling them what he was looking for, and had received assurance of a welcome.

Dr Moustapha Hassan was as good as his word: 'Dr Shareef,

it's a great pleasure to meet you,' he said in Arabic when Kelvin arrived.

'Likewise, Dr Hassan. It's good to be back in Egypt.'

'I've got good news for you,' Dr Hassan continued. 'I've traced all thirteen references you sent me. Seven are here; I have a museum map showing where they are. Four are in the Luxor Museum, and two are in Aswan.'

Kelvin knew that the size of the Cairo Museum was 13 000 square metres, and to find anything needed catalogues and maps. 'Is there still no date for the new museum's opening?'

Work on the Grand Egyptian Museum sited a few kilometres from the country's greatest monuments and the only remaining wonder of the ancient world, the Pyramids of Giza, had begun in 2005, but its completion had been repeatedly delayed, first by the Arab Spring in 2011 and more recently by the Covid pandemic. When it finally opened to the public, it would be the most extensive archaeological museum complex in the world and host to more than 100 000 artefacts – including, for the first time, King Tutankhamen's entire treasure collection on display.

'I'm afraid not,' Dr Hassan said. 'We live in constant anticipation, for all the most spectacular items have already been moved there. However, everything you want is here. What else can I help you with?'

'I'm taking a boat ride up the Nile, something I haven't done before, and I'll visit any accessible historical sites during the cruise. Would you have a list of them?'

Dr Hassan nodded. 'I can email you a copy of the historian's guide to the Nile.'

'Can I buy the book?'

'No, it's out of print, but we have a scan of it in the library.'

'That will be a great help.'

'How long do you have?'

'The boat leaves in five days, but I can visit again after it returns.'

'Then keep the map of the museum, and I'll leave you to look for your references. Here's your researcher's pass; it will allow you to take photographs, but of course without artificial lighting or flash.'

'Of course. Thank you.'

Kelvin checked out of his hotel three days later and took a taxi to the pier with his suitcase and Gladstone bag. The Gladstone – the badge of an English GP – immediately identified him as the doctor to a crew member, who came to collect his suitcase.

The first officer met him at the entrance. 'Dr Shareef. Welcome aboard. I'm First Officer Youssef. I'll show you to your cabin, and Captain Galal will meet you in a few minutes. Boarding times are busy.'

Kelvin had finished hanging up his clothes, checked out the examination couch to one side, and inventoried the medicine cupboard, when he heard a knock on the door. It was the captain, wearing an impeccably tailored white uniform with shoulder stripes. He was dark-haired, tall and lean, with a neatly trimmed Egyptian moustache. 'Welcome aboard, Dr Shareef.'

Kelvin shook hands as the captain continued.

'If there's anything you need, please let me know. The passengers are due to board for lunch from twelve-thirty, although some will come later. If you would like to join me and the officers in reception, you'll have a chance to meet them. You are free for the next two days. We sail early the day after, so I recommend you stay the night on board.'

'I'll be here, Captain. I've checked out of my hotel. I'll visit a pharmacy this afternoon. I may need some items I haven't seen in the medical cupboard.'

'I'm surprised. The stock list should be complete.'

'It is, Captain, but one of the couples on the passenger list is young; on her booking form, the wife says she's three months pregnant. I need to buy some items in case of complications.'

'I never noticed. Thank you for mentioning it, Doctor.'

'Captain, each of us has an area of responsibility. I would be a poor doctor if I didn't look. Several aged passengers have listed medicines they take routinely. I know why they take them and will alter any treatment accordingly.'

The captain nodded his understanding. 'This is a small boat, where all the crew participate in keeping the passengers happy,' he agreed.

'There is one thing, though,' Kelvin added. 'I may need the assistance of a woman. I want to know I can call her if I must treat a woman and her husband objects to her being with me alone or if a female patient needs help to undress.'

'I'm reassured, Doctor. There is indeed a female crew member assigned to the cabins here. I'll tell the first officer to introduce you to her.'

Fifteen minutes later, the first officer arrived, accompanied by a woman wearing a yellow dress with white cuffs. Her name tag had the annotation 'Cabin Service' underneath it. Kelvin thought she was about forty, dark-haired, with what he thought of as a friendly face with laugh lines. The first officer introduced her to Kelvin as Neith.

Kelvin explained to Neith why he may occasionally call on her services, and she responded, 'I'll be happy to help, Doctor.'

'Then I've another service to ask,' Kelvin said. 'A young woman has booked into cabin 216. A friend thinks she's shy and has suggested I give her an Egyptian evening dress to wear as a surprise. After she arrives, can you check her dress and shoe size, and tell me where to buy a suitable outfit?'

'Of course, Doctor. I shall check as soon as possible.'

As the passengers arrived during the afternoon, the first officer collected their passports for safekeeping, then a crew member showed them to their cabins.

Kelvin was there to greet them, too, in his official capacity as the ship's doctor. He welcomed most of the passengers in English, but those who had ticked Arabic as one of their languages, he greeted in Arabic. This included Kate who, Kelvin noted, was as pretty in the flesh as she looked in her passport photograph. *She's tall, a metre eighty-four in heels.*

Kate looked at him in surprise and answered in Arabic. 'Pleased to meet you, Doctor, but how do you know I speak Arabic?'

Kelvin's broad smile, and his grey eyes twinkling in amusement, charmed her. She smiled in return, her emerald-green eyes sparkling, when he said, 'Your Iranian surname would be enough for me to assume you spoke Arabic, but I must admit that I read the passengers' answers to the booking form questionnaire.'

She laughed, said, 'Mystery solved,' and moved forward to the first officer as Kelvin turned to greet the young couple behind her.

Later, most passengers, including Kate, left for a tour of Cairo's Khan Al-Khalili, the city's biggest bazaar market. Only a few passengers stayed on board.

Kelvin visited a nearby pharmacy to buy pills for pregnancy-induced morning sickness, then found the dress shop that Neith had recommended to him, at the same time as she'd discreetly handed him a slip of paper noting Kate's dress and shoe sizes.

The salesperson asked for the colour of Kate's eyes and hair, and selected a dress accordingly.

When she returned to her cabin, Kate found a folded piece of paper on her bed with 'Kate' written on it. She opened it and read, 'Look in the cupboard. I hope it fits.' It was unsigned.

She tried on the gloriously embroidered deep red dress and the shoes with rhinestone buckles, then, holding the beaded handbag, she looked in the mirror. *That's not Kate. I don't know who it is, but she's beautiful.*

She took a selfie and sent it to Marylyn, then called her.

'Hello, Kate. Are you on board?'

'Yes, and I've found your present.'

'What present?'

'Have you looked at your WhatsApp?'

'No, hang on a moment. Yes, I see the photo. You look stunning. But what's the present?'

'The dress, shoes and handbag.'

'They're not from me, Kate. I wouldn't know where to buy those clothes. You must have a secret admirer. Was there a note?'

'Yes, it just says, "I hope it fits". In English.'

'Well, then you have a secret admirer and a mystery to solve,' Marylyn laughed. 'I think you're off to a smashing start. Wear the dress and see who's pleased.'

'Thanks, Em.'

12

THAT EVENING, MANY COUPLES had decided to spend the evening on land, taking advantage of the offered evening tours or dinners with exotic food and dancers, and a stream of taxis whisked them away. The catering staff served pre-dinner cocktails in the restaurant lobby for those who stayed on board.

Kate was one of them. Wearing the dress, she entered the lobby area to find the captain, the first and second officers, the chief engineer, the doctor and a man wearing a Pharaoh Tours badge, the agent's representative, standing in a receiving line. The agent stepped forward with a smile. 'Miss Mansoumi, I'm Hasani Sharif, the agent's representative. Welcome to our tour, and if you need anything, please call.'

'Thank you,' Kate said. 'Is Sharif a common name in Egypt, or are you related to the famous actor or our doctor?'

'Certainly not the actor, although I wish I were,' the agent smiled. 'Let's ask the doctor if he knows of family ties.'

He turned to Kelvin and asked, 'Doctor, do you know if we are related?'

'Not to my knowledge.' Kelvin bowed to Kate. 'I would rather be related to this lovely lady.'

'Flattery won't work, Doctor,' she responded. 'I know that this dress disguises all my faults.'

Kelvin smiled. 'I believe that even if you were dressed in a potato sack, your beauty would shine through.'

The agent turned away to greet a new arrival as Kate, slightly flustered, came up with a reply. 'I might make allowances with other men, but I believe doctors are incapable of diagnosing unless they undress a woman, so what you say is unreliable.'

Kelvin's response was swift: 'You are incorrect. Doctors can only judge a skeleton accurately. A woman would have to lose more than her clothes.'

Kate gasped, then laughed, and Kelvin grinned. 'Come, have you met the other passengers?'

'No, none of them.'

'Then let me introduce the ones I know.'

With long experience in keeping passengers happy, the captain whispered something to the first officer, and at dinner time, Kate found herself at a rectangular table beside Kelvin, who sat in the centre of one of the long sides.

'Is this chance, or did you arrange for me to sit next to you?' Kate whispered to Kelvin.

'I suspect the captain decided to handicap me,' he replied.

'So now I'm a handicap, am I?' Kate said, laughing.

'If you'd been seated opposite me, your beauty would have had me mesmerised, and I would talk to no one else, so the captain has blocked my view of you.'

Giggling, Kate said, 'Can you say *anything* that is the truth? Or is that impossible?'

'I never tell a lie. The gentleman sitting opposite you is a retired cruise ship captain – ask him.' Catching the attention of the white-haired gentleman with a white beard and magnificent handlebar moustache seated across the table from Kate, Kelvin said, 'Captain Marsden, may I introduce Miss Mansoumi? She wants to learn about shipboard etiquette.'

'With pleasure, Doctor. Miss Mansoumi, I adore beautiful women. How can I help?'

Kelvin turned slightly to look at a woman opposite him to his right; beside her was the other woman who made up the couple. 'Miss Jones, may I ask why you've joined us on our cruise?'

'Please call me Bridget, Doctor.' Indicating the woman beside her, Bridget said, 'Belinda, my partner, and I are dance instructors in Paris. We plan to watch as many belly dancers as possible during our trip, so it's part business and part tourism.'

Kelvin grinned. 'I approve of the first. I can call the agent and ask if he can have a belly dancer join us at each of our stops, give a demonstration, and perhaps provide lessons for the ladies.'

'Are you also the entertainments officer?'

'No, but I shall recommend belly dancing as a good exercise to promote the health of our passengers.'

The other diners had heard the exchange, which brought guffaws of laughter, and there were masculine murmurs of 'Damn good idea' and 'Hear-hear'. When one of their wives said, 'Henry, behave yourself,' the laughter was general.

Sitting across the room, the captain looked at the merriment at Kelvin's table and smiled. He had made the right decision.

Kelvin asked, 'Bridget, as dancers, I expect you also teach yoga?'

'We both practise daily. Belinda is the teacher.'

'Then may I suggest that you offer classes for any interested ladies? You can use one of the sun decks for lessons. Then, with your permission, I'll post a notice asking anyone interested to join you in the lounge on the morning of the first sailing day after breakfast to agree on a programme. I shall say it's the doctor's recommendation for good health!'

'And I assume you will be joining us?' Bridget asked, flirtily.

Kelvin grinned. 'Of course. And if Miss Mansoumi comes wearing a leotard, you couldn't keep me away!'

This brought more hilarity, especially when Henry's wife said, 'Henry, you're too old to go and watch. The doctor doesn't want to treat a heart attack!'

When dinner ended, at Kelvin's table – the noisiest in the ship's dining room – all were friends, and Kate was still trying to decide who was the most likely passenger to have given her the dress.

After breakfast the next day, Kelvin left for another day at the museum.

The passengers, including Kate, took an organised tour of the same museum, after which they visited the pyramids, had their photos taken riding a camel, saw the Sphinx, and, on the return journey, called in at a shop that sold perfume essence.

Climbing off the bus on the dock, Kate didn't reboard the ship. Instead, she took a taxi to a dress shop recommended by Neith, the housekeeper serving her section of the vessel. She didn't know it, but it was the same one Kelvin had visited.

There, Kate bought three complete outfits. The salesperson, helping her choose matching accessories for them, produced a pair of shoes identical to those Kate had received in the surprise gift.

'I already have a pair of those,' Kate said.

'Are they new?'

'Yes, but I've only worn them once.'

'Are you from a cruise boat?'

'Yes. Why?'

'We delivered a dress and accessories to a cruise boat with a pair of those shoes yesterday. Was the delivery for you?'

'I think it must have been. Who was the buyer?'

'I don't know. I didn't see the buyer. I was out. The salesperson who made the sale is away today.'

Kate was a little disappointed, and the salesperson misread her expression. 'Don't worry,' she said, 'the mystery buyer didn't take an Egyptian tiara with a snake emblem. Would you like to try one?'

Kate felt daring. 'Why not?'

She positioned it carefully on the crown of her head and studied herself in the mirror. 'Do you think it suits me?' she asked the salesperson, who looked at her admiringly.

'Yes!' she said. 'If you straightened your hair and wore one of those scarab necklaces, you'd look like a goddess!' She pointed to a picture hanging on the wall.

'Who's that?'

'Hathor, the goddess of love.'

Kate then had an idea. 'I'll take it. And a scarab necklace. And have you any leotards?'

'Yes, several. Do you want plain or exotic?'

'What do you recommend?'

The salesperson looked at her shrewdly. 'I have a couple that do wonders for almost any body type, and your figure is already stunning, so you'd look amazing.'

'Then I'll take them.'

'Do you have makeup to match the dresses?' the salesperson asked. 'The tiara needs dramatic eyes.'

'Probably not. What do you suggest?'

'Let's look. I'll put a packet of the cosmetics you choose for each dress in the bag, and I'll include the manufacturer's makeup guide. What are you wearing during the day? Do you have kaftans?'

'Do you have plain ones with simple embroidery?'

'Hundreds, all Cairo styles. Wear one, and you will be part of the crowd.'

'Then I'll take three. Choose some for me to look at.'

I haven't had as much fun in years, Kate thought as she returned to the boat laden with her purchases.

She called Marylyn.

'Hello, Kate.'

'Hi, Em. How's Darryl?'

'Being elusive, but I'll trap him. He's a dish.'

'So he's a handsome hunk?'

'No, Kate, just an over-intelligent and funny guy I love deeply. I'm beginning to ache.'

'So you're not sleeping with him?'

'No, although I want to. I'm determined to be difficult this time. Did you wear the dress and uncover your secret admirer?'

'I did wear the dress, but I can't confirm who the admirer is, although I think the only candidate is a fantastic character.'

'Why?'

'He's the ship's doctor. His name is Shareef, but he speaks English perfectly. Last night I sat at his table. When I accused him of arranging things so I ended up sitting next to him, he gave me a story about the captain handicapping him so he couldn't look at me because I was so beautiful. I told him I didn't believe him, so he introduced me to Captain Marsden, a retired cruise ship captain, and said I must ask him about shipboard etiquette. The captain backed him up, so I don't know what to think.'

'Kate, you sound happy. Are you having fun?'

'Yes, Em, more than I've had in years. Our group includes a yoga teacher and a dance teacher. The doctor had us all laughing

– promised belly dancers on board as often as possible and then persuaded the yoga teacher to give yoga classes on the sun deck. And I've bought three more dresses and two sexy leotards for yoga, and an Egyptian tiara with a snake in the front so I can look like the goddess Hathor.'

'Go for it! Have lots of fun. That's all that matters.'

At dinner that evening, Kate learnt something more about Kelvin. The guests around their table compared notes on what they had seen on tour, and then Captain Marsden asked Kelvin, 'Doctor, we didn't see you today. What did you do?'

'I was at the museum, in one of the underground crypts, burying myself in ancient Egyptian scripts. I'm researching ancient medicines.'

'Can you read the hieroglyphics?'

'More or less, with the help of my portable scanner and computer. The tour guides show you the hieroglyphics, the most visible writings, but for every line of hieroglyphics carved into the stone, there are dozens more, handwritten in a script called Hieratic. When the manufacture of papyrus became common, Egyptians kept records on papyrus in Hieratic script. Demotic script, somewhat simpler and easier for everyday things, came into use later for everyday notes and messages, like letters and emails today.'

'Can you give an example?'

'Possibly; how about I say the same thing in all three? Would that work?'

'Try.'

Kelvin looked at Kate and said, 'Beautiful princess, I, Grand

Vizier of the temple of Hathor, send you a hundred doves as a sign of my love.'

Kate blushed. Captain Marsden laughed, and the table followed. 'Doctor, you've embarrassed Miss Mansoumi.'

Kelvin smiled. 'Now, if I wanted to write the same thing, there would be a little picture of the sign that denotes a beautiful woman, a movement sign in the correct direction, the sign for a hundred, one for a dove, the cartouche for Hathor, the goddess of love, and then my cartouche, that of the Grand Vizier. I believe it's where the saying "A picture is worth a thousand words" originated.' Kelvin paused and winked at Kate to show he was joking. 'Hieratic script written on papyrus is simpler and more practical than carving a stone tablet, which would be difficult to slip into her bodice.'

As the laughter died, Marsden asked, 'How would you say the Hieratic version?'

'That's easy: "Lots of love from Vizier."'

'Got it. And Demotic?'

Everyone could see the devilish grin on Kelvin's face as he turned to Kate and said, 'I'd slip a little card into her bodice with a heart emoji and the doctor's caduceus, the winged staff and serpents.'

Kate blushed again, and laughter re-erupted around the table.

When dinner ended, and the other passengers began drifting off to their evening's entertainment, Kate remained sitting alone with Kelvin. He offered to walk her back to her cabin, and on the way, she asked, 'Doctor, why did you say those things at the table? Were you trying to embarrass me?'

'Not at all, Kate,' Kelvin assured her, using her shortened name for the first time. 'If I had said them privately, what would you have thought or said?'

Kate looked at him with steady eyes. She had noticed his use of her name. 'That you're a flirt,' she said, quietly.

'Well, perhaps I am. But I also never lie, as I told you yesterday. Good night, Kate.'

Half an hour later, lying in bed, waiting for sleep to claim her, she thought about Kelvin's use of her name and concluded sleepily, *It must be he who gave me the dress.*

13

AT BREAKFAST ON DAY THREE, Kate asked Kelvin directly. 'Doctor, you called me Kate. How'd you know my name? My passport says Kathleen.'

Kelvin grinned at her. 'Have a look at your suitcase.'

'Oh, hell!' Kate said, and laughed. 'Of course! I wrote my name on it at the airport with the crayon the tour bus driver gave me.' *He's observant; I suppose researchers are like that.*

'So what's your name? If you're calling me Kate, I can't see why I must keep calling you Doctor Shareef.' She gave him a naughty smile.

'My name's Kelvin.'

Kate, surprised, said nothing. *That's an English name.*

After breakfast, Kelvin returned to the museum while Kate and the other passengers boarded the bus for an Islamic and Coptic Cairo tour. Kate wore one of her daytime kaftans.

Kelvin lost himself in the texts he referenced. When hunger pangs alerted him that it was time to eat, he visited a café for a quick sandwich, then returned to work.

Kate wasn't overly interested in the mosques and churches. However, when they had lunch at a restaurant in front of a market, she and five other women decided to spend the afternoon exploring. As the only Arabic speaker, she became the unofficial tour guide –and dressed as she was in a kaftan, like other Egyptian women, the boutique sellers assumed that was exactly what she was.

Kate soon learnt of the guides' problem keeping tabs on a

group, so she adopted a management strategy. After the first few minutes, she told the group, 'Ladies, we'll lose ourselves in this market and may never find the boat again. If that happens, ask anyone to help you find a taxi and give the driver our boat information. However, cooperating allows us to see more than wandering around alone. Let's agree on what we want to see, like clothing, food, trinkets, decorations, jewellery or artisans, and I'll ask where to go. Where shall we start?'

They started with jewellery. Kate asked for that area, and a boy took them there.

Halfway through the afternoon, the women agreed to take a break and found a coffee house. Opposite, across the narrow alleyway, was a tiny boutique and what seemed a strange activity by men stopping there. The women's view of what was happening was intermittent as the crowd strolled and pushed along the alley, so when they were ready to leave, Kate said, 'Ladies, I think something interesting is happening over there. It seems to be only men, so let's drift to the left with the crowd and try to get closer.'

The little boutique was selling tobacco, with packets on a shelf behind a wrinkled, aged man sitting at a table, hand-rolling cigars on a pad before him. When he finished three long thin cigars, he twisted them around each other into a single cigar and laid them on a shelf to dry. After drying and unwinding the bundle of three, a metal jar on one end of the table held the finished product – individual cigars with a spiral shape like a corkscrew.

'This is fascinating!' said one of the women. 'I've never seen squiggly cigars.'

'Nor have I, Mabel.'

Another said, 'But did anyone see what the buyers were doing? One man came, took a cigar from the jar and sucked on it, then put it back, then tried another, and it must have worked better because he bought it.'

'Urrgh! How can they do that? Surely it must spread disease?'

'I would freak out!'

'I'll tell Henry not to buy cigars that aren't in sealed packets.'

Kate said, 'Ladies, I've seen something similar in England several times.'

'In England? Never!'

'Have you never seen a tramp ask a stranger with a cigarette in his mouth for one and see the stranger give him the one already half-smoked? Have you never seen two men passing a lit cigarette back and forth between them?'

After a pause, Jennifer exclaimed. 'Well, I'm glad I'm not a smoker.'

After Kate found the market entrance where they met the bus, they returned to the boat carrying dozens of multicoloured packets.

Kelvin returned to the boat later and was pleased to see a reception notice announcing Takht music and a belly-dancing display. The agent had made good on his promise.

That night, as he was about to dress for dinner, Kelvin thought of Kate and what she might wear, and he chose an evening jubbah in red with gold embroidery. His mother had bought it for him when they had gone to an embassy cocktail party, and he had brought it with him for the cruise in case he needed formal evening wear.

Kate arrived wearing one of the gowns she had bought, in a lovely deep green. As she descended the stairs to the restaurant lobby, she looked over the people in the hall and felt disappointed that Kelvin wasn't there.

She joined Bridget and Belinda, who were standing to one side.

'Kate, you look beautiful in that dress! Where did you buy it?'

'Thank you. A shop not far from here. I felt English clothes were unsuitable in Cairo.' Looking around at the hubbub of people, she continued, 'I'm looking forward to the music and belly dancer tonight.'

'Oh, yes, you must be familiar with Arab music. Have you ever tried belly dancing?'

'When I was a little girl, with several other girls, I attended dancing classes. Belly dancing was one of their courses, but I didn't have the hips. I did learn a bit in my last two terms at school. It's super exercise. If I had continued, I might have become much better.'

Belinda asked, 'Are you coming to the yoga session in the lounge tomorrow morning?'

'Of course! I must return to yoga practice; it's been years.'

'Then maybe we can do some dancing as well.'

Kate replied, 'That might be fun, but I'm probably as stiff as a board.'

Belinda looked up. 'My gosh, your doctor looks handsome.'

Kate looked at the stairs; Kelvin was halfway down. 'Wearing that suits him, but he's not my doctor.'

'I think he is, Kate, but he's good at hiding it. When he talks to you, don't listen to what he's saying; look at the expression in his eyes.'

Kelvin had to work through the crowd to reach the three women, and Belinda observed, 'There, look, he's being polite, but he's coming straight to you.'

'Ladies, you look lovely tonight. Kate, in that dress, you are ravishing.'

'And without it, mister flatterer?'

Kelvin grinned. 'If you took it off, I would have to think up some esoteric descriptions to avoid being politically incorrect.'

His eyes are laughing and tender. The thought gave Kate a funny feeling.

'Well, your jubbah makes you into a virile man. I want a photo.'

Kelvin looked surprised. 'Why?'

'I'll send it to my company's marketing department for a new perfume advert. I shall call the perfume "Undress Me".'

Kate could see he was embarrassed, but it was for only a few fleeting seconds before he answered with a broad smile. 'When can I buy some? It may be the solution to my problem.' Then, ignoring Kate's momentary puzzled expression, and indicating the way with a hand, he added, 'Come, it's time to eat, listen to the music and stir the emotions of the people on board.'

The Arab music, played by a quartet, was familiar to Kelvin, Kate and the crew, and possibly to some of the passengers, but it was entirely new for Captain Marsden and his wife.

'Doctor, what can you tell us about it? To me and my wife, the music is unfamiliar.'

'You mean it sounds like caterwauling cats.'

Marsden laughed. 'If you say so.'

'Well, that's not far from an accurate description. Western ears recognise music played on a fixed scale. The maths of sound defines an octave as the change between one frequency and another that is double or half. The West has adopted a standard to make different instruments that produce the same frequency sounds, like the piano, which can make twelve sounds in an octave. The piano has eight equal divisions and four semitones in each octave. It allows the instruments to play together. Other cultures define a different number of notes in an octave, so it sounds terrible if you are unused to their music. Cats have no agreed standard; they might have thirty or forty divisions, so they're appalling.'

Everyone laughed, and Kelvin continued, 'The Takht ensemble uses quarter-tones and whole and semi-tones. Interestingly, it gives musicians the freedom to express feelings that Western music isn't usually capable of, except by altering the volume of each note or the speed at which they play a piece. The closest to it is probably jazz, where a trumpet player purposely distorts a musical note. Sit back, close your eyes and listen. What is the music trying to make you feel?'

Kate thought, *The doctor reveals something new every day. I think he adores music.*

As the dessert arrived, the music changed, switching to a different tempo, and a voluptuous woman appeared, with a riq, or tambourine, in one hand. Barefoot and wearing ankle bracelets with tiny bells, she was dressed in an embroidered brassiere, with a belt decorated with coins around her hips holding up a diaphanous skirt of a dozen strips. As the tempo increased, she whirled and wheeled, making her foot bells ring, and then shimmied her hips so the coins gave a distinctive sound.

Kate looked at Bridget and Belinda. Unlike the others, whose gazes were riveted on the writhing woman, they were looking around discreetly at the passengers. Bridget caught Kate's eye and raised an eyebrow. Kate shook her head slowly. She sensed that Bridget, like herself, classed the performance as tourist-amateur. Nevertheless, they all applauded when the woman finished.

The boat left at four the next morning. The engines started while most passengers were asleep, and a shore crew cast off.

However, two or three did wake and found their way to the top deck to watch Cairo moving slowly past the boat, the lights on both banks reflecting in the Nile water. Kelvin was one of them. He understood that leaving Cairo before a mass of ferries and other watercraft shot back and forth over the river was a smart move. He stayed on the top deck until just before breakfast, showered and then went to the restaurant.

The diners were discussing various things, including the meeting proposed in the lounge at ten to discuss yoga classes, the visit to the Temple of Heryshef after lunch, the boat's arrival at Beni Suef, and the trip east into the desert to a place where they could see men training falcons.

Approaching lunchtime, three groups had formed: those staying on board for a relaxing day, those going to the temple, and a small group who wanted to see the falcons.

Kate was sunbathing on the top deck when she saw Kelvin walking towards her.

'Hello, Kate. I don't see your name on the tour lists. Are you staying on board?'

He's looked to know where I'm going. 'I haven't decided yet. What are the merits of each?'

'The temple is not impressive. Although occupied for centuries, the inhabitants have recycled most of it, using the stone for new buildings. It's also in the middle of the town. If you've never seen falcons flying, it's worth seeing them; feeding them is an exciting experience. It's a good one for photographers.

Usually, a guy there takes high-speed photos and mails them to you.'

'Is feeding them dangerous?'

'No, not if you obey the rules. They give you heavy gloves and a safety helmet, although the latter is probably unnecessary.'

'Which tour will you go on?'

'I must accompany the group to the falcons. There are ambulances in town but none in the desert.'

'What's dangerous there?'

'This is Egypt. If you read the early history, most of the medical information dealt with bites and stings by snakes and scorpions, although you're unlikely meet one out there nowadays; it's too close to civilisation.'

'Thanks. I'll think about it.'

Kelvin rechecked the lists before the boat docked and saw that Kate and seven others had signed up to see the falcons.

14

THE RIDE WAS FAST across the Beni Suef Bridge in a small van to visit the falcons, and only ten minutes later, they reached a vast open desert space with four white tents. A dozen men wearing white galabiyas sat beside a tent or stood around; two had falcons perched on heavily gloved arms. The falcons had little leather helmets that blocked their vision. A boy of about fourteen years old attended a small brazier, heating a kettle of water for tea or coffee.

Once the men had greeted their small group and gathered them together on the desert sand, one of the falconers pulled on a pair of heavy gloves and hung a bag around his neck. 'Hold the sack with your left hand, then use your right to reach in and take a piece of chicken,' he instructed. 'Pull your hand out in one movement and hold it up high before you. The falcon will collect it. I shall show you. Please, everyone, observe.'

Stepping forward four paces, he did what he had described. His hand wasn't up for more than five or six seconds before a swooping falcon hit the glove with its claws and left with the piece of meat in its beak.

An excited Captain Marsden volunteered to go first. He pulled on a pair of heavy gloves and placed a yellow plastic helmet on his head. Then one of the men hung a cloth sack around his neck and explained the procedure once more.

Half an hour later, four passengers had done the same thing, and a man with a camera had taken a photograph every time.

Kate stepped forward for her turn, donning the gloves and the helmet and waiting while a falconer hung the bag of chicken around her neck. Then he stepped back and indicated that she could go head.

Kate tried to push her gloved hand into the bag of meat chunks hanging from her shoulder, but the heavy leather made it difficult and awkward. On the third try, when the glove caught on the bag again, she pulled off the glove and reached in to remove a chunk, thinking she could put the glove back on before offering the meat to the falcon flying above her. But she hadn't even raised her hand past her waist when she felt a shocking, solid impact from the left front. It lifted her from the ground, and she lost her footing.

She fell onto her back on the sand with a resounding thump, with something on top of her. 'Ooomph.' She lost all remaining air in her lungs and greyed out. Her last thought was: *A bus hit me.*

She didn't see the swoop as the falcon braked or feel the wind of its wings as they brushed Kelvin's back.

Kate heard a voice speaking Arabic from far away as the weight pressing her down eased. 'Are you all right?'

She couldn't speak. Her chest and lungs seemed paralysed.

Lips.

Eeaaaahhh...

Lips gone.

Kelvin looked at her worriedly. He placed an ear on her chest. *Her heart's okay. Chest muscle paralysis – I struck her hard. I must deflate her lungs.*

Hand on my breast.

Sighhh...

Lips on mine again.

Eeaaaahhh...

Lips gone. Hand on right breast, pressing.

Sighhh...

'Good. Inhale.'

Kate tried to gasp. It hurt.

Lips again.

Eeaaaahhh...

Lips gone. Breast again.

Sighhh...

'Try again. Inhale.'

Kate tried, managed a little, and the grey began to lift. The face only centimetres from hers with the worried eyes seemed familiar.

Hand pressing on my right breast.

'Good. Breathe out.'

Kate tried but couldn't.

Press.

Sighhh...

Lips again...

Eeaaaahhh...

'Exhale.'

Kate's chest muscles, finally recovering from the shock of the impact, manage to work.

Sighhh...

The worried face became clearer. *It's the doctor.*

'Muhammed, continue with the tour and call a taxi. I'll take Miss Mansoumi back to the boat and check her out. Kate, don't try to move. Just shut your eyes and breathe steadily.'

The pain was still there, but each breath seemed easier.

Kate lost track of time as she lay there, concentrating on her breathing, and then she heard Kelvin say, 'The taxi is here. Don't try to move. I'll carry you.'

Kate felt his arms push under her, then the sensation of rising and moving. *He's strong.*

Kelvin carefully laid Kate on the back seat of the taxi, turning her gently on to her right side.

Once the taxi reached the boat, two crew members with a stretcher helped transfer Kate to the medical cabin, where they laid her on the bed.

She was beginning to feel better. 'What happened?'

'I tackled you out of the way of the falcon,' Kelvin said. 'I'm sorry I hurt you, but it was better than losing your hand.'

Sitting beside Kate, Kelvin explained what had happened. 'When you put your hand into the bag to remove a piece of meat, a falcon saw it and began a dive to strike. Without the glove, if the falcon had hit your hand, the least damage would be losing a finger; any lacerations from its claws would have meant a certain infection. I did the only thing I could – I knocked you out of its flight path.'

'Oh.'

'Now. Are you breathing better?'

'Yes. It's still hard, though.'

Kelvin told her, 'I'm going to inject you with a muscle relaxant and a pain killer.'

'What will that do?' Kate asked.

'It will relax your muscles and make you drowsy. If you want to sleep, do so.' Working quickly and methodically, he administered the medicine.

'And then?'

'Later, I must look at your ribs on the left side, the sternum, where your ribs join in front, then at your hip and spine. I want to make sure there aren't any cracks or fractures. I'll need to remove your clothes. I'll call a woman to help if you wish.'

Kate already felt the effect of the drug. ''S okay. I was married once.'

Seconds later, she was asleep.

Satisfied that he would cause her no pain, Kelvin conducted his examination, and then left her sleeping while he reported to the captain.

15

KATE WOKE TWO HOURS LATER, her bladder bursting.

'Welcome back.'

Kelvin came into view.

'I need the toilet.'

'Shall I fetch the bedpan? I'll give you a surgical gown and call the woman attendant if you wish?'

'No time!' Kate insisted.

'Right. I'll help you,' Kelvin said, removing the sheet covering her.

My god, I'm naked!

'Swing your legs off the bed. I'll help you sit up. Good. Now, use your right arm to support yourself on mine, and try to walk.'

Moving carefully and gently, Kelvin helped Kate onto the toilet, then left the small bathroom.

Some minutes later, Kate called, 'Kelvin, I can't stand.'

He went back into the bathroom, helped her up, then supported her as she walked back to the bed. He piled up the cushions and pillows, instructed her to lean against them, and then replaced the sheet.

'Kate, I examined you while you were out, and I could find nothing broken. You have severe bruising on the left side of your rib cage, a bruise at the bottom of your spine where you hit the sand, and another on the edge of your hip. I've treated them with arnica ointment. I'll give you a sleeping pill later and rub in another layer of ointment in the morning. Tomorrow you may feel tender, but you will be fine.'

'I haven't thanked you for saving my hand. Thank you,' Kate said, 'I don't know how I would have lived with only one.'

Kelvin patted her shoulder. 'I love rugby-tackling beautiful women and don't often have the chance,' he said.

Kate tried to laugh, but the pain in her ribs cut it short.

'Sorry, I must avoid making you laugh. You've missed lunch. Would you like something to eat? I'll ask the kitchen to bring a meal on a tray.'

'Something light, like a shorba soup or bread and hummus.'

'I'll go and see what the kitchen can do.'

Kelvin was back within a few moments and said, 'The kitchen will send a tray; I told them to add a bottle of sparkling water to the order.'

'How do you know I like sparkling?'

'I noticed you always order it at dinner.'

He must have watched me.

Kelvin sat down at the tiny desk and opened his laptop. 'Your food will be here in a moment, and I have something to write for the captain.'

'A report on the incident?'

'No. I've already done that. I'll compose an instruction sheet to hand to all passengers feeding the falcons to avoid the same thing happening again.'

Surprised, Kate asked, 'Is that something usual in a ship's doctor's life?'

'No, but I'm not a permanent ship's doctor. I think it's better to avoid accidents than fix the consequences.'

Puzzled, Kate asked, 'If you're not a ship's doctor, what are you?'

'I'm a doctor, although I don't practise as one. I've never registered. These ships on the Nile don't have permanent doctors. Unlike the big cruise liners, these boats are never far from a town.

They offer all-expenses-paid holiday jobs for young doctors. I'm going up to Aswan and back to Cairo.'

'So what do you do when you aren't holidaying on the Nile?'

Just then, Kate's food arrived. 'Eat your lunch, and we'll talk after I finish this instruction.'

Kate cleared the tray. *I didn't know I was so hungry; maybe it's because I've just escaped a future with only one hand.*

She sat back against the cushions and watched Kelvin. *Could he be the person who gave me the dress? He has an English name and speaks English.*

The waiter returned and collected the tray. Kate thanked him and continued to look at Kelvin. *He has grey eyes; I remember them being worried. He's kind.* Then she recalled him carrying her. *He's strong, and I felt safe.*

Kelvin closed his laptop. 'I've finished it, Kate.'

'What will you do with it?'

'I've sent it to the first officer and asked him to print copies to distribute to the passengers.'

'They'll probably just attach copies to the boarding pack.'

'I've asked that they hand out the info to the passengers before visiting the falcons. Of course, that might not happen.'

I'll switch to English. 'So, Kelvin, who and what are you?'

Instead of answering, he asked. 'Can you laugh now, Kate?'

'I think so. Why?'

'Because there's nothing we can do except laugh when fate intervenes. People always laugh at the unexpected.'

Kate frowned. 'You must explain that. Whenever I expect something and the opposite happens, I'm disappointed. I don't laugh.'

'I'll give you an example. Imagine we're walking in a field, and we arrive at a wire fence. I lift a strand and push down another so you can bend and step through the space.'

'Where's the unexpected?'

'Well, I'm a hero, and I believe I can jump the fence easily, so I try, but my foot catches the top wire, and I fall on my head.'

'I would be worried that you had hurt yourself. What's funny about that?'

'Nothing. That's a negative expectation; your mind had already added it as a possible result. Now, imagine the scene if I jump the fence, but while doing so, my pants split down the back.'

Kate managed a strained giggle. 'That would be funny, especially if you were wearing pink underwear!'

'That's because you would have had no expectation of it happening. Now, imagine if I wasn't wearing any underwear.'

Kate began to laugh but forced herself to restrain it. 'Oh God, Kelvin, I can't laugh that much.' She had tears in her eyes. 'It hurts.'

'It's good exercise for the muscles,' Kelvin said with a chuckle.

As Kate's laughter subsided, she said, 'Okay, now you know I can laugh. Tell me.'

'I have a medical degree, then I did another as a pharmaceutical chemist and became an explorer. I look for chemical compounds that pharmaceutical companies might use, and I'm travelling the Nile valley to discover what plants the ancient Egyptians used for medicine.'

'Where does fate come in?'

'You are an English Iranian working in marketing; I'm an English Egyptian scientist and explorer, and we meet on a Nile cruise. I cannot imagine a more unlikely thing to happen, but fate decided we should meet, and sealed the deal by throwing a hungry falcon between us.'

Kate laughed.

'You get it,' Kelvin said. 'I can tell a woman's fate-has-intervened laugh. It makes her breasts go up and down.'

Kate looked down to see that the sheet had dropped below her breasts. She pulled it back up. 'You're trying to change the subject.'

Kelvin grinned at her. 'I'm not. That was the truth.'

Kate couldn't help it; she laughed again. 'Kelvin, I haven't laughed as much for months.'

'That's good. Laughter is the best medicine. Now I've revealed all my secrets; how about yours?'

'Oh, I'm ordinary. I'm a marketing director for a company that promotes beauty products for women. I'm responsible for Europe.'

'That's not ordinary, and especially not if you say, "I'm a beautiful, intelligent marketing director". But why are you in Egypt on a Nile cruise?'

He's the first man to flatter me with the word 'intelligent'.

'I don't think I can tell you.'

'So I must guess?'

'For the moment, yes.'

Kelvin thought about her; he didn't realise he was frowning. *Where do I start? And what do I know?*

While he was marshalling the facts he knew and what he didn't into a satisfactory order, Kate watched him. *I don't know why I like him so much, but he has an expressive face; I can almost see what he's thinking. Maybe I'll learn what he thinks of me when he tells me his guess, whether he's far out or not.*

'Okay, Kate, I've worked it out; what I know fits together.'

'Then tell me. It should be fun. I'll laugh when you get it wrong.'

'Do you want me to use Arabic or English?'

'Kelvin, let's agree to use Arabic except when we are with English speakers.'

'Okay.'

'Let's see. You're twenty-seven – I know that from your passport and your passenger data – and your twenty-eighth birthday is in four months. You are female, beautiful and intelligent.'

'My passport doesn't say "beautiful and intelligent".'

'No, but I can see you, and you are. You have an English first name and speak English but also speak fluently in Arabic with an Iranian accent. And your surname is Iranian, so your father is probably Iranian.' Kelvin paused while Kate nodded, then continued. 'You said, "I was married once," and I deduce it was a short marriage when you were still young, possibly with some parental influence. "Once" also means you haven't married since, and you are here alone, from which I deduce that you have no boyfriend.'

Kate smiled but said nothing.

'Now, the data is speculative. You are the marketing director of a major corporation and have worked your way up to this position because of your intelligence. I eliminate the possibility of rapid promotion because you slept with the boss, as I know that promoting women's beauty products is a business that employs women or gay men primarily. Macho men selling beauty products don't match the stereotype of men boasting about their achievements in a golf club bar. Therefore, reaching the marketing director position has been years of hard work in a woman's world. I admire that.'

Kate thought, *He's brilliant, honest, and admires successful women. That's rare.*

'Ergo, a short marriage with no children indicates either a sterile husband, a decision not to produce children or a catastrophic marital failure, and this, followed by a life in a woman's world, indicates few male relationships. Add to this your age, when most women become aware of a fundamental desire to become mothers. The simple solutions are a few minutes in bed with a virtual stranger or a visit to a sperm bank, but years of raising a child alone follow. Raising a child alone is not your style; you probably have siblings, so expect a family life.

'Therefore, you are looking for a man to love and who will love you, so you decided on a cruise. You chose this one because it takes two weeks – long enough to convince yourself if a man is worth pursuing.' Kelvin gave Kate a querying look. 'That's my analysis. How did I do?'

Instead of answering, Kate said, 'You know, because we're on the Nile, you remind me of someone.'

'Who?'

'We're going to Aswan. The Cataract Hotel is there. Agatha Christie spent time there writing books where Hercule Poirot, her detective, used his little grey cells to work out solutions, as you've just done. You could be a detective.'

'I'm a researcher, Kate, like a detective. I told you I was. So how close was I?'

Kate grinned at him. 'I won't ruin your dream world. Will we marry, have many kids and live happily ever after?'

'The gods will decide, but I've serious doubts about it happening.'

'Why?'

'I might tell you one day, Kate.'

'Spoilsport,' Kate retorted, with a cheeky grin, then changed the subject. 'I haven't had a shower today, and I think I'm strong enough to do so. Will you take me back to my cabin?'

'If you wish, it might be better for you to shower here, where I can keep an ear open for a cry for help.'

'Then take me to my cabin, and you can read a book or

whatever while I shower. I need all the magic creams that turn me from Cinderella into a princess.'

'Leave the bathroom door open,' Kelvin instructed her once they reached her cabin.

'So you can watch? That would be a new experience for me.'

'I will if you want to strike that off your bucket list. But, seriously, if you fall against a closed door, I'll have a hell of a job getting to you.'

'Why must you be so practical? You've half-carried me, naked, to the toilet, and although I don't remember it, I'm sure you've had a good feel all over when you did your physical examination of me, so watch all you want.'

'I'm very moral, Kate. I only felt where I had to for medical reasons.'

'Then I'm disappointed,' Kate joked. 'I can't be as beautiful as you tell me.'

'I never lie, Kate. If you like, I'll feel you all over with pleasure once you've showered.'

'Wow, I've something to look forward to,' Kate said as she stepped into the shower.

Kelvin sat on the little settee in Kate's cabin, reading a magazine while she showered. Soon, she called, 'Kelvin, can you pass me a towel, please? I don't want to step onto the slippery floor with wet feet.'

Turning his back to her so he didn't appear to be ogling her, he passed in a towel.

When Kate came out of the bathroom, scrubbed and with brushed hair, and walked towards the wardrobe, Kelvin felt a sudden tightness in his chest and gut. *My God, she's beautiful.* 'Are you coming to dinner tonight?' he asked, straining to keep his voice casual.

'I think I should, Kelvin. If I don't, the ship may start gossiping about immoral activity on board, so I should show everyone I've recovered.'

'Kate! How are you feeling?'

'Maybe a bit fragile, Bridget, but I'm fine. Our doctor screwed all the bits back together after dismantling me.'

The whole table, including Kelvin, burst into laughter when Bridget, with a broad smile, said, 'A fine choice of words, Kate. Congratulations.'

Realising the unintentional pun, Kate blushed, and everyone laughed even harder.

Kate looked at Kelvin, saw the grin and twinkling eyes, and said, 'And you could be a gentleman and deny any involvement instead of grinning like a Cheshire cat!'

'Kate, you know I never tell lies,' he responded, causing even more laughter.

'Everyone, I propose a toast to the most marvellous couple I've ever met,' Bridget said, raising her glass. 'To Kate and Kelvin: may they keep us laughing to the end of the voyage.'

Kate thought. *It's only been four days, and they've decided we're a couple.*

'So what happened to Kate?' Henry asked. 'We've heard rumours, but we'd like to hear it straight from the horse's mouth.'

'Well, to train the birds, the falconers use a dead chicken or duck on the end of a rope and whirl it around in a circle, and then someone lets a falcon fly without it seeing the lure. It must climb, then circle to look for prey, and when it spots the whirling chicken, it must judge its trajectory and that of the chicken, then dive and strike. The young falcons often fail to hit the lure, but after repeated practice, they succeed.

'What we experienced today was not training; it was direct feeding. The falcon was up in the air, the meat virtually stationary, and the falcon knew where the meat came from. So it began its dive as soon as Kate put her hand in the food bag. Fortunately, I saw her remove the glove and knew what might happen, so I took evasive action.'

'How did you know what would happen?' Bridget asked.

'Falcons represent Horus, the ancient Egyptian god of kingship – there are many falcon statuettes in the artefact collections. And falconry is an ancient practice. In the Sinai and Arabia, it's the sport of kings, and many people practise it. I spent a day in the Sinai some years ago, with men training falcons.'

As dinner ended, Kate said quietly to Kelvin, 'After dinner, can we go up to the top deck alone and talk?'

Sitting in two armchairs on the top deck, with a 360-degree view of the city lights, the reflections in the Nile ahead and a myriad of stars above, Kate and Kelvin sat in silence for a few minutes, nursing their glasses of wine.

'It's so beautiful,' Kate said. 'It fills me with a feeling of peace and happiness.'

'Yes, I feel the same. The slow drift of the river generates in me a feeling of eternity.'

After another few moments of silence, Kelvin asked, 'Kate, what do you want to discuss?'

'I'm confused,' she admitted. 'In just four days, I've changed from a sad single woman into an excited, laughing woman in a relationship. At least, that's what Captain Marsden, Bridget and the others think of me. I'm no longer sure of who I am, and it's entirely due to you. I feel I'm different when I'm with you. I don't know why, because I know so little about you.'

Kelvin looked at Kate with soft eyes. 'I feel the same,' he said quietly. 'I was a stodgy researcher hoping for the excitement of new scientific discovery, and now I've found excitement in discovering you.'

'Kelvin, please tell me. The first afternoon on the boat, I found a dress, shoes and a handbag in my cupboard. Did you give them to me? And if so, why?'

'Yes, that was me. I can tell you why. I have a doctor friend, Ahmed Badawi, who has taken holiday jobs on the cruises between Luxor and Aswan for years. Those cruises last three or four days, and he did them because it was a way to meet young women without a strong attachment. Although he practises in England, he's currently in Cairo because his mother has found a young woman that Ahmed might like sufficiently to marry, so he's not working on a boat. He suggested I should make this trip because I could see all the historical sites I wanted to visit, and he said I might meet an attractive young woman.

'When I saw the passenger list three days before you boarded, I called him and said he should stop hoping I would meet a woman because there was only one on the list – you. So he told me to see what you looked like and, if you were worth pursuing, to buy you a dress.'

Turning to Kate and putting his wine glass down, Kelvin took her hand. 'Kate, I thought you were beautiful the moment I saw you, and that's why I followed Ahmed's advice about buying you a dress. And that evening, when you arrived for dinner, I knew I had chosen well, for you were stunning and visibly thrilled.'

'I was. And your taste is superb,' Kate said. 'It made me want to continue feeling like that, so I bought more dresses.' Pressing his hand, Kate continued, 'Kelvin, when I'm with you, I feel alive, and it seems we fire up each other when we talk, and that's why the others think we fit like a couple, but that's confusing because I should know far more about you than I do.'

'Kate, are you scared?'

'Yes.'

'Why?'

'Do you remember when you made your Hercule Poirot deduction of my situation? It was incredible, Kelvin; you were extremely accurate, especially about my marriage. It was indeed quick and catastrophic.'

'Do you want to tell me about it, Kate?'

'No, but I'll say that although I'm not a virgin, I've never had an orgasm, and I've never met a man I want sexually – including my ex-husband.'

'So why did you marry him?'

'I was a virgin, and I thought that came later.'

'Kate, are you trying to say that our feelings for each other are completely new to you, and you need to know more about me before you can understand them?'

'Yes, Kelvin.'

'Then, excuse the pun, we are both in the same boat. What would you like to do about it?'

'Instead of going on the tours whenever the boat stops along the Nile, can I come with you? Maybe I can help somehow, but I might learn enough to make me feel more confident.'

'I'd adore that, Kate. Now, let's call it a night. I'll leave my cabin door unlocked, so you can come and ask if you need any medicine.'

At midnight, unable to sleep, Kate rose, wrapped the sheet around her, and slipped into the corridor. Tiptoeing along the quiet passage, she walked a few paces to Kelvin's cabin. As promised, he had not locked the door.

He was fast asleep, naked, without a sheet, and the window blinds were open. The light from the town lit up the room.

Kate dropped her sheet and lay down on the bed beside him. *I feel safe here.*

Within minutes, she was sleeping soundly.

16

KELVIN WOKE, BRIEFLY WONDERING where he was. He recalled a fragment of his dream in which he had followed a falcon across the desert.

He lay in bed, remembering the day before, the smell of Kate's perfume still in his nostrils. It took him a minute or two to realise that the scent was too strong to be merely a lingering remnant. He turned his head to look at the pillow beside him; there was an evident depression where someone had rested their head.

He bent forward and sniffed the pillow. *Kate slept here!* It gave him a warm feeling, one he had never experienced before. He lay revelling in it for a while before checking the time, then realised it was early enough for the small gym to be empty.

He put on shorts, a sleeveless T-shirt and gym shoes, and spent thirty minutes exercising before returning to his cabin, showering, and dressing for breakfast.

On his way to the breakfast room, he knocked on Kate's door, holding a tube of arnica ointment.

'Yes, who is it?'

'The health inspector.'

'Oh, then come in.'

Kate was still in bed, sitting with the sheet pulled modestly to her neck. She had slipped out of Kelvin's cabin early that morning while he was still asleep.

'Did you sleep well, Kate?' he asked with an extremely broad smile.

He knows I slept beside him! 'Yes, but I had a weird dream,' she said.

'You too? What was it?'

'I left my bed and went to another cabin, where there was a pharaoh on the bed, lying like a mummy, with his hands crossed on his chest. I lay beside him in the same position, just like the stone statues in the Cairo Museum.'

'That's bad, Kate.'

'Why?'

'Sleepwalking can be dangerous. Imagine if you had walked off the boat and fallen into the river.'

'Wouldn't that have woken me up?'

Deadpan, Kelvin replied. 'Maybe not quickly enough to avoid a crocodile. We must agree on a cure or prevention.'

Her smile became a grin. 'And what do you suggest, Doctor?'

'I must think about it. Meanwhile, here's the arnica. After you've showered, rub it onto your sore spots.'

Kate found a different solution. 'Go back to your surgery,' she instructed. 'I'll shower, and in ten minutes, I'll come to your surgery for the arnica treatment. Then we can go to breakfast together.'

'Kate! How are you this morning?'

'Much better, Bridget. Our doctor has changed my medical treatment.'

'What's he doing now?'

'Well, he's smeared so much arnica ointment on my damaged parts that I believe he's trying to glue me back together.'

'I've heard about that treatment,' Bridget said, laughing. 'A doctor did the same for a friend of mine, and she stuck to him for a week!'

Everyone at the table joined in the laughter.

'Kate doesn't need to worry, Bridget,' Kelvin chimed in. 'I use surgeon's gloves. At most, she'll have a couple of gloves stuck to her bruises for a week!'

Grinning, Bridget turned back to Kate. 'Are you coming to yoga?'

'Yes, Bridget. I may have to avoid some exercise positions, but it will benefit me.'

'And you, Doctor?'

'I've no choice, Bridget. I must be there in case Kate falls apart. I'll bring my glue.'

Breakfast continued with happy laughter.

After the meal, Kate returned to her cabin to change into her leotard. At the same time, Kelvin examined his data on the necropolis of Tuna El Gebel and the ancient Egyptian cemetery of Beni Hassan, which they would visit the next day. He wanted to see where he might find the best hieroglyph panels.

Kate left her cabin an hour later, wearing one of the new leotards and flip-flop sandals, with a towel wrapped around her waist, and climbed the stairs to the top deck. She was the first passenger to arrive.

The staff had laid out twenty yoga mats in four rows. A small table held a jug of iced lemon-flavoured water with glasses.

Kate chose a mat in the first row, dropped her towel onto it to mark it taken, then poured herself a glass of water and walked to the railing to admire the view.

'Hello, Kate,' Bridget said, walking up the stairs. 'I'm glad to see at least one person has come. Where's your doctor?'

'He's coming, Bridget, but he's not my doctor.'

'You might not think so, but you're his princess. He said so at the first dinner we had.'

'He was joking, Bridget.'

'Well, he's not joking now. We only have one chance in our lives for great love. I thought I had lost mine but got a second chance with the same man when his wife died. Don't let that chance go by. Grab and hold on to it, and don't listen to others or conventions.'

Just then, the other yoga enthusiasts, including Kelvin, arrived in a group, chatting excitedly as they chose their mats.

Once everyone was in position, Belinda walked to the front, counted those present, and said, 'Everyone who signed up is here, so I'll start with the first position. Bridget will demonstrate it for those unfamiliar with the position, and then we'll do it together.'

For an hour, Kate forgot Kelvin as she followed the lesson. She managed most positions but had twinges with one or two, and Belinda saw her hesitation. 'Kate, if there's pain, don't push past it. There's always tomorrow.'

She heard Belinda ask, 'Doctor, have you suffered from a recent injury on your left side?'

'Yes, six months ago. Four broken ribs and a broken leg.'

'Then you are doing very well. You are still stiffer on that side but work slowly at it, and it will improve. Let me show you. When you twist, you compensate for the left by moving your hips more. Keep them straight and force the twist in your upper body to work. And keep your knees together: don't let them slide when you twist to the left, and you'll recover the flexibility in the lower leg muscles again.'

'Thanks, Belinda. I thought swinging a golf club had fixed it.'

'It would have helped, but a golf swing includes turning the hips, which means different muscles at play.'

Belinda called a halt. 'Okay, everyone, that was great. Our next yoga class will be the day after tomorrow, but you can do some practice in your cabins if you have a moment.'

Everyone thanked her, and Bridget asked Kate, 'Do you want to try a belly-dance exercise?'

'I can try. What should I do?'

'There are three basic movements. The first is a sideways hip movement. Keep your hips facing forward and bend your spine so one side rises and the other drops, then smoothly go back to straight up, and then on to the other side. Do it slowly while you count, five each way. Watch me. One, two, three, four, five.'

Bridget's hips swung through what looked like an impossible angle. 'Then five back, and five the other way. Do this until your hips move through at least forty degrees, twenty each way. After that, you can increase it by lifting one leg onto your toes, and finally, you make your count faster. Try it.'

Kate complained, 'I feel stiff. I can't move far.'

'I think you're doing well, Kate. A few hours of practice and you'll soon be there. Now, the second movement is the forward and backward one.' Belinda grinned. 'You know what that simulates? Try it: the lower spine must curve forward and then back. The count is three forward and three back. Watch.'

'That's sexy,' Kate observed.

'It is. It's what we do when we dance to Latin rhythms. Try it.'

Kate tried and said, 'I think I'm worse at this one than the sideways one!'

'It's easier to develop this movement than the sideways one; just dance to Latin music, and it comes. Now, the third exercise is a combination, side to the right, then smoothly into a forward, slide into the left, and back. Although two movements, it looks like you're rolling your hips in a circle. Watch.'

Bridget gave a perfect demonstration of a belly dancer's rolling hips.

'Where's the belly come in?'

'When you roll your hips forward, suck in your tummy; for hips backwards, push it out. That woman dancing the other night was sucking and pushing her belly without enough hip movement. She was an amateur.'

Bridget looked over Kate's shoulder. 'Doctor, I think you can dance. Am I right?'

Kate spun around; she'd thought Kelvin had left with the others.

'I learnt the samba in Brazil,' Kelvin said. 'You can't go there and not dance at the festivals. Many will dance the other rhythms, too, especially the Argentinians.'

'Then find some music, and come up here every evening, play the music and teach Kate the samba.'

'That will be a pleasure! Kate, are you in?'

Kate didn't reply immediately – it seemed an invitation to plunge into the unknown with him. Then she saw his smile and sensed that the plunge would be a pleasure. 'I'll wear gym shoes, so I don't stab your feet.'

'Then we'll dance tonight after dinner. I'll download some music. Let's go for lunch.'

'I must shower and change out of my leotard.'

'Okay, me too.'

'Kate, what do you want to do this afternoon?'

'I'd like to go up to the sundeck, relax, watch the people on the banks, sunbathe and maybe snooze. Do you have something to do?'

'I haven't finished my list of the hieroglyph panels we will see tomorrow. But I can finish my list later and join you on the sundeck.'

'Don't forget to download the Latin music.'

Kelvin smiled. 'I'll do that now and meet you upstairs later.'

When Kelvin made his way to the sundeck an hour later, he found Kate wearing a bikini, her folded kaftan on the table beside her, sunglasses covering her eyes. She had arranged two loungers side by side.

Kelvin removed his kaftan and, wearing only gym shorts, lay down on the empty one.

Kate turned to look at him. 'Kelvin, tell me how you broke your ribs and leg. I can see the scars.'

'Kate, I wish I could lie to you.'

'Why?'

'Because then, like any man lying beside a beautiful woman would, I'd tell you a story that made me seem like a hero, like how I jumped in front of a runaway truck to rescue a terrified little octogenarian who was about to die, and when I leapt out of the way I landed on the walkway edge with the lady on top.'

'So you weren't a hero?'

'No, Kate, I was sitting in my rental car in New York when a runaway truck rammed into the back of the car. I spent over two months in hospital and a convalescent home.'

'That must have been traumatic.'

'It was.' *And I only learnt later how traumatic.*

'Thanks for telling me, Kelvin.' Kate lay back and closed her eyes.

Half an hour later, Kelvin's voice woke her up. 'Kate, you've had enough sun on this side.'

'Okay, I'll turn. Please can you put the sun lotion on my back?'

He did as she'd asked, revelling in the smooth feeling of her warm skin under his fingers. He heard her sigh with pleasure.

Lying down on her tummy, her head turned to face him, Kate said, 'Tell me what we'll see tomorrow and what interests you.'

'First, I must check that my photos include all the hieroglyphics. There are almost certainly many images of the same panel in different museums, and, short of visiting all those museums, I don't know if my photos are complete.

'The first, in Ashmunein, is the oldest. Unfortunately, it is of little interest. Modern buildings now surround it. Tuna El Gebel is much later, the New Kingdom to Greco-Roman times, but it does have tombs with hieroglyphics. However, the panels are all photographed and documented, and I don't expect to find anything new there. The tombs of Beni Hassan we visit in the afternoon will be more interesting. They are twelfth dynasty onwards. They are well documented, but reading about them differs from a visit.'

'What made you want to visit these sites?'

'I wish I could tell you, but I don't honestly know. My geologist father said that herbs might grow anywhere but that those that grow in harsh conditions have much higher concentrations of chemicals in their leaves. He thinks the irrigated sides of the Nile are an unlikely source and suggested that in antiquity, the lands to the south, referred to as Nubia, were a more likely source.'

'So why come here?'

'Egyptian history is a confusing collection of snippets, and often different researchers disagree on interpretations. The first king of the Beni Hassan area in the twelfth dynasty, Amenemhat I, may have been Nubian. A literary text called the Prophecies of Neferti suggests that Amenemhat's mother was a queen from Ta Seti, and Nubian, or the daughter of a Nubian from Elephantine.

Elephantine was a mini kingdom near Aswan, absorbed by the kingdom of Ta Seti. Possibly, the area had a high population of Nubians, and they got their herbs from further south. There might be a mention of herbs there, or anywhere between here and Aswan.'

'Kelvin, I'm as confused as Egyptian history! So, you are looking for ancient herbs used by the Egyptians; they might have a hieroglyphic mention but could have come from the far south?' When Kelvin nodded, Kate said, 'That's worse than finding a needle in a haystack!'

'I know, Kate, but sometimes, if you look, you find the needle. We found each other, after all.'

Kate had no answer for that. Instead, she asked, 'So what do I wear for Latin dances?'

'As little as possible! Shoes with low heels and a full skirt. I'll wear a shirt and trousers. We can dress like that for dinner.'

'Okay, Kate, I have some music. Let's go to the top deck and samba.'

The two of them, dressed for dancing, had had another enjoyable dinner at their usual table, with plenty of gentle teasing about their outfits. Now, on the top deck, Kelvin began his instruction.

'The samba has the advantage of being as simple or as complicated as you want to make it – that's why it's so popular,' he told Kate. 'Once you can dance the basic steps, you can expand the number of additional steps in your repertoire. We'll try to do the basic and maybe get to the reverse basic tonight. Watch my legs and feet.'

Kelvin demonstrated the simple forward and back steps with a wiggle of his hips. 'Now, hold my hands and follow my feet.'

Kate did, and Kelvin said, 'More wiggle, Kate. The samba is a very expressive dance. That's it! Now, let's try it to the music.'

For the length of a tune, they stepped backwards and forwards with a wiggle each time, and Kate slowly relaxed as she began to feel the rhythm. *I like wiggling my bum to music.*

'Okay, now let's learn the reverse; it should be easy for you.'

Kate followed his steps, and for another song, they danced, combining the two steps, with Kelvin leading. Kate stopped watching Kelvin's feet and became aware of him. *He has a very sexy wiggle. I must wiggle more.* By the tune's end, they were moving seamlessly together, guided only by the music.

'Let's dance one more tune. Like the tango, the samba is a dance where the partners use their bodies to express desire. Let's try.'

By the end of the dance, they were much closer, brushing together all the time.

'Kelvin, that was fun, but I'm now sweaty.'

'Me too, Kate. We can go and shower. The tour leaves early tomorrow, so we must sleep. What shall we do to stop your sleepwalking?'

Kate looked at him. *Is there a slight smile on his face?* Then she remembered Bridget's words. *Don't listen to others or conventions.*

'If you leave your door unlocked, I can fetch a sleeping pill. I'm sure that will do the trick.'

Kelvin lay on the bed. He couldn't sleep, wondering if Kate would come.

Ten minutes later, he heard the cabin door open quietly, then close, and he sensed more than saw Kate's shadow in the light that filtered through the curtains as she came to the bed and lay down beside him.

'Kelvin, if you're awake, kiss me good night,' she whispered, 'and then I'll sleep without sleepwalking.'

He turned towards her, and, sensing his turn, she did too. In the pale light, he needed only to move forward slightly to kiss her. It lasted an eternity.

Kate felt a tension in her legs, and her toes curled before he moved back.

'Good night, Kate.'

'Good night, Kelvin.'

17

BY THE TIME THEY HAD thoroughly explored the temples and monuments of Tuna El Gebel, Kate thought she was an expert. Whenever they found a hieroglyphic panel, Kelvin selected a photograph to give her, and Kate did a check. First, she carefully checked that the top row matched the photo, then she worked down the right side, studying the first two or three carved letters or cartouches for clarity, and then she did the left, checking the last ones. Finally, on her knees, if necessary, she studied the bottom line, even scraping away a bit of sand to see if there were more lines.

She found four panels with fuzzy photo edges, and Kelvin took new pictures. They also found a piece with no matching photo in Kelvin's pack.

'Kelvin, that was interesting and fun, but the research differs from what I expected.'

'Most of it is, Kate. I've often thought it's like the exercise parents give their kids, the precursor to the jigsaw puzzle.'

'Which one is that?'

'The box with different shaped holes – round, square, triangle...'

'...And half-moon, star and hexagon?' Kate finished.

'Yes. The kid picks a block and must find the hole through which it will fit. Often, research is like that: we find something, like an unknown hieroglyph or a carving with a carbon date, and then we search the literature to discover if anyone has seen it before. That's when the problem begins. We must find where it fits, but it's also like a giant jigsaw, and we find a place where it would fit, but if another researcher has used that place for something, then it's a fight between two researchers over whose bit belongs in that place. Sometimes there are three or four claiming their bit fits best.'

'But where do researchers get that motivation?'

'I can't answer that, Kate. I suppose it's that some minds try to find order in chaos, but behind it, the force is the same one that drives others to climb a mountain.'

Their next stop was Ashmunein, and after they'd spent twenty minutes looking for hieroglyphs, Kate said, 'You were right, Kelvin. There's not much here.'

'This town, originally named Khemenu, grew to become the city of Thermopolis and was once a Roman Catholic diocese. It's built mainly with limestone; burning the stone to make cement was common. Now that restorers are re-erecting the columns, we can see that Thermopolis was extensive, but there's little left of ancient Egypt.'

Packing his belongings into his bag, Kelvin said, 'Let's go back to the boat for lunch, then visit the Beni Hassan tombs.'

'Kate,' Bridget asked at lunch, 'what are you doing with our doctor at the ruins?'

'I'm trying to learn something – so far, without success – although what I've found out about a tomb we'll see this afternoon gives me hope.'

'What do you want to learn?'

'Have you taken a good look at him, Bridget? I only woke up to it when he picked me up and carried me after the falcon incident.'

'If you mean he's well built, of course, I have; I'm a woman. But what does that have to do with tombs?'

'He's Egyptian, and when I was looking on the web to find out about him, I learnt that Egyptians have won many gold medals at the Olympics for wrestling, then I discovered it was a popular sport here four thousand years ago.'

Bridget was smiling and said suggestively, 'Well, then, you can look forward to some unusual wrestling.'

Kate grinned. 'I know nothing about wrestling; he'll outclass me. But the website included information on tombs with pictures showing the wrestling holds they've used for thousands of years. I want to learn a couple, so if he tries it again, I can escape.'

Kelvin intervened. 'What do you mean "again"?'

Kate smiled sweetly at him. 'You've already conveniently forgotten that the last time you wrestled with me, I ended up with bruised ribs. I'm taking precautions.'

The others at the table laughed, and Bridget said, 'Doctor, watch out. Next thing you know, Kate will learn how to wield a sword.'

'Then I shall wear padding.'

The laughter became raucous when Kate said, 'Make sure you wear it in the right place.'

'Kate, this is the tomb of Amenemhat, the guy I told you about yesterday who may have been Nubian. You can find some of the wrestling pictures you're looking for. I've photos of the paintings made from them over a hundred years ago. You may be disappointed because the paintings have deteriorated since then.'

'Are we doing the same as before?'

'Yes, Kate, but the decorations are beautiful. I want to see the scenes of burials and funerals, particularly those in the tomb of Khnumhotep II, where there are scenes showing preparations for his funeral and reincarnation.'

'Okay, let's get to work.'

They worked through the hieroglyphic panels in Amenemhat's tomb before going on to the next one.

'This is Khnumhotep's tomb,' Kelvin explained. 'You check the photos, and I'll look at the funeral preparation scenes. Then we'll visit Baqet's tomb. It has the best wrestling pictures.'

'Khnumhotep must have been an important man to have a tomb like this. It's magnificent!'

'Important is one thing, rich another,' Kelvin said. 'The cult of offerings to the divine ruler began early and, although supposedly religious, the offerings did often serve to build the king's wealth. I believe it's no different today, where taxes can be considered an offering to the state's rulers and administrators. It may have been easier then, for the priests could tell anyone refusing to make an offering that the gods would strike them down.'

The two worked in companionable silence for about half an hour, and then Kelvin said, 'Kate, I've finished. Have you seen enough?'

'Yes. I've checked all the photos.'

Kelvin smiled. 'And learnt to wrestle?'

'No, but I understand now how a wrestler yields victory: he slaps the ground three times.'

'How did you work that out, Kate?'

'Look at this photo – these two pics and the squiggle that means three.'

'Kate, you're brilliant. Well done!'

Back on the boat, Bridget quickly sought out Kate and asked in a feigned whisper, 'So, did you learn to wrestle?'

Smiling proudly, Kelvin replied for her: 'She didn't, Bridget, but she did manage to decipher some of the wrestling descriptions by herself.'

'What was that?'

Kate smiled. 'How to get away any time a wrestler holds me down. I tap three times on something, and he must immediately let me go.'

'That's something worth knowing.'

Kelvin remarked, 'Kate, there's a flaw in your thinking.'

'What?'

'I may be Egyptian, but I'm not a wrestler.'

The table burst into laughter again when they saw Kate's grin as she said to him, 'Then I'll use one of those pictures that show illegal moves, like a knee between the legs.'

As the laughter died, Bridget asked, 'What other illegal moves did you decipher?'

'Biting off a nose, ear or nipples – not to mention other parts.' More hilarity reigned for minutes.

After dinner, as they sat together on the top deck, Kelvin said, 'Kate, I'll never hold you down like a wrestler. Dare I leave my cabin door unlocked?'

'Please do. I feel safer in your cabin than alone. Maybe it's that I feel less lonely. I'm trying to figure it out, Kelvin; it's been years since I slept beside anyone. Maybe I didn't know I was lonely.'

Kelvin nodded understandingly, then said, 'Tomorrow, the boat leaves at four in the morning. We stop early at Tel Al

Amarna to look at some famous tombs and the city of Akhenaten before continuing to Asyut.'

'Do you think we'll find something?'

'I don't know, Kate. Abydos may be better. But the story of Akhenaten and his city is a key to Egyptian history, and I want to see the tombs. Something may trigger an idea.'

Kate came to his cabin again, and Kelvin kissed her as he'd done the night before, although it seemed to Kate to last even longer. She felt her toes curl again and tension in her legs before she said, 'Enough, Kelvin. Let's sleep.'

At breakfast, while the boat motored south to Tel El Amarna, Captain Marsden asked, 'Doctor, I read about Akhenaten last night. How do modern Egyptians view Akhenaten? I read that his successors did their best to destroy his legacy.'

'I don't believe modern Egyptians have a common view, Captain Marsden. Some know some salient facts, and the scholars know more, but piecing together the history of his reign is ongoing, hampered by the vandalism of those who opposed his reforms. We have no proof, on papyrus or stone, that Tutankhamen was his son, although many believe it to be true.'

'What do the scholars believe?'

'We know that Tutankhamen may have married his aunt, and Akhenaten may have fathered a child with his daughter, but this was common practice among the rulers to keep a tight-knit family. Some believe the medical analysis of mummies and pictorial evidence indicate inherited degeneration, but it surprises no Egyptian. Pharaohs had dictatorial power; they were considered gods, so even if he had a manic mind, the people would excuse not only his desire to have and be associated with one supreme god but to build a new city from scratch for his worship. Being nuts enough to try and maintain their rule and lives through incestuous marriage was insignificant. But Akhenaten did leave a lasting legacy.'

'What was that?'

'He had a massive impact on art. You can read about Amarna art on the web, and once artists learn something new, you can't take it away from them. When you look at the tombs today, think of the tombs you've seen in the past, and you will notice they are different.'

'What should I look for?'

'Before Akhenaten, the paintings and glyphs tried only to tell a story. The size of a man in the image depended on his status; a pharaoh was bigger than a vizier, who was bigger than a worker, for example. After Akhenaten, the artists tried to bring feelings into the characters, using different postures and body forms. Some we can interpret as surrealist. Before Akhenaten, a sheaf of wheat and two corn cobs indicated a quantity of each; afterwards, they were arranged into an attractive garden.'

Bridget asked, 'How did they treat their women?'

Kelvin said, 'Well, life was hard and short for everyone, and most women didn't survive long through and after their childbearing years. Only upper-class men avoided death in battle or accidents on a journey. Children and feeding them was the role of women, although they had respect and equality at a level that women haven't enjoyed since. Look at the paintings in the tombs, and ask the guide: the upper-class men had several wives, and each had children, and the wives became powerful figures alongside their husbands, who revered them. Cleopatra is the ultimate example, and we know as much about Nefertiti as her husband Akhenaten, for they appear together in paintings.'

'Kate,' Bridget asked, 'what's your opinion on all this?'

'I'm going to sit for a sculpture of myself as soon as possible,' Kate declared, grinning. 'A photo in a wallet is not enough!'

When they saw Kelvin's surprised expression, everyone chuckled.

Kelvin asked, 'Kate, head and shoulders or full size?'

'Full size, of course. Then my husband can cuddle my statue when I'm away.'

The laughter grew louder, then became hilarious when Henry's wife said, 'Now that's a good idea. I should have one made of me and put it to bed in the spare bedroom, so Henry will sleep there if he snores.'

The laughter was louder when Henry retorted, 'Get the sculptor to make it from our wedding photo, and then I'll sleep there every night!'

'Akhenaten must have been at least a little mad to build a new city,' Kate remarked to Kelvin as they stood on a high spot viewing the site of Amarna, Akhenaten's city.

'Why do you say that?'

'I'm trying to imagine what this city was like. It's a shame the successors destroyed it, for it must have been beautiful. I can see it, with trees, marble roads and green grass.'

Kelvin agreed. 'You have the right picture; they might even have had fountains. I believe he built it as a physical symbol that the old religions were dead, but those gods didn't let him kill them off. Let's go and see the tombs; I've work to do.'

While Kelvin studied the inscriptions, Kate admired the paintings. 'You're right, Kelvin. I can see these murals are different. They seem much less formal. The artists have added a touch of surrealism, as if they are trying to stir feelings instead of just telling a story. I can feel them.'

'I'm all in favour of stirring your feelings, Kate,' Kelvin joked, then grew serious again. 'I'll show you the photos taken years ago before they deteriorated.'

'When?'

'After we go to bed.'

'I don't know if that's a good idea, Kelvin. Stirring my feelings when I'm in bed with you may have consequences!'

'You stir mine the moment you get into bed with me, so it's only fair I stir yours.'

'Yes, but stirred feelings are something completely new for me, and we only met a week ago.'

'So you won't come to my cabin tonight?'

Kate had to think about it. *I want to, and he's gentle; and I'll never get anywhere if I don't try.* 'I'll come, Kelvin, but I may not stay.'

That night Kelvin, afraid she might leave, shortened their goodnight kiss, and Kate wondered, *Why do I feel dissatisfied?*

18

AFTER BREAKFAST ON DAY EIGHT, Kate and Kelvin went onto the top deck to look at a plan for the Abydos Temple.

'Kelvin, there are many temples and buildings at the Abydos complex; it will take days to find hieroglyphics.'

'Well, most of the day, anyway,' Kelvin agreed. 'I have a document from the Museum that lists the panels. We'll take a taxi in the morning, before the boat sails to Al Banyana, and then rejoin the boat when it stops there to collect the passengers after they've finished their second temple tour.'

'Why do you think it's a good place to look?'

'Because it has many old tombs. It's an ancient city, with centuries of occupation. Unfortunately, over those centuries, as regimes changed, the citizens destroyed and replaced much of it with new buildings, but archaeologically it's important, and it has something other places don't.'

'What's that?'

'Don't laugh, Kate, but I think Abydos holds a memory of the gods of the past.'

'Why do you say that?'

'Seti I, the pharaoh before 1300 BCE, who fathered Rameses the Great, built a temple and inscribed on the wall a list of the kings of Egypt from Namer onwards. Namer lived two thousand years earlier. How's that for memory? Before Namer, there's little but legend. Also, only about two kilometres into the desert is Umm El Qu'ab, where the tombs date back to the period of Nagara, five thousand years ago, when recorded history began.'

'But where do the gods enter your picture?'

'Egypt's polytheist religion was at its height until Rameses II, despite Akhenaten's attempt to create a monotheistic religion based on the sun god Ra, but only thirteen hundred years later, after surviving for four thousand years, it had ended. Abydos existed over the entire period, so if records or writings mention ancient medicines, it is where the people revered those ancient gods and goddesses that we should look for them.'

Kate nodded her understanding. 'Let's mark on the Abydos plan where we can find your list of hieroglyph panels. We have all day on the boat on the way to Sohag to do that, and we have yoga class this morning and belly-dancing practice after lunch. I'd like a sunbathe as well.'

At dinner that night, Bridget asked, 'Kate, are you going to practise a Latin dance tonight?'

'I don't think I should,' Kate said, putting a protective hand on her lower back. 'I overdid the belly dancing earlier, and I have a slight pain here.'

'Then you need a massage. Doctor, have you studied physio?'

'Yes, but I'm afraid I neglected the subject in favour of osteopathic methods.'

'So you crack bones?'

'Some osteopaths do, but I don't. I should have gone to more physio lessons.'

'Why didn't you?'

Looking slightly embarrassed, Kelvin admitted, 'The lessons were packed with female students, so the men went to osteo.'

Kate asked, 'Why? And remember, you never lie.'

'Because the physio teacher was a handsome young lecturer who used the students for demonstrations.'

With a wicked grin, Bridget jumped to a conclusion: 'And the osteo teacher was a sexy woman who cracked the bones of the male students?'

'Not overly sexy, but she was strong, and the lessons could be painful.'

Everyone laughed, including Kate, who said, 'Then I won't ask you to massage me. It hurts enough already.'

When she slipped into his cabin later, Kate said, 'Kelvin, I would love you to massage my back – but please be gentle.'

'I'll try, Kate. Lie on the bed on your tummy.' Kelvin started massaging her legs.

Kate giggled when he arrived at her thighs. 'You can press harder. That's too gentle – it's almost like a caress.'

'It's what I want to do, Kate, but I'm trying to be a doctor.'

Thirty minutes later, after he had done her bottom, back, arms and neck, Kate was feeling an entirely new experience: it was as if the bed was no longer there, and she was floating in a warm pool. 'Kelvin, I'm no expert, but I think you're good at this. Do the rest of me.'

She turned over, and he began again on her legs. Fifteen minutes later, when he bypassed her breasts and reached her neck, she said, 'Kelvin, I said all of me.'

Half an hour later, after he had massaged the muscles around her breasts, carefully avoiding her nipples, Kate thought, *I'm so relaxed that if he makes love to me, I won't be able to resist.*

But Kelvin just said, 'Your massage is complete, Kate.' Then he kissed her and lay down next to her.

To her surprise, Kate felt a sharp pang of disappointment. *I wanted him to.*

The next day, at breakfast, Bridget asked teasingly, 'So did you have a massage last night, Kate.'

Seeing Kate's expression, Kelvin jumped in. 'Of course, she did, Bridget. A passenger in pain is my responsibility, and it was my duty to try to relieve that pain. It did get me thinking, though. Can I ask you something?'

'Please do.'

'Considering the number of passengers on board and their ages, would they make sufficient use of a professional masseuse to justify the cruise company employing one?'

'Now you suggest it, I do. It's a brilliant idea.'

'Then perhaps you could suggest it to the captain? You can say I agree for health reasons.'

Bridget, now diverted from the subject of Kate's massage, replied, 'I will, as soon as I can.'

Realising how skilfully Kelvin had diverted Bridget's interest in her, Kate thought, *He's protecting me.*

She and Kelvin left the boat at seven in a taxi for the fifty-kilometre drive to the temple. There, they repeated what they had done at the previous ruins, Kate checking the hieroglyphic panels against his photos and Kelvin looking at others.

Five hours later, Kate had enjoyed the morning. She found having an expert to answer her questions compared to a canned speech by a guide made a huge difference. And Kelvin found that Kate's constant questions didn't slow down his survey; to the contrary, they helped him concentrate on the glyphs.

They passed a refreshments counter when walking from one panel to another, and Kelvin said, 'Kate, I must buy more water. Do you want some?'

'Please. Let's take a short break in the shade.'

They'd found a convenient stone in the shade of a wall to sit on while they sipped the cool water when Kate pointed and said, 'Look, there's the group from the boat.'

'I'll ask when they are returning to the boat. If we don't catch the bus, we have a hundred-kilometre drive in the opposite direction to catch the boat at Quena.'

Kelvin did, returned and said, 'We have a bit more than an hour, Kate. We can do the last two panels. Let's go.'

Kelvin stood reading the glyphs at the panel's top while Kate did the same as she had done for every photo. She stood back from it and checked that the image included everything she could see. With his head craned back, Kelvin didn't see Kate drop to her knees beside the wall and begin excavating with her bare hands; she was trying to make a small valley along the base of the stone.

He only noticed her when he bumped into her. 'Kate, what are you doing down there?'

'The photo's incomplete, Kelvin. The camera was far from the panel, and the sand blocked the view of at least one line of hieroglyphics.'

Kelvin dropped to his knees. 'I'll start at the other end.'

Fifteen minutes later, another line of glyphs was visible. 'This seems to be the last line, Kate. I'll photograph them.'

Kelvin took several pictures by lying on the sand close to the wall, with his camera as low as possible. 'Kate, you're marvellous! You deserve a prize! After lunch, we can look at the images on my computer screen and try translating them.'

'Okay, hold on to that thought.'

'What thought?'

'That I deserve a prize.'

'I'll think about one, Kate.'

Back on the boat, the two huddled around the screen in Kelvin's cabin. Kate's perfume kept invading Kelvin's senses; he thought it was doing its best to sneak up his nostrils into his brain.

He called up the photo on the screen, then fetched a carefully bound document. 'This is a reference to hieroglyphs; I would typically refer to it on the web, but on a moving boat on the Nile, comms is a problem. I printed it from a Pennsylvania University document. Let's take the glyphs one at a time and copy what the university says each one means.'

As he sat down beside her, the heady perfume distracted him again. 'Kate, have you sprayed on a bit of extra perfume?'

'Of course.'

'Why, "of course"?'

'I'm not going to let you forget your promise of a prize.'

'I won't forget,' Kelvin reassured her.

They worked together, referring to the photo and then the document, with Kelvin making notes, for about forty minutes, before Kate said, 'This is impossible, Kelvin. We've only found one, and even that's doubtful.'

'It's possible, but it will take a long time. Let's try something else. This first one is a cartouche, so it must be the name of someone. Turn to the section that lists known people. There are only a couple of hundred.'

After another twenty minutes of searching the document, Kelvin said, 'This one looks right, Kate.'

'Yes, I agree. Who is it?'

'Anedjib. A high official, I think, but I can confirm that later. The next sign I recognise. It means something like "fall" or "came down". Look in the verb section.'

144

'So it says Anedjib fell?'

'No, it reads right to the left, more like something fell on Anedjib.'

'What did?'

'Probably the next glyph.'

'If you can't search directly, can you send the photo to someone who can do it for you?'

Kelvin thought of Zorah. 'I could ask a woman at the British Museum, but I don't want to.'

'A girlfriend?'

'I never made love to her, Kate, although she's young and a good friend.'

'Then why don't you want to send it to her?'

'The less chance anyone else knows what we find, the better. Getting someone to pay for information depends on its being exclusive, and she may have to ask someone else. Later tonight, when the boat is stationary, I can try to connect to Penn University. That may work.'

Kate nodded. 'But if you can't translate it tonight, you must send it to your British Museum woman tomorrow.'

Later, after the yoga class, Kelvin remained on the deck watching as Bridget, Belinda and Kate practised the belly-dancing movement.

'You're getting there, Kate,' Bridget said encouragingly. 'Your forward and backward movement is nearly enough, and the sideways swing has improved. Lift onto your toes on the rising side as a smooth movement, don't wait to reach the end of the hip movement. Slow down, don't shake. Think of a Balinese dance, where it's all movement and no bells.'

Kate did, and Kelvin thought, *I should have a raging erection now.*

When the class ended, Kate approached Kelvin, who was

waiting at the rail. 'I'll take a shower and dress for dinner,' she said, mopping her sweaty face with a small towel.

'That can wait,' Kelvin said. 'Quena is ahead, and we must pass the Nag' Hammadi Bridge. Let's stay up here and watch.'

'What's special about it?'

'It has to swing out of the way.'

Kate reached out and took Kelvin's hand. *I feel tense, like we're arriving at a place we've seen before.*

When the ship swung around the island in the bend of the Nile seven kilometres before Quena, Kate saw a bridge. 'Wow, that's a long bridge,' she commented.

'It's the railway bridge, and it's actually only half a kilometre long, but it probably seems longer, because there's nothing to compare it with for scale.'

'But how do we get past it? I don't see any bit that will swing away.'

'This one is high enough to go under. The swing bridge is still coming, a bit more than two kilometres further.'

Fifteen minutes later, as they passed under the rail bridge, Kate could see the next bridge ahead.

Kelvin said, 'You can see all the bridge sections connect on top of a column. Look for the one that has a column in the middle.'

'Yes, I see it, towards the right.'

'That section will rotate on the column in the middle, leaving a passage down each side for boats. This boat's builders built it to a specification to allow it to fit through the space.'

'Where will we moor?'

'On the other side. There's a mooring for cruise boats on the West bank.'

19

AFTER DINNER, IN KELVIN'S CABIN, after the boat had tied up in Quena at the riverside dock, Kate sat staring at the hieroglyph photo while Kelvin logged in and connected to Pennsylvania University.

'There, I'm connected. I must download the photo in the requested format to get a translation...' Kelvin trailed off as he noticed that Kate was staring at the photo and looked pale. 'What is it, Kate?'

'Kelvin, pass me a piece of paper and a pencil.'

Kelvin passed her a notebook, 'Here.' He watched as she carefully copied four glyphs.

'What do these say?'

'In ancient Egyptian, they are the equivalent of "hwn't".'

'How would you pronounce that?'

'The "hw' as "a", and the vowel would be "i" between the "n" and the "t", so "Anit".'

'When I looked long enough, I just felt I was looking at the name of something.' Kate shook her head in confusion – she didn't know how the idea had come to her. 'Cut the photo into three, a first and last part before and after "Anit", and download those.'

Kelvin downloaded the first, and a message popped onto the screen: 'Searching for a match – image one. Estimate twenty-three minutes.'

It took nearly thirty minutes while Kelvin and Kate searched his data for references to Anit – if it was medicine, it should appear in the ancient pharmacopoeia. Then a list of six alternate transactions with percentage accuracy rolled on to the screen.

'Well, that seems pretty conclusive,' Kelvin said: 'Either "despite" or "although", followed by "treated with" or "treatment with", "anointing with" or "administering".'

'Do the last bit.'

Kelvin uploaded the second image, and the message popped up: 'Searching for a match – image two. Estimate eighteen minutes.'

The result appeared in seven. Kelvin read, '"Calamity fell on Anetjib." The alternatives are "disaster", "catastrophe" or "came to".'

'And that footnote?' Kate pointed at the screen.

'Use of "death" instead of "calamity" would normally be the cartouche of Anubis.'

'So the whole translation is, "Although treated with Anit, calamity fell on Anedjib"?'

'Yes, Kate, and you did it! You are a wonderful, marvellous, fantastic woman!'

'It wasn't me, Kelvin,' Kate said, her confusion evident. 'It was something or someone else that prompted me to find it.' Then, to his surprise, she said, 'Kelvin, I'm tired. I think it's time I got some sleep. We can discuss the next steps tomorrow.'

'Okay, Kate,' he said. 'You deserve a good-night kiss.'

She could feel his passion when he kissed her; she sensed he didn't want to release her from his arms, and the shiver of fear she'd experienced earlier at Kelvin's excitement, and which had led her to say she wanted to retire for the night, returned.

She didn't sleep in his cabin that night.

When Kate arrived in the breakfast room the next day, Kelvin, already seated, had made a start on a bowl of fruit.

Pulling out a chair, Kate sat down next to him. 'Morning! So are we going to the Dendera temple today?'

'Yes, Kate, not to study but just to visit.'

'Why?'

'I've been there several times and I know there's nothing to find. It's a complex that covers a long period in Egypt's history, but there are four places that I want to visit. Most important is the Temple of Hathor, then the temple of the birth of Isis, and then there's the sacred lake and the sanatorium.'

'Is there a personal reason for your interest?'

'Yes. I haven't asked you about your attitude to religion, but I'll tell you mine. I believe there's much we don't know about the universe and that without that knowledge, people have, since they first looked at the stars and wondered, created gods to explain what they don't know. I don't believe the gods of any one group of humanity are any more legitimate than any others. I believe the stories surrounding them all are fictional, created mostly by citizens, either with good intentions or to enrich themselves, or both.'

Kelvin looked at Kate to see if she was following him, and she nodded. 'So I'm entitled to choose which gods I shall pray to,' he continued, 'and I chose Isis and Hathor, for those were the names given to them by my ancestors. Isis is the force of healing, and Hathor is the force of love. If I pray, it is not to an entity but to those forces.'

Kate nodded again. 'You've just put into words what I've felt for years,' she said. 'I shall come to the temples with you and pray. And where does the sacred lake fit into your theory?'

'It's a genetic memory. Humanity has always needed water to survive, so water has become a precious symbol of life for everyone. We evolved from the sea, our blood is salty, and we carry the memory of that water throughout our bodies.'

He's a philosopher. 'Kelvin, what you say simplifies everything, and I feel good.'

'A truth can do that.'

As they approached the entrance to the temple complex, Kate said, 'This is magnificent!'

'I don't think that's the right word, Kate, it's more than that, but I don't have a better one. What do you feel when you look at it?'

'That thousands of people had to believe in building this. It's like the great cathedrals of Europe, like York or Notre Dame. The people who built this must have believed deep down in Hathor and Isis.'

'This is the gate of the Roman emperors Domitian and Trajan. They believed, although they were Roman emperors.'

'Then shouldn't they have built a temple to a Roman god?'

'Domitian might have begun building the temple to appease the people, but then Trajan appears pictorially as a pharaoh making offerings to Hathor, possibly because he recognised Hathor as the goddess who predated Aphrodite and Venus in people's beliefs. That's purely speculation on my part; we will never know what he thought. Let's go through and explore the temples.'

Two hours later, having examined all the surrounding temples, they stood together in the Temple of Isis. When Kelvin bowed his head, Kate did too. She reached out and held his hand. She didn't hear his prayer, but she thought, *Isis, support this man who has dedicated himself to healing; he's worthy of your help.*

Twenty minutes later, after their prayers, they arrived at the back of the temple behind the sanctuary, alone in front of the shrine of Hathor. Kate prayed. *Hathor, bless my love for Kelvin, for I shall not waver.*

She didn't hear Kelvin's words, but when she turned to look at him, he turned to her, and she saw the glow in his eyes. She stepped forward into his arms, looked up, and kissed him.

On the boat's top deck, after lunch, Kate asked, 'What do you plan for Luxor, Kelvin?'

'We have a day and a half there. I want to visit the Luxor museum. I've four medical references to items in the museum that I must look at. There are two more in the Aswan Museum.'

Kate nodded and said, 'I had an idea last night while I was trying to sleep: now that we know the name of a medicine, maybe we can ask the local herb sellers if they have seen it?'

'I think it's worth a try,' Kelvin said, then looked at Kate with concern. 'Didn't you sleep well last night? I didn't, either. Why didn't you come to my cabin?'

'I was scared, Kelvin. I don't know why.'

'Please don't be scared, Kate. I would never harm you.'

'Then I'll try tonight.'

Kate slipped into Kelvin's cabin that night and joined him in bed. Cuddling up to him, she whispered, 'Kelvin, I've thought about last night. I'm the problem.'

'What is it, Kate?'

'Yesterday, I had two conflicting feelings: I wanted to make love to you, but the thought scared me.'

'I think that's just uncertainty, Kate,' Kelvin said. 'You aren't sure if your feelings are real or just stirred up by time and place. Don't worry about it. I won't make love to you. Kiss me, then go to sleep.'

The kiss lasted long enough for Kate to think, *I'm being stupid,* before Kelvin turned away.

'Kate, I'm going to the Luxor Museum this morning, then this afternoon and tomorrow morning; I'll look for herb sellers. Do you want to take the day tour to the Valley of the Kings with the other passengers on the cruise? Then you and I can look for herb sellers in Edfu the day after tomorrow.'

'I said I wanted to stay with you, and that's what I want to do,' Kate reminded him.

'Okay. I suppose the temples aren't going anywhere, so we can visit them another time.'

He thinks there'll be another time. So do I.

At the museum, after Kelvin had introduced himself to the curator, Dr Gamal, using Dr Moustapha Hassan as his referee, they found themselves with a dedicated expert guide.

When Dr Gamal learnt they had missed a guided tour to the Valley of the Kings and Queen Hatshepsut's temple to visit the museum, he assured them, 'You made the right decision. All that's left in the tombs are the wall decorations. We have the contents here and in Cairo, and far better photos of the walls than seeing them in dim light, but the tourists like descending into a tomb.'

Dr Gamal found the four references Kelvin sought. The tablets mentioned a medical treatment, treating a snake bite on two and scorpion stings on the others.

Kate asked, 'Doctor Gamal, why were snakes and scorpions such a problem in antiquity?'

'First and foremost, people went barefoot or wore simple sandals. Also, only the wealthy had beds; the masses slept on the ground. Second, people and fauna had to share a narrow strip of land beside the Nile, so the likelihood of encountering something dangerous was high. Since then, the growing population has displaced the snakes and scorpions except on the fringes of civilisation. Come with me; let me show you painted scenes of daily life, and you will see barefoot men reaping and women threshing and winnowing corn. Disturbing a snake or scorpion often led to a sting or bite.'

After admiring the paintings, they thanked Dr Gamal and went for lunch at a restaurant in the Winter Palace hotel.

'Kelvin, this hotel is fantastic.'

'It stems from an era when few people travelled, and most of those who did were extremely wealthy. Wait until you see the Old Cataract Hotel in Aswan. It has character.'

As they polished off the last crumbs of a delicious lunch, Kelvin said, 'Let's find a taxi driver and ask him to take us to a herb seller.'

They visited four herb sellers. Three were in markets, manning stalls with piled boxes of dried herbs and roots and some other items that, to Kate, looked like dried-up bits of animals. When Kelvin showed them the name of the medicine they were looking for, all shook their heads.

The fourth was in a small mud-brick shop on a dusty street, with a collection twice the size of the first three. Looking at the glyph, the aged man inside said, 'I've seen that sign only once. A man once offered to sell me some leaves, but when he couldn't tell me what they were for, I refused to buy them, and he left. He was a stranger, a Nubian.'

Excited when they left the shop, Kelvin said, 'Kate, we're getting warm. I can feel it.'

'Me too! We must try some more tomorrow. We'll tell the taxi driver we want to visit herb sellers south of Luxor.'

'Why south?'

'Nubian travellers coming from the south would meet them first.'

'Kate, if we to manage to find Anit, it'll be due to you.'

Before Kate left her cabin to join Kelvin, she thought to herself, *Kelvin won't take advantage of me, so I must overcome my problem.* She didn't put on her nightie before wrapping the sheet around her.

Kelvin kissed her again, and it left her wondering. *Did he notice I'm naked?*

Kelvin had noticed but said nothing. *It's the first time. Take it slow.*

After an early breakfast, they left the boat at the dock in Luxor. The taxi driver took them to five herb sellers that gave them no new leads, and, getting back into the taxi after they visited the fifth, Kelvin said, 'Kate, I think this is hopeless. Let's go back to the boat.'

'Where's the explorer and researcher gone to, Kelvin? I thought you never gave up.'

'I'm not giving up, Kate. I'll return to the hieroglyphics. There are lots to check and translate.'

'Come on, let's try just one more herbalist. If you don't want to come, I'll go alone.'

'Of course I'll come.'

And the sixth herb seller turned depression into euphoria. 'I don't have any of this herb, but I know who does, or at least who did,' he said. 'Nakia Khali in Edfu had some when I visited him years ago.'

'Do you know what it does?'

'He told me it made a nice tea.'

'Where do we find him?'

The herb seller gave them directions, then said, 'Tell him that Bithiah Sallom sends him good wishes and that I would visit if my arthritis allowed me to.'

Kelvin said, 'We thank you, and may Allah grant you every wish.'

In the taxi back to the boat, Kelvin said, 'Thank you, Kate.'

'What for?'

'Insisting on a visit to another herb seller. Without you, I would have buried myself in old documents again.'

'You would have got there in the end, Kelvin,' Kate reassured him, squeezing his hand. 'I'm just playing hunches.'

After lunch, they went to the upper deck to watch the activity on the river as the boat motored to Edfu.

'What will we see at the Edfu temple?' Kate asked Kelvin.

'Apart from the herb seller, the temple is dedicated to the marriage of Hathor and Horus.'

'Then we must visit it. Hathor is waiting for us. Are you excited?'

'Trying hard not to be, Kate. I know the herb seller we want to see may no longer be there, and he may not have any Anit if he is. But we have taken a small step forward.'

'I feel that too, and with every step you take, I'll try to take a small step too.'

'You'll sleep with me tonight?'

'Yes, but only a small step.'

It was a repeat of the night before, although the kiss lasted longer, and Kate wrapped her arms around him. Naked, she pressed her breasts against his chest. *Now he knows I'm nude.*

Kelvin thought, *She wants more, and so do I, but I can't.*

20

THE FOLLOWING DAY THEY JOINED the passengers on the buses to the Edfu temple but didn't go into it. Instead, excited, they crossed the car park and the main road, found the side road the sixth herb seller had told them about, and soon stood before a small shop.

The roller shutter was down. On it, in Arabic, they could read 'Healing Herbs' in faded green paint.

'This is disappointing, Kate.'

'Very disappointing,' she agreed. 'Maybe it opens later. Let's ask someone.'

Three shops further along the dusty street, they found a baker, and Kelvin asked. The reply was even more depressing. 'No, it won't open. Nakia Khali had an accident three weeks ago while crossing the road to the temple. The shop is now up for sale.'

'Was he killed?'

'No, but he can't walk. His wife sold everything in the shop. I can tell you where to find him if you want to buy the shop, but he's asking too much.'

'Please, we would like to talk to him.'

'Take a taxi to the Falafel restaurant on the Aswan-Giza road. There's a small street beside it. Walk to the end and ask someone for him.'

Finding Nakia Khali proved easy: the first young man they came across, sitting against the wall of a house, pointed across the road and said, 'That one there.'

The older woman who opened the door a crack first looked

suspiciously at Kelvin, then, when she saw Kate, relaxed and opened the door further.

Kate stepped forward and said, '*As-Salaam-Alaikum, sayidati.*'

The woman replied, '*Wa-Salaam-As-Alaikum.* How can I help? Do you want to speak to my husband?'

'If possible. His friend, Bithiah Sallom, sends his good wishes.'

'Then come in. My husband can't walk but is otherwise well and will be pleased to hear of his old friend. I shall make coffee.'

Nakia Khali was sitting in a comfortable chair, his legs on a stool. Kelvin and Kate greeted him politely while his wife bustled off to make the coffee.

Kelvin repeated, 'Bithiah Sallom sends his good wishes.'

Nakia asked, 'How is he?'

'He's well. Complaining about his arthritis, but he'll live many years.'

'That is good to hear, but I'm sure you didn't come here just to bring his wishes.'

'That is true. We asked Bithiah Sallom if he had some Anit, and he sent us to see you.'

'I wish I had some to sell you, but I've none left; I used the last three years ago.'

'Can you tell us where to get it?'

'No, for it came from Nubia. Once, I had a regular supply, but it became rarer as the years passed. If there is anyone who has any, it will be a Nubian in Kom Ombo.'

'There are Nubians there?'

'Many came from the Nubian valley when the high dam flooded it. Perhaps one of them still has links with Nubians in the south.'

Khali's wife entered the room, carrying tiny cups of strong black coffee on a tray.

As she sipped hers, Kate asked, 'Why are you selling your shop? Have you no children to run it for you?'

The man proudly said, 'I've four sons, but they are all educated and work in cities along the Nile. One is a doctor in Cairo. None of them is interested in selling herbs.'

'That is sad.'

'Inshallah, times must change. The baker waits for me to drop my price before he buys my shop.'

They thanked both Nakia Khali and his wife, and returned to the Falafel restaurant on the highway. Kate looked at her watch and realised they'd missed the boat's departure. 'Kelvin, we must take the taxi to Kom Ombo, the boat's next stop.'

In the taxi, Kelvin admitted, 'I'm beginning to give up hope.'

Kate put a reassuring hand on his thigh and said, 'I learnt something interesting when I studied sales and marketing, Kelvin.'

'What was that?'

'We learnt that salespeople should count their failures to get an order, not the successes, and as managers, we should count the number of failed calls they made to measure their success.'

Interested, Kelvin asked, 'Why?'

'Because no salesperson can achieve a hundred per cent success. On average, they may have one success in ten calls. I'm counting our failures to find Anit, and each makes me happier, for the tenth one is closer.'

'Kate, remind me about your prize.'

'I don't have to, Kelvin,' Kate said with a warm smile. 'I think you might be it.'

Their searches in Kom Ombo produced four more failures, but three of the four all said the same thing. 'To find an ancient herb, try Luxor or Aswan.'

They reboarded the boat for dinner, and afterwards, Kelvin said good night to Kate, kissed her at her cabin door, and then went to his cabin. He filed the photos he had taken, then undressed, showered and lay down on the bed.

He couldn't sleep; his imagination began to build images of what he would find in Aswan.

The door opened quietly, and Kate, wrapped in a towel, slipped in. 'I can't sleep,' she whispered.

'Me neither. I guess it's the excitement. Come, get into bed.'

She dropped the towel and was under the sheet beside him a moment later.

He turned to her. 'May I kiss you?'

'Please, Kelvin.'

The kiss lingered, and Kate felt warm and relaxed, naked in Kelvin's arms. He stroked her back. The cabin faded away, and it seemed she was somewhere else as pleasure flooded her.

Suddenly, Kate heard wings; moments later, a dark shadow descended over her. Frightened, she pushed Kelvin away, and then the cabin returned, and she was once again in the bed.

'What's the matter, Kate? Did I do something wrong?'

'No, I think it's me. I felt wonderful, and then I seemed to be floating in your arms and joining somehow with you. Then I heard wings, and something dark came to me. It scared me.'

'Kate, maybe it's something from your past. When you relax completely and stop thinking, those old memories can push themselves up from what we call the subconscious. Can you think what it might be?'

'I never told you why my marriage failed.'

'You don't need to, Kate. You already said it was quick and catastrophic.'

'Well, that may be the problem. My husband had sex with me three times. The first time was before the marriage, possibly contributing to my marrying him. I didn't have an orgasm, so the fourth time he proposed to tie me up. He said punishing me for not having an orgasm would bring it on. When I saw the glitter in his eyes and the expression on his face, I felt he was cruel. He terrified me, so I left him. It was less than six weeks after our marriage. I haven't had sex since, and have never been in bed with another man until you. When men have proposed sex, I haven't felt fear, just no desire. With you, I feel desire.'

'Kate, I think I must tell you something.'

'What?'

'I told you about the accident months ago that broke my ribs and leg and how I spent over three months recovering?'

'Yes, I remember.'

'Well, since that accident, I've had erectile dysfunction. I can't achieve an erection, so I can't have sex.'

A feeling of disappointment tempered with sympathy filled Kate. *The first man I want to make love with can't!* 'Is it permanent?' she asked gently.

'No. Physically, I'm fine. I still have erections in my sleep. The problem seems to be psychological.'

'That's a relief,' Kate said, then asked, 'How do you know you're having erections if you're asleep?'

'The doctor gave me a test. When I went to bed, I stuck a paper band on my penis and found the band broken in the morning.'

Kate absorbed this information, then asked, 'So where does that leave us?'

Kelvin sighed. 'If some night in the future, we reach the same point we did tonight, you can try to remember that I would never hurt you. Maybe the black shadow won't come. And that may also help me recover.'

The boat stopped the next day in Aswan, and Kate and Kelvin joined the group tour.

On the bus to the ferry that would take them to the island where the Philae temple stood, Kate asked Kelvin, 'So, what's special about this one?'

'The builders dedicated it to Isis, the goddess of healing. I need healing, so a visit and a prayer seem appropriate.'

'Then I shall pray for you too.'

The tour guide described how the island of Philae, since the 1900s after the completion of the Aswan low dam, flooded annually. Then, in the 1960s, the temple on Philae island was deconstructed piece by piece and carefully moved half a kilometre away to the higher Agilkia Island. The reason for this was the construction of the Aswan Dam at that time and a massive international project to save the ancient temples and ruins.

When they arrived, Kelvin and Kate headed for the temple of Isis. As they walked, Kelvin told Kate about the temple.'It dates to about 550 BCE. At first, it was a small kiosk dedicated to Isis. Later, Ptolemy II built the temple we see today and dedicated it to Isis, Osiris and Horus, but it's known as the temple of Isis. For centuries, pilgrims came to worship Isis.'

In the far back of the temple, Kelvin took Kate's hand as he prayed silently. *Isis, goddess of healing, heal my ill that I may honour Hathor with the love I feel for the woman by my side.*

Kate squeezed his hand as she offered up her own silent prayer: *Hear my plea, Isis. Heal this man who has dedicated his life to you so we may honour Hathor through our love for each other.*

They visited the temple of Imhotep and then the temple of Horus, where Kelvin pointed out the hieroglyph panels. 'Kate, Christianity and the Byzantines have a lot to answer for. The early Christians, and then the Iconoclasts after Egypt fell under Byzantine rule, scratched out these hieroglyphs. But if you look carefully, you will notice that images of Horus have not suffered as much.'

'Why?'

'Historians speculate it's because of parallels between the stories of Horus and Jesus. They are tortuous arguments. Come, our group is collecting for the return. Let's join them.'

On the boat, Kelvin asked, 'Kate, will you sleep with me tonight?'

'Yes, Kelvin, but let's not tempt fate. We must give the goddess time to help. Just a cuddle and a kiss, like a long-married couple.'

After dinner and a turn on the deck to look at the lights of Aswan, she went with him to his cabin.

'Kelvin, we have two more days to find herb sellers before you must be on board when the boat leaves for Cairo. I'm supposed to leave tomorrow morning with the others before the new passengers arrive for the return-to-Cairo cruise. I'll delay my flight by two days and book the Old Cataract Hotel for the last night so I can help. Will the captain allow me to spend an extra night on board with you?'

'I'll ask, Kate. I'm sure he'll agree.'

21

AFTER BREAKFAST, KELVIN SAID, 'I can't go into Aswan, Kate. I must stay to say goodbye to our passengers as they leave, then meet the new passengers after lunch. But the good news is that the captain agreed you can stay with me for an extra night.'

Kate smiled. 'Great. I'll move my stuff into your cabin now, then go into Aswan to look for herb sellers.'

Kate stood with Kelvin to say goodbye to the passengers as they debarked. They all had nice things to say to them, but Bridget was the most forthright. 'Doctor, Kate, this is the best holiday I've ever had. Thank you. You have our address and numbers, so please call if you're in Paris. And send us a wedding invitation and photos of your kids! They'll be beautiful.'

'What makes you think we're getting married?' Kate asked with a laugh.

'When the gods decide, we don't have a choice, and I know it's inevitable.'

'Thanks, Bridget,' Kelvin said. 'I hope you're right.'

Later, Kelvin wrote his medical report for the captain to send to the agent: apart from two crew members who had cut fingers and a passenger couple who had diarrhoea after eating street food, and, of course, Kate's incident with the falcon, there had been no medical incidents of note. He then studied the list of new passengers, looking for any that were likely to need abnormal care and noting those passengers taking routine medicine who he should interview to be sure they had sufficient medication for the trip.

The passengers began arriving at three. The onboarding procedure was identical to the one in Cairo, with one significant difference: Kelvin was no longer looking for a potential partner.

Kate ordered a taxi and asked the driver to take her southeast of Aswan to find herb sellers. He took her to an area where the maze of narrow passages surprised her.

'This seems very old?' she remarked.

'It is, *Sayidati*. The temple builders first occupied this area.'

'But how do I find herb sellers?'

'Just ask, *Sayidati*. Someone will know, or they will send you to someone who might. I cannot drive down these passages – they are too narrow. I will wait for you here.'

In the fourth shop where Kate enquired, the owner said, 'My son will take you to see the herb sellers. There are five. He knows every street here, as he delivers my produce.'

At each of the first three, Kate asked, 'I wish to buy some of this herb. Do you have it, or can you tell me where to get it?' but got no joy.

She needed a break, so she told her young guide, 'Find a place that sells cool drinks. I'm sure you would like one too.'

He took her to a café, and they sat at a small table with tall glasses of lemonade. The boy asked, '*Sayidati*, this herb you ask for, where does it come from?'

'I don't know. It is an ancient herb. I'm hoping to find some, although it is not common.'

'Then asking the young men selling herbs is no good. We must ask an ancient man.'

Smiling at his description of a man as ancient, she asked, 'Do you know any?'

'There is one I know. Before the man sold his shop, he would give me a sweet when I delivered his vegetables. But I don't know if he's still alive.'

'Can you take me?'

They wound through five narrow streets to a cul-de-sac, and the boy knocked at a small house at the end. The woman who opened the door recognised the youngster.

When he asked for Jaddo Hamed, she showed them into a small room, where a man with silvery hair and a deeply lined face sat in a chair with a blanket over his legs. When he opened his mouth to speak, Kate saw only three teeth.

'*As-Salaam-Alaikum.* Why have you come here?' he asked.

Kate bowed her head to him. '*Wa-Salaam-As-Alaikum*, great grandfather. I am looking for an ancient herb.'

Jaddo Hamed had to hunt under the blanket that covered his legs to produce a pair of wire-framed spectacles with powerful lenses, then fumble them onto his ears. Then he looked at the paper Kate showed him with the word 'Anit' written on it, both as a hieroglyph and in Hieratic, and whispered, 'Anit. I've not seen that for many years.'

'So it is no longer available?'

'I do not know. Only one man I know of may have some: Babu Fadel.'

'Where do I find him?'

'My granddaughter can tell you.'

He sent Kate's guide to summon a young woman to the room. She had a conversation with the boy, and when he had repeated the instructions to be sure he had understood them correctly, Kate thanked them both, and they left.

'It is a long way, *Sayidati*.'

'But you are a strong boy. We will go.'

The walk took forty minutes. Finally, the houses began to thin out, and the invading desert sands made the going more difficult.

The home, surrounded by a wall, was visibly old, but inside the walls, once they passed through the gate, was a small but luxuriant garden, and surrounded by the plants and flowers was a man in a wheelchair.

As Kate and the boy approached him, he watched with bright eyes that gave the lie to the wrinkles and white hair.

'*As-Salaam-Alaikum*, Babu Fadel.'

'*Wa-Salaam-As-Alaikum*. What brings a goddess to my house?'

Kat decided to be direct. 'The need to buy Anit.'

'Then I cannot help you. The last time I bought a few leaves was many years ago. I used it for myself.'

Kate thought, *At least I'll learn what it does.* 'For what reason?'

'To make a tea that kept me and my wife healthy when others became ill.'

'Where did you get it?'

'A Nubian sold it to me, but he has not come for fifty years.'

Perhaps he knows where it grows. 'Where did he come from?'

'From far south. The Nubian rode a camel. Perhaps his people no longer grow it. The dam flooded the Nubian valley. If they grew it there, it no longer grows.'

'Thank you,' Kate said. 'I will continue my search.'

'Then try further south, where camels can walk.'

When Kate returned to the boat, Kelvin told her, 'Kate, I don't want to eat dinner on board. I'd rather have you to myself. The ferry to Elephant Island is a three-minute walk from here. Let's take it and go for dinner on the island.'

'That's a great idea! Give me ten minutes to change.'

During their dinner on the terrace of the Movenpick Hotel, Kate told him about her search for the herb.

'Kate, it's always the same,' Kelvin said despondently. 'It exists, came from the south but comes no more.'

'Yes, Kelvin, but now we know it still exists.'

'Only maybe.'

'I believe it does.'

Later that night, when they climbed into bed, Kate asked, 'So now you've seen the passenger list for the return trip, you can tell me: how many beautiful sexy young women will there be?'

'None, Kate,' Kelvin said with a laugh. 'There are two women, aged thirty-three and thirty-four, but they're not beautiful and sexy. They're travelling together.'

'Then I hope they are a lesbian couple,' Kate teased.

'Kate, even if I could physically, I cannot imagine either of them replacing you. You're marvellous. And anyway, they have no chance of luring me away from the work I must do.'

'What work?'

'Instead of going on excursions on the return journey, I'm going to translate the hieroglyphics on the photos we took.'

Reassured by his response, Kate said, 'Darling, please, love me like the last time.'

It was like the last time, but when Kate felt the pleasure flooding her, the dark shadow didn't come. Instead, her body tingled all over, and then she felt Kelvin and herself, locked together in their embrace, lifted into the night sky, and then the sound of wings as it seemed they rested on the green grass of a small valley with a tinkling waterfall and a small pool. Kate felt waves of ecstasy flowing through her as Kelvin caressed her, and a fire began below her tummy. As it grew, the heat made her pant. Suddenly, Kelvin was there in her mind, and she was in Kelvin's; their bodies seemed to be one, and then she shuddered as unbearable pleasure flowed up her spine and down to her curling toes.

Now I know what an aerial orgasm must be like.

Afterwards, lying in a stupor, with her eyes closed, she asked in a whisper, 'Kelvin, have we returned to your cabin?'

'I don't know; I haven't looked,' he whispered back.

After another few moments of lying together in silence, Kate said quietly, 'Kelvin, we're all sweaty. We should shower.'

'Okay, my love, you go first.'

'No, you go. I'm not sure I can stand.'

Kelvin showered, and while waiting for Kate to do the same, he changed the damp sheets on the bed. *I want to marry her, but I'm only half a man. If I ask and she says yes, how long will it last? Less than an hour after an orgasm is not the right time for a rational answer.*

When Kate returned from her shower, towelling her hair dry, he said, 'Kate, that was wonderful, and if I were a whole man, I would ask you to marry me. I'm afraid that if I do, you'll say yes without thinking about it.'

'I don't need to think about it. I know what I want.'

'But you may feel different in the future. Unless I get better, you may slowly become frustrated. You will think fate has mistreated you, and we will no longer experience what we did tonight.'

'Kelvin, I've lived without sex for over six years but now have had the most incredible orgasm imaginable because I love you. I think that's enough. I don't need more.'

'Kate, I love you too, but we've known each other only two weeks. You must return to work, and I must finish my contract, then I'll return to England as soon as possible. Then, if we can continue and live together for a few months, perhaps you can be sure.'

'Do you think you can recover?'

'Yes, Kate, and now I'm determined to do so.'

'Then do it with me.'

'I will do, Kate, so I can be sure we'll give our children a good home.'

'You sound like Darryl.'

'Who's he?'

'My friend Marylyn's boyfriend. She wants to marry him. He's a statistician at Cambridge University and won't ask her until the probability of a successful marriage is over ninety-five per cent.'

Kelvin laughed. 'I think I'd like him.'

22

THE FOLLOWING DAY, as they left the boat after breakfast, Kelvin said, 'Everything we've learnt indicates that the plant comes from far south. It may be so far south that it's across the border in Sudan, and I may need to visit the Khartoum Museum for more information. I think we'll learn nothing in the towns or villages that didn't exist before the dams. The southernmost settlement before the Aswan damming a hundred years ago is Manteqet as Sad Al Aali, just before the high dam. We can get a taxi to the Sad Al Aali market and begin our search there.'

The taxi left them at the side of the road near a typical market with a haphazard array of stalls under awnings supported by poles and ropes connected to nearby buildings.

The first stall they approached sold vegetables; an older woman sat at one end, behind the veggies, on a box.

'*As-Salaam-Alaikum*,' Kate greeted her.

'*Wa-Salaam-As-Alaikum*. You don't look like vegetable buyers.'

Kate replied, 'We are not. We seek someone who sells herb medicines.'

'Do you know what you want? Or do you need advice?'

'Someone who could give advice might be best.'

The woman turned to look at a young man, probably in his mid-teens, at the far end of the stall. 'Mohammed, take these visitors to Doctor Makeen.'

'Thank you, *Sayidati*,' Kate said.

A ten-minute walk down winding lanes brought them to a small building with a sign outside that read 'Doctor Makeen,

Natural Medicines'. The inside was an Ali Baba's cave of plants, roots, and pieces of bark and flowers in shallow wicker trays. Kate wondered what else hid in dark corners. *I don't want to know!*

There was no counter, but on a single chair beside a small doorway sat a beautiful young girl. When they walked in, she said something they couldn't hear to a person in the room behind a door, listened for a reply, and gestured for them to go through the door.

A little light came from two small windows in the room, revealing a small, aged man sitting upright in a chair. He had a dark-skinned bird-like face, silver hair and a full silver beard. When he spoke, Kelvin was surprised; his voice was soft and mellow, that of a much younger man.

'Wa-Salaam-As-Alaikum,' Kelvin said, and the man cocked his head to one side, as one does to hear better. 'I'm Doctor Shareef, and this is my partner, Miss Mansoumi.'

Kate stepped forward and said gently, 'As-Salaam-Alaikum, *aljadu al'akbar.*'

The old man looked at Kate, smiled, and said, 'Great grandfather was a good guess,' referring to her greeting. Then, turning to Kelvin, he asked, 'Are you a medical doctor or a scientist?'

'Both. I research natural medicines.'

'So why have an Egyptian doctor and his Iranian consort come to visit me?' the old man said, making an accurate assessment of their ethnicities from their accents.

Kate immediately thought, *He thinks we are more than friends.*

Kelvin's thought was different: *He has travelled and has met Iranian speakers.* Then he took the piece of paper from his pocket with 'Anit' written on it and handed it to the old man. 'We are searching for this plant.'

His reply was abrupt. 'You won't find it. Where did you find this name?'

He knows it!

'I can show you a photograph of a hieroglyphic panel on a temple at Abydos. I've translated the text: "Although treated with Anit, calamity fell on Anedjib." It is the word "treated" that drew my attention.'

'Thank you for that information. I did not know the name was mentioned anywhere.'

Kelvin asked, 'Why do you say we won't find it?'

Doctor Makeen didn't reply. He looked at Kate. 'I must first know the answer to a question.'

'Then ask,' Kate said.

'Have you felt the presence of a god?'

At first, a puzzled Kate had no answer, and then she remembered the previous night. *I might have.* 'I do not know, but twice I've dreamed of wings above me, and the second time they carried me to a place where I saw a waterfall.'

'Isis has blessed you, for you have heard the wings of Isis and will feel the touch of Hathor. I can tell you this, for I know you will tell no other.' Then, addressing them both, Doctor Makeen continued, 'My grandfather inherited this business from his father, who inherited it from his father and his grandfather before him. My grandfather was young when he saved the life of a fellow · herbalist when a scorpion stung him. He could not charge a fellow herbalist, but his friend brought him a small packet of leaves a month later. He called the plant "Anit" and told him it was a tonic, that if he felt tired, he should take a quarter of a leaf brewed as tea.

'For two hundred and fifty years, the man and then his child and then their children and children's children have come irregularly and brought the same leaves to my grandfather, father and me. I asked one of them where the leaves came from, and he said that men, Nubian desert dwellers, occasionally came alone to buy cloth, silks, cotton of different colours, and sometimes a scarab. The Nubians accepted no money and had none, but traded the leaves for whatever my friend bought for them.

'I've asked where the Nubians come from, and he told me one man had said he came from Dehmit. My friend said he did not believe it, for the Nubian was a desert man and came on a camel.'

'So that's why you say we'll never find it?'

'Yes, and because of a legend that has passed from father to son in my family for untold generations.'

'Can you tell us this legend?'

'Yes, for I know you will tell no one else,' the old man said again. Then he closed his eyes and began reciting the legend. Kelvin had heard it several times before: it was the Egyptian Genesis, about how Nut, the goddess of the sky, had created the world. But instead of ending the story with Isis breathing life back into Osiris, to Kelvin's surprise, Doctor Makeen continued.

'Isis called on her mother Nut to implore her child Geb to give her a small wadi where the people could grow her plant to protect all, and this Nut did. Isis worked her magic to ensure Seth would not find the wadi, making it invisible, and allowing no one in, and only one man to take the plant to the people when she sent a sign.'

Opening his eyes, the old man said, 'I've never seen the man who comes, and I've never looked for the wadi. Since those times, the desert has dried. If the plant grows, little can be there. The wadi must lie in the desert, and as the man does not cross the Nile, it must be south and east of here, where no one lives. The legend says Isis made it invisible; perhaps, if it did exist, today, it has filled with sand.'

'Your legend, apart from the plant and the wadi, concords with Ancient Egyptian mythology,' Kelvin observed.

Dr Makeen shrugged. 'The legend is far older. Once people

believe, they do not change their beliefs unless their world changes. Storytellers are known for changing the stories they pass on.'

'You say the plant promotes good health?'

'Yes. But it does not prolong life, except perhaps for gods. How old do you think I am?'

'I guessed ninety when I saw you and seventy-five when you spoke.'

'I'm a hundred and two, but I've drunk the tea since I was a baby.'

Kate asked, 'And your great granddaughter?'

'She's twenty-two. She has two brothers. My eldest great-grandson is thirty-one, and, if I'm lucky, I'll be a great-great-grandfather soon.'

Kelvin said, 'Thank you, Doctor Makeen. I assume it would be an insult if I offered to pay for your time. What service would you ask of us?'

'None,' the old man said, then grinned, 'but bring me six leaves if you find the plant.'

'Why six?'

Quietly he whispered. 'Three for eternity: a quarter of a leaf for good health, a half to cure, a whole leaf to bring back life. Plus, I have a wife.'

On their return journey, Kelvin asked Kate what she had thought of the aged doctor.

'He knows more than he told us,' she said.

'How do you work that out?'

'First, he knows we're in love and suspected I had felt the presence of a god. I saw his eyes light up when I mentioned the waterfall. He knows there is one.'

'So you think it's a real place, not just in our imagination?'

'Maybe it isn't there now, but it once was. Dr Makeen did say that his story was two hundred and fifty years old; it may be much older.'

'Okay, what else?'

'When he told us about the wadi, he added that it had probably filled with sand, but he doesn't believe that.'

'Why?'

'Because he never said that his supply of Anit had dried up or run out. It might still come to him. He told us just enough for us to try and find it. He wants six leaves, so his supply may be only two or three at a time, and he uses them to keep healthy. Also, he dangled a carrot. He said that I would feel "the touch of Hathor". He knows that any couple in love would want that, so we will continue to search.'

'I feel very much the same, Kate, and when I said that the ancient mythology doesn't include the wadi, he lost no time explaining why it doesn't. He's a believer, Kate. His family have believed for three hundred years, perhaps thousands. There is another reason to keep it a secret, although I don't know what it is. I suspect there are other herbs, but as we know of Anit, that's the lever he's using.'

'Kelvin, we know Anit exists and believe the wadi exists. How will we find them?'

'I must think about it, Kate.'

23

THAT EVENING, KATE WOULD STAY at the Cataract Hotel in Aswan – she couldn't remain on board with Kelvin, as the departure time for the boat the following day was an early four am. Kate's Egypt Air flight was at seven the same morning.

As agreed, Kelvin joined Kate that afternoon in her hotel room. Kate didn't unpack; she just removed and hung up her gown for the evening. 'I've booked at 1902 – we'll dine in style,' she told Kelvin as she did so. 'But it's too early for dinner now. Let's go for a drink on the terrace. I've asked the hotel hairdresser to come to my room to do my hair later.'

Kelvin nodded his agreement. 'While you're having your hair done, I must visit the boat and check in with the captain. I said I would be on board for the departure, so I must tell him I'll be boarding late.'

Later, on his way to the boat, Kelvin stopped at the 1902 restaurant, and the maitre d' came to him. 'Doctor Shareef, it's good to see you again. Are you dining here tonight?'

'I am. I'm accompanying a young lady who's a guest, Miss Mansoumi. She's made a reservation. I have a tuxedo, but I prefer to wear a dress jubbah; would that be permissible?'

'Of course, sir. I'll see you later.'

When Kelvin returned from the boat early that evening and knocked on the door of Kate's room, the hairdresser opened it. Wearing a bathrobe, Kate, seated at the dressing table, called out, 'Kelvin, my hair's nearly done. You go and shower.'

He did as he was told and fifteen minutes later, wrapping a

towel around his waist, stepped back into the bedroom. The hairdresser had left, and Kate, still in her bathrobe, had her back to him.

He busied himself dressing, aware that Kate was doing the same on the other side of the room, but purposefully not looking at her to give her privacy. When he heard her say, 'How do I look?' he finally turned to her.

She was wearing the red Egyptian gown he had given her. Her deeply shadowed eyes were smudged in dark purple with a deep green outline. Around her neck, she wore a large green scarab on a gold chain, and on her head, a golden headband secured her black hair, which fell straight to her shoulders. With its head facing him, a golden snake with jewelled eyes reared from the headband.

He stared, amazed. 'Goddess, where is Kate?'

'Right here, my love.'

'I must be the only man alive who's held Hathor in his arms.'

'Stop teasing,' she laughed.

'I never lie, Kate. If Cleopatra were here, you would outshine her.'

'The power of makeup!' she said, with another delighted laugh.

As Kelvin followed her out into the corridor, her scent entranced him. 'What's the perfume?' he asked.

'It's oud, with sandalwood, amber and cinnamon. Perhaps Hathor used it. The ingredients were available thousands of years ago.'

Kate was surprised when they entered the restaurant, but Kelvin expected it. The sounds died instantly to complete silence, and the staff froze where they stood, staring entranced at the magnificent couple. The maitre d' was the first to recover, taking a deep breath and coming forward to bow. 'Doctor Shareef, if I had known you were accompanying the goddess Hathor, I would have arranged music.'

Kelvin smiled. 'I'm grateful you didn't. I have little time to discuss affairs with the goddess before she returns to her realm.'

'Then please, follow me.'

As they did, a man with a camera stepped forward and took a photo.

As they sat, the sounds in the restaurant, although hushed in the low ambient lighting, returned to normal.

'How did he know you were coming?'

'I've been a regular visitor, Kate. I'm Egyptian, and the maitre d ' has a phenomenal memory. I also passed by when I went to the boat to check if it was fine to wear the jubbah.'

Kate chuckled. 'Why did he compare me to Hathor and not Isis?'

'Every person who looks at us can see our love.'

Looking at him, Kate felt that warm feeling again. *It's contentment.* Taking a sip of the white wine the sommelier had discreetly poured for them, she asked, 'So, what are your plans?'

'I sail with the boat tomorrow, and as it's with the river's current, it takes two days less than coming south. So I'll be in Cairo in thirteen days, and then I must see the agents and sign off. I'll stay at the Ramses Hilton, my favourite in Cairo, and research for a week or two. I shall try to dig up maps and charts of the Nile and its surrounds, south and east of the Aswan High Dam, two thousand years ago. I may try Athens and Rome for maps too, but I've someone at the British Museum who might help, at the Met in New York and Browns. I'll ask the Cairo Museum myself. Then, assuming I have solid leads, I'll fly back here and arrange an expedition.'

'So you will return to Britain in four to six weeks?'

'Can you hold out that long, my love?'

'I must, but be careful. I now know what an orgasm is like, so don't delay!' Kate gave him a devilish grin in the candlelight.

'I certainly won't, my darling. And what will you do during that time?'

'I've emailed my office. They should have delivered my paper inbox and schedule to my parents. When I arrive in the afternoon, I'll go and see them and spend Sunday going through everything. Then, on Monday, it's back to the grindstone. I have one idea: I'll find out why we don't promote men's perfumes and learn the answer to the question, "Who buys them, men or women?" Do you remember I said I would send your photo for an ad? That gave me the idea.'

'I do remember, but I hope you won't. I'd be a bad actor. My answer to your question would be that it's women – first mothers, then girlfriends, then wives. I don't think I've ever bought any, except once or twice as a student.'

'That's what I suspect, and I'm willing to bet that we have a better idea of what women buyers will choose than the current promoters,' Kate said, then continued, 'then I must call Marylyn. She'll be dying to know what I've been up to.'

Kelvin said, 'That reminds me, I must call Ahmed. I'll do that tomorrow.'

As they left the restaurant, the maitre d' thanked them for coming and handed Kelvin an SD card. 'The photo is on this, Doctor. I hope to welcome you and the goddess again.'

'You can count on it.'

As they walked to Kate's room, she asked, 'Darling, I might need to survive without you and an orgasm for six weeks. Please come to bed with me. You can still return to the boat with plenty of time before it leaves.'

Kelvin grinned. 'I was about to suggest that.'

Kelvin took his time undressing her but left on the serpent circlet. And this time, if anything, the flight to the grassy bank beside the pool took longer, the waterfall flowed stronger, and the finale took Kate to heights she had never experienced.

Kelvin left her sleeping just before one. He said at the hotel front desk, 'Please, Miss Mansoumi must catch the seven o'clock flight to London. She'll need forty-five minutes and a strong coffee before departure. Can you arrange a taxi?'

'For a goddess, sir, nothing is impossible. I shall have a personal attendant wake her and assist with her packing. The hotel limousine will be ready for her. Right now, it is waiting to take you to the dock.'

At the airport, Kate was surprised at an upgrade to first class, and also at how the cabin attendant greeted her. 'Good morning Miss Mansoumi. I'm sorry you are alone. We were hoping your partner was also travelling with us.'

The flight attendant gave Kate the morning edition of the *Aswan News*. The photo taken in the restaurant covered the front page with a banner headline, 'Hathor, goddess of love, visits the Cataract Hotel.'

Oh, hell! I hope that picture doesn't go any further than Aswan. I expect Kelvin won't see it. We can do without a horde of paparazzi following us.

24

KELVIN MANAGED SIX HOURS of sleep before he went for breakfast. The passengers at his table included the two young women he had met when they boarded – the ones Kate had asked about.

Fortified with food, he returned to his cabin. For twelve days, he intended to work through all the photographs and data he had collected on the southbound trip with Kate. He sat down to begin, but every time he looked at a photo, the memory of Kate with him when he clicked the shutter diverted his thoughts.

He called Ahmed.

'Hi, Kelvin. I saw the *Cairo Times* this morning. Where did you find a goddess? You must have turned the hotel upside down,' his friend said, by way of greeting.

'What are you talking about?'

'Haven't you seen this morning's newspaper?'

'No, I'm on the return leg of the cruise. We left Aswan at four this morning.'

'Then you've missed seeing the headline in the *Aswan News*. It's also in the *Cairo Times*, their sister newspaper.'

'What is it?'

'It's a picture of you and the most beautiful woman I've ever seen, taken in the Cataract Hotel; I recognise the 1902 restaurant décor. The banner headline says "Hathor, goddess of love, visits the Cataract Hotel".'

Shit. I wonder if Kate saw it.

'Ahmed, I know who took the photo; I have it on an SD card. I didn't know he had sold it to a newspaper.'

'Well, tell me about her. It's obvious from the photo you're in love. Have you proposed?'

'We are in love, Ahmed. She's the woman I told you about on the cruise, Kathleen Mansoumi. She's Iranian, speaks Arabic, and I call her Kate. The dress she's wearing in the photo is the one I bought for her at your suggestion.'

'Well, you said it was like taking the bull by the horns,' Ahmed laughed. 'The depiction of Hathor in mythology is a cow, or a woman wearing a headdress with horns, so you evidently earned Hathor's help. When is your marriage, and can I be the best man?'

'I haven't proposed. Agreeing to marriage after two weeks on a cruise with a romantic atmosphere would be foolhardy – although Kate did say she would marry me when I asked. When it happens, you will be the best man.' Kelvin paused to gather his thoughts and added, 'I told her about my problem with erectile dysfunction.'

'I'm surprised you aren't over that and suffering instead from priapism!' Ahmed said, with feeling. 'Is she still with you?'

'No, she left for London yesterday. I'll join her after I finish my contract on this boat and do some research in Cairo.'

'Then we must meet in Cairo.'

'We will do, Ahmed. How is Ameena?'

'That's off, Kelvin.'

'So when are you returning to London?'

'Not for a while. Ameena has a sister who's three years older. Soraya is qualifying as a paediatrician, so she told her mother she was not interested in marrying until after she was qualified. I met her on my third visit to see Ameena, and we fell in love. We're trying to determine how to marry before she qualifies.'

'Kate's parents are paediatricians – Amin and Yara Mansoumi.

They live near Elstree. He's a surgeon, and she studied in Cairo. Tell Soraya to look them up on the net. I bet she could work in their practice if Soraya's good enough and Kate recommends her. If Soraya is interested, I'll speak to Kate.'

'Kelvin, you're a star. When you arrive in Cairo, I'll tell my mother she owes you hamam mahshi for dinner, and you can meet Soraya.'

The two friends said goodbye, then Kelvin looked for the SD card, downloaded the picture of him and Kate onto his computer, and then sent it to Kate as an email attachment, with a note saying, 'I would frame this and hang it in my cabin if I had a printer. All my love, Kelvin.'

When Kate arrived in London on Saturday afternoon, sleep deprived after her early flight and lengthy trip, she went to her parents' house. They were keen to hear all about the cruise, and when her mother asked, hopefully, if she had met any attractive men, Kate replied, 'There were no single men among the passengers, and the crew were all Egyptians. The doctor on board was great. I'll tell you later how he saved me from losing my hand, but first I need to sleep.'

After she woke to the morning song of the garden birds in their garden, she made herself a cup of coffee and got back into bed. She switched on her laptop. Kelvin's email was the top item in her inbox. It raised her spirits, and although she had already seen the photo, she looked at it, smiling, lingering for several minutes on the memory of their last night together.

She didn't notice her mother quietly entering the room.

Yara couldn't see the screen clearly, but she could see Kate's face, and she had never seen her daughter smile in this way; there was something special about it. She knocked discreetly on the open door.

Kate looked up. 'Morning, Mother,' she said.

'We've been waiting for you to serve breakfast. When are you coming down?'

Kate pulled on a tracksuit and, as she followed her mother from the room, she hesitated momentarily, then picked up a folded newspaper.

'Hello, Dad.'

Her father was sitting at the breakfast table, reading a newspaper. 'Sleep well, did you?'

'Yes, I was more tired than I thought.'

'A drop in adrenalin, too, I imagine.'

Her mother asked, 'Kate, what would you like? Yoghurt, fruit, eggs, coffee?'

'After two weeks of Egyptian food, I must learn to eat English again,' Kate laughed. 'Scrambled eggs on toast, grilled bacon, and more toast with marmalade.'

While her mother bustled around, preparing the food, Kate sat at the table and addressed her father. 'Dad, have you and Mother been busy, and how are Ava and the kids?'

'Nothing much has changed in two weeks, Kate. I've had to do two cleft palates in succession. Ava is planning a course in advanced dentistry; she wants to do implants.'

'Good for her.'

Kate tucked into her eggs while her parents ate yoghurt and fruit – they liked the thick yoghurt from the Middle East.

Pausing between spoons, Amin said, 'Kate, you promised to tell us about your hand.'

Kate took a deep breath. 'Before I start, I want you both to look at yesterday's *Aswan News*.' She handed the folded newspaper to her mother.

Yara opened it, saw the headline, and then looked at the picture. Stupefied, she stared, unmoving, until Amin reached over and took it.

Yara finally found her voice. 'Kate, is that you?'

'Yes, Mother.'

Amin then said, 'My god, you're beautiful. Where did you find the pharaoh? He's the epitome of a god.'

'That's the man who saved my hand.'

'The ship's doctor?'

'Yes, although he's more than that. He's also a pharmaceutical chemist and a research scientist. He was on the ship as a locum. His name is Kelvin Shareef.'

While Amin absorbed this, Yara asked, 'Where did you buy that magnificent dress?'

'He gave it to me. I didn't know it was him – it arrived as a gift from an anonymous admirer – but after he saved my hand, Kelvin admitted it and said he gave it to me because he thought I was beautiful.'

She then told her parents about the high points of the cruise, saying Kelvin photographed hieroglyphics to translate without going into the details of his research. 'I know Mother will ask, so I may as well get it out of the way,' she said finally. 'Before leaving me at the Cataract Hotel, Kelvin said he wanted to marry me but wouldn't formally ask because two weeks on a holiday cruise was not long enough to learn everything about another person. I told him I knew enough and would marry him immediately, but we agreed to continue together and find out more about each other when he can come to England in a month or two.'

'Does he want children?'

'Yes, Mother, that's why he wants us to be sure.'

'That's an incredible story, Kate,' her father said, 'and I think he's the kind of man I would like.'

Kate left the breakfast table to work through her papers and emails. It was on her way up the stairs to her room that she thought. *I didn't tell them he's English and his parents live near Gatwick. I'll let them know at lunch.*

Ava arrived for lunch with her husband and children. Yara excitedly showed her the newspaper, and Kate had to tell the romantic story of the doctor she had met on her Egyptian cruise all over again.

She forgot to tell her parents that Kelvin was English.

On Sunday night, Kate packed up and drove to her flat in Canary Wharf, where she unpacked and then went to bed.

The next morning she arrived at the office early and, for three days, didn't have a minute to spare as she attended meeting after meeting, catching up on everything. However, she did find enough time to instruct her secretary: 'Brenda, I want a jpg picture printed privately, a large print. If I give it to our media guys, it'll make the rounds in the company, and I would like to avoid that, so find out to whom I must send it. Then I want a survey to answer the question, "Is it men or women who buy men's cosmetics, especially colognes and deodorants?" Lastly, I want a list of the companies that market cosmetics for men, ordered by sales turnover of those items and, if possible, sales turnover for the last five years.'

'Yes, miss, I'll find out.'

'You're a gem, Brenda.'

25

JAMES BROUGHT A NEWSPAPER to Kelvin's grandfather, Lateef, at the Shareef family home. He had subscribed to the *Cairo Times* when he immigrated to England and still enjoyed reading it, for most of it was in his mother tongue, Egyptian Arabic.

Handing it to him, James said, 'Sir, it appears your grandson has made headlines in Cairo.'

Lateef took the paper eagerly. 'Has he, by heaven? What the devil has he been up to?' After a long look, he said, 'Not Cairo, James; the Cataract Hotel is in Aswan. Let me read the paper, then you can give it to his mother. The woman in the picture does resemble a goddess; my grandson must have my genes.'

When Darius and Layla returned that evening, James gave Layla the paper. She took one look and said, 'Darius, our son seems to have joined the gods. Look at this.'

'She's beautiful,' Darius said, studying the picture. 'Kelvin must have done more than research. I hope she has the character to go with her beauty.'

'I'll find out,' Layla said. 'I'm going to give Ahmed a call.'

Ahmed was surprised to hear from Layla, but things fell into place when she told him the reason for her call. 'I'm sure you know what my son is up to. I've seen the photo in the *Cairo Times*, and I want to know, who is that beautiful woman?'

'I've never met her, but when I saw that picture, I told Kelvin he should marry her. But I think he should tell you about her, not me.'

'Is she Egyptian?'

'No, she's Iranian English. Her name is Kathleen Mansoumi. Her parents are paediatricians. They live near Elstree and have a practice at the Barnet Hospital.'

'Is Kelvin going to marry her, Ahmed?'

'I hope so. I think they are deeply in love, but he said he'd continue to court her after returning to London because he thinks they should have more time before deciding.'

'Thanks, Ahmed; I won't ask for anything more. Kelvin did tell me your mother was trying to arrange a marriage. Did she find the right girl?'

'No, but I'm in love with her elder sister and trying to persuade her to marry me.'

'It seems to be the marrying season,' Layla said. 'Good luck!'

Ending the call, Layla quickly opened her laptop. Finding Doctor Yara Mansoumi on the hospital website took a few minutes.

She called the number provided and spoke to the secretary. 'I'm Doctor Layla Shareef, mother of Doctor Kelvin Shareef. Can you ask Doctor Mansoumi to call me on this number? Tell her it's about her daughter, my son and the *Cairo Times* photo.'

'Certainly, Doctor.'

She didn't have a long wait for the call. The voice was pleasant and excited. 'I'm Kate's mother, and I've seen the front page of the *Aswan News*.'

'Yara, I'm glad you called. I think that picture may appear in English newspapers once they discover that Kate and Kelvin are both English. Then we'll have reporters calling us.'

'I thought Kelvin was Egyptian?'

'Well, he's English-Egyptian,' Layla said. 'His father, Darius, and I live south of Gatwick.'

After a pause to absorb this new information, Yara said, 'Kate will be with us here at home this weekend. Would you like to come for lunch on Sunday and meet her? Then we can discuss a common strategy if reporters start calling.'

'Yara, that's very generous of you. Unless my husband has an unbreakable commitment, I'll twist his arm. When would you expect us?'

'Would twelve be too soon? We'll have lunch at one. I'll message you our address.'

'That would be perfect.'

'Are you both happy with Egyptian food?'

'Of course!'

'Darius, we have lunch on Sunday with Kate's parents.'

'Who's Kate?'

'The goddess Hathor.'

'Well done, my darling. Where?'

'Near Elstree.'

'Then Muammar can drive us there. We must allow an hour and a half for the journey.'

'Amin, we have important guests for lunch on Sunday.'

'Who, my dear?'

'Kelvin's parents, Darius and Layla Shareef.'

'Good heavens, how did you manage that?'

'Layla called me. They live in England.'

'Amazing things keep happening when the gods are involved.'

'Kate, I know you're coming for the weekend, but I called to tell you not to duck out of it. I've invited two guests for lunch on Sunday who you must meet.'

'Okay, Mother, I'll be there. I must rush, I'm late for a meeting. Bye.'

As Kate ended the call with her mother, wondering briefly who the mystery guests might be, Brenda popped her head into the office. 'Miss Mansoumi, do you have a moment?'

'Yes, Brenda?'

'Here's a website address; register and download the photo file to them, select the size you want and the number of copies, then pay online. They'll deliver in the London area.'

'Thanks, Brenda.'

'Here's the quote for the survey data you wanted. The quote for the list of companies will come tomorrow.'

Kate looked at the quote. 'This is exceptionally low. I expected a much higher figure.'

'I asked my boyfriend how he would do it. He works in data mining and has many contacts. The attached sheets describe the data sources and how they will sort it.'

'Great, Brenda. I'll look at it tonight.'

The cruise boat was in El Banyana, and the tour for the morning was the visit to the Abydos temple. There was no reason for Kelvin to go on it, for he had visited the temple with Kate on the southward trip, but after four days of poring over photos of hieroglyphics, he decided he needed some air and sunshine.

He sat beside the bus driver on the way there to avoid discussion with the passengers. As the two single women travelling together had shown no interest in him since departure, Kelvin had decided that Kate might have been right, and they were a lesbian couple. It meant he could relax in their presence.

When the bus arrived at the temple, Kelvin told the guide that he would look at the hieroglyphics, and not to wait for him if he wasn't back at the bus on time – he would take a taxi to Sohag.

'Do you want another guide?'

'Not unless there's someone who can translate hieroglyphics.'

'There is Kadeem Bakir. He's been here for decades.'

'Where do I find him?'

'He often sits in the sun outside the museum. If you see an old man with a beard, that will be him.'

Kelvin found Kadeem Bakir exactly where the guide had said he would be.

'*As-Salaam-Alaikum.* Are you Kadeem Bakir?'

'*Wa-Salaam-As-Alaikum.* I am, sir. How can I help you?'

'A guide told me you might help me translate some hieroglyphics.'

'That will be a pleasure. Can you show me the writings?'

'Come with me.'

Standing at the panel Kelvin photographed, he said, 'I've translated the last line we can see. My translation is, "Although treated with Anit, calamity fell on Anedjib."'

'I haven't translated that, although I've translated nearly everything else. Perhaps I never saw it because sand covered it. Let me have a look.'

Kelvin thought he could hear the old guide's bones creaking as he sat, then lay down on the sand to look at the line of symbols carved on the stone. He scooped away the sand in front of it, then carefully blew away the remaining dust.

For three minutes, he mumbled to himself. Kelvin could hear him saying, 'Is that "treatment", "cleaning" or "purification"?' Finally, he said to Kelvin, 'Your translation is excellent. If there is an error, it is in the sign you have translated as "treated". An alternative is "anointed"; it does not have quite the same meaning.'

'Can you tell me, what is Anit?'

'I don't know, but I've seen that sign elsewhere. I'm not sure where, but we can look for it.'

'Then we shall do so.'

Three hours later, after following the old guide from one hieroglyphic panel to another through the ruins, Kelvin suggested they buy food from an itinerant seller and sit somewhere to eat. He was beginning to think his guide was dragging out the visit to earn a high bonus.

While munching on a hawawshi, a spicy meat-filled pita bread that Kelvin found delicious, the old guide asked, 'What is your interest in Anit?'

'I'm a chemist, and I have a list of ingredients used in ancient Egypt that appear in papyrus texts. One-third have a modern equivalent, but the others have no identification. Anit is one of them. If I can find out what it does, perhaps I can suggest a modern equivalent.'

'Let's find that symbol, then I'll tell you of a man who might have your answer.'

An hour later, before a funerary text beside a tomb, the guide exclaimed, 'There! The seventh line down.'

Kelvin could see the symbols for Anit, the pharaoh and Isis. 'How do you translate that?'

'Pharaoh was anointed with Anit, invoking the protection of Isis, before the embalmers carried him away.'

'I would have said "bore", not "carried"; the symbol shows the body on the bearer's shoulders. But your translation is excellent.'

Photographing it, Kelvin thought, *That line supports what Makeem told Kate and me.* 'I appreciate your help,' he said to the guide. 'What should I pay you for today's excellent assistance?'

The guide named a figure, and Kelvin paid him three times the amount. The old man bowed in gratitude, then said, 'Kind sir, there is a seller of herbs opposite the Alhoashim Mosque in Nagaa Al Ghabat. I buy my medicines from him. He is old and might tell you what Anit can do.'

Kelvin took a taxi to the mosque. He negotiated a price for the onward trip to Sohag and asked the driver to wait for him. Then he entered the shop.

'Old' is an understatement, Kelvin thought when he saw the shop owner.

After the usual polite greetings, the shop owner asked, 'What can I do for you?'

'Kadeem Bakir, a temple guide, suggested I should see you. I want to know what Anit does.'

'I'm afraid I can't tell you. I bought some once, just a tiny packet. The man who sold it to me promised that someone would come and tell me what it does, but no one came. I've never sold it because I was worried it may be poison. Most herbs are harmless in small doses, but high doses can kill.'

'I know. Do you still have it?'

'I can look. Please, wait.' The shop owner limped through a rear door.

Ten minutes later, he returned. 'Here is the packet. It is still unopened.'

Feeling a terrible tension that he managed to disguise, Kelvin picked up the packet. It looked like dry goatskin covered in wax, with a small label with the symbol he recognised. Keeping his tone even and casual, he asked, 'Will you sell it to me?'

'Of course, although it will be without any recommendation for its use and no guarantee it is still viable, as many years have passed since I bought it. Let us say twenty Egyptian pounds.'

'That's expensive, but my taxi is waiting,' Kelvin said, as he found the notes in his wallet.

The ancient smiled as he accepted the notes. 'I should have asked for more, but thank you.'

Kelvin reached Sohag as the boat docked. Excited about his find, he was about to call Kate when he looked at the time – six pm. *Two hours' time difference, she won't be home. I must call after ten.*

He showered and changed for dinner. The reception announcements board said the evening was Egyptian, and galabiyas were de rigueur, so he dressed in one.

Feeling cheerful, he joined the passengers for the evening's events: a wine tasting, an oriental buffet dinner and a party. The wine tasting quickly became more like a wine-drinking session, so dinner passed pleasantly, with everyone in high spirits.

After everyone had eaten, Kelvin remained seated at the table with a glass of wine, discussing with the passengers what they had seen at Abydos. He did notice the two single women paid him more attention than they usually did, especially Ms Morgan, and he decided it was probably because of the relaxed dress, not to mention the free-flowing alcohol. *Tomorrow I had better have a supply of headache powders available!*

An hour later, he was back in his cabin, undressing for bed, when someone knocked at his door. He put on a bathrobe and opened the door. Ms Morgan, carrying her shoes, was outside. 'Doctor. I think I hurt my foot. It's swelling, and my shoe is tight.'

'Come in and lie on the table. I'll have a look.'

She did, and he pulled the chair to the end of the surgery table and sat down. Carefully examining her foot, he didn't notice that she had lifted her gallabiyah above her knees.

Kelvin felt confused: there was nothing wrong with the foot. Then, looking up, he found he was looking between her spread thighs, and she was not wearing panties.

'Doctor, can you see anything?'

'Yes, Ms Morgan. Why are you not wearing panties?'

'Because I feel horny, and doctors give me the hots because they know how to treat my problem.'

'Ms Morgan, that's an affliction I no longer treat. I'm engaged to be married.'

'Oh, well, I tried. You wouldn't consider a quickie with no strings attached?'

'No, Ms Morgan.'

'Right, I'll be off then. If you change your mind before the end of the trip, tell me you want to check my foot.'

'Good night, Ms Morgan.'

Closing the door behind her, he thought. *That's odd; I never once thought I was incapable, but I did say I'm engaged.*

It made him remember that he had to call Kate.

'Hello, my darling! I've waited four days for you to call. You're taking a big risk – I might forget all about you!'

'Kate, I'm sure you were busy, and so was I.'

'With the two single women?' She laughed.

'No, with research – although I've just declined a blatant offer.'

'Tell me.'

Kelvin did, and Kate said, 'Marylyn told me she had met women like that. I can't imagine ever doing something similar. Sex without affection is only a fraction of being together. Poor girl probably hasn't known anything any better.'

'My sentiments exactly, Kate. But I've got something much more exciting and important to tell you. I returned to Abydos this morning to see if I could find something more.'

Kelvin told her every detail, up to and including the amazing discovery of an actual sample of Anit.

'Darling, that's fantastic! So now we finally have some Anit. What will we do with it?'

'Nothing now. Apart from being a tonic, as Makeen said, I want to follow up on its use, but I'm not going on any more tours; I shall send queries to obtain maps. But what have you been doing?'

'Meeting after meeting for three days. But I'm organising a survey to confirm that women buy men's perfumes and an investigation into the companies that market them. I'll make that TV ad, with you as a star. You turned me into a goddess, so I'll make you a pharaoh.'

'Are you writing the screenplay?'

'It's called a script for ads. I'll write it, and you can approve it.'

'I look forward to it,' Kelvin said, then changed the subject. 'How are your parents, Kate? You haven't mentioned them.'

'They're fine, although Dad says my mother is working too hard. I'm visiting them this weekend. They've invited some mystery guests for me to meet.'

On hearing that Kate's mother was overworked, Kelvin thought, *I shouldn't have told Ahmed that Soraya might study with her parents.* He said, 'Kate, you've just killed an idea I had.'

'What idea, my darling? Your ideas are usually brilliant.'

Kelvin told her about Ahmed and Soraya and explained, 'I told them that maybe you could recommend her to your mother, but that might overload your mother more.'

'Darling, I'm not sure you're right – Soraya may prove to be a help. Would Ahmed bring her to England for a short period to meet my mom?'

'I imagine he'll jump at the chance.'

'Then, when I talk to my parents, I'll put that forward as a suggestion.'

26

ON FRIDAY, KATE AUTHORISED the survey. She didn't need approval from her boss, as it was within her marketing budget. Kate also received the quote for the company list; it was low, so Kate approved it.

She returned home, packed what she needed for the weekend, and then had a pizza delivered before going to bed. She checked Kelvin's schedule, found he was in Minya, and dreamed of him – Minya reminded her of their first kiss and how her toes had curled.

Kate slept late the following day. There was no hurry to go to her parents, so when she woke, she made a cup of coffee, returned to bed and called Marylyn.

'Hello, Em. Have I woken you after a night of debauchery?'

'I wish. I'm alone in my flat. Are you back?'

'Yes. I returned a week ago, and I've been snowed under at work.'

'Did you meet the love of your life?'

'Yes to that too, Em! And when he returns to England in four or five weeks, I'll introduce him to you.'

'Wow, Kate, love at first sight! If I weren't so determined to pin down Darryl, I would book a cruise right now!' Marylyn joked.

'It wasn't at first sight, Em; it took four days.' Kate chuckled. 'So you've made no progress with the mathematician?'

'I'm seeing Darryl more often, and I've given up the others; I'm a one-man woman now. But he hasn't proposed.'

'So you're sleeping with him again?'

'No, Kate, I told you, no candy until he proposes. In the meantime, I'm trying another approach: the way to a man's heart is via his stomach. My mother is teaching me fancy cooking. Can you come to Cambridge next Saturday evening and join us in his rooms for dinner à la Marylyn? You can tell me if I'm making progress.'

'That would be wonderful. I'll call you on Saturday morning to confirm.'

Saying goodbye to her friend, Kate showered, ate muesli for breakfast, and then left for her parents' place.

Over lunch, Kate asked, 'So, who's visiting tomorrow?'

'You don't know them, Kate,' her mother said, with an inscrutable smile.

Kelvin's question about writing a screenplay popped into her mind, so she spent the afternoon thinking about what she would do. The most important thing was not to imply the man was virile and handsome but to show that a woman wanted him; she concluded that she must deliver an interaction between a man and a woman that leads to success, or at least an implied success.

She sat down and typed a script, then sketched a storyboard. She thought a pro might do it better, but she wrote the storyline she had thought of on the cruise.

Desert scenario: Handsome man in a tent, seen spraying on deodorant, who then mounts a horse and rides across a dune.

Switch scene.
The man arrives and rides down a dune towards a veiled young woman watching over a herd of goats. He dismounts and approaches her. 'Where is the owner of this herd? He has stolen four of my goats.'
 'My father has gone to market with goats to sell.'
 'Then I shall take four of your goats.'
 As the man nears the young woman, she smells his scent. Her body

language opens up and her eyes sparkle. Breathlessly, she whispers, 'Take me instead.'

'Come.' The man remounts his horse and hauls her up before him.

Final scene: Man's tent. The horse stands beside it, still saddled. Pieces of a woman's clothing fly from the tent, and the camera zooms in to a close-up of panties and a bra. Horse rears and screams.

Fade out to a picture of a perfume bottle: phallic symbol or clothed male. Caption: 'Undress Me: The perfume that works.'

Kate thought *Corny, but it might be effective* as she hit the 'save' key. *Now I must ask someone for another opinion.*

That evening, she dreamed of Kelvin again. She was in the desert when he arrived on a horse, said, 'Come,' and took her to his tent.

When she woke, she didn't remember what happened after that.

After a late breakfast, Kate returned to her room to bath and dress. It took a long time because she spent almost an hour with the photo of Kelvin and her at the Cataract Hotel on the screen, daydreaming.

After her bath, thinking about how Kelvin would like to see her dressed, she eschewed her usual weekend tracksuit and chose a pretty dress instead. She brushed her hair and carefully applied a minimum of makeup.

She had just finished when she heard her mother call up the stairs, 'Kate, our visitors are here.'

Yara and Amin met their guests on the front steps of their home. Layla was first out of the car when Muammar opened the door, stepping forward with a bouncing step and saying, 'Yara, I want a hug!' then following her words with action.

'Layla, I love you already,' Yara said.

Layla then turned to Amin, who asked, 'Do I get a hug too?'

'Of course!'

Darius said, 'Yara, please excuse Layla's exuberance. She's been looking forward to this meeting for years.'

'I know what you mean! Me too! Do I get another hug?'

Darius embraced Yara and then shook Amin's hand vigorously. 'Amin, I think we have extrovert wives.'

'It's common in doctors, Darius. That's why we marry them,' Amin laughed.

Yara showed their guests to the terrace, where Amin organised drinks, and Kate found the foursome when she came down the stairs from her room to meet the mystery guests. One glance at them was enough for Kate to know who they were – the family resemblance was unmistakable.

She went straight to Layla and said, 'May I have a hug?'

A minute later, they separated, tears in both women's eyes. Still holding both hands, Layla said, 'Since Kelvin was ten and told me he had a girlfriend at school, I've lived in terror of meeting the woman who would marry him. I should have had more confidence in my son. Welcome to our family!'

Kate then embraced Darius, stepped back and looked from one parent to the other. She said, 'Kelvin is part of you both. I love him and can't help loving you.'

'And we already love you and your parents too, Kate. Now, I

must admit to ignorance. Kelvin has not told us anything. He's left us in the dark.'

'Let's sit down. I'll have a Campari, Dad, and I'll tell you about it.'

She told the story from the beginning. Layla watched her as the tale unfolded, feeling warm and happy. Kate was so obviously in love. Darius, by nature more cynical, was slightly less accepting. He thought she was outstandingly beautiful, inside and out, and understood why Kelvin would fall for her. But then, why had no other man snapped her up years ago?

And he had another reservation: he judged Kate's love as great as a teenage girl's obsession, and his experience told him that obsessive love was dangerous.

Concluding the story of her and Kelvin's whirlwind romance, Kate looked at her watch and said, 'The boat should have docked in Cairo about now, and Kelvin should be on board. I'll call him.'

When she got him on the line, she told him, 'You're on speakerphone. I'm on the terrace at my parents' place, and we're about to have lunch with some special guests.'

'Who are they?'

'Your parents! We're all here together and want to talk to you.'

'Good god, how did that happen?'

'Your parents are detectives like you, my darling. Your mother organised it.'

'Am I in trouble?'

'No, except we all want you back here, especially me.'

'Hello, Kelvin,' Layla cut in. 'I'll start by warning you: you're in trouble. From now on, if I must take sides in any argument, I'm on Kate's side. I already love her like a daughter, and I'm sure your father does too.'

'Okay, Mother. I'll rely on Kate's parents' support.'

Everyone laughed.

'When are you coming back?'

'Soon. Kate can tell you what I'm doing.'

After another fifteen minutes of happy chatting, the house-keeper announced that lunch was ready. The conversation over the meal flowed smoothly, with lots of laughter.

After Layla and Darius had left, later that afternoon, Kate brought up the subject of Soraya. 'Kelvin's friend, Ahmed Badawi, is courting a young woman called Soraya in Cairo. She's just finished her final year as an intern doing paediatrics and needs another year in practice. Dad said you were working too hard, Mother. If Soraya comes here for a week or two and decides she likes it, and if she proves herself competent, perhaps you can take her on as an assistant with a student visa? Then she can relieve you of the routine treatments.'

'That's a great suggestion, Kate,' her father said. 'Yara, you should go for it.'

'Where would she live?'

'It's only for two weeks. Soraya can stay in Ava's room,' Kate said. 'If you invite her to stay and you talk to her mother, I'm sure it will be fine.'

When Kate left her parents alone to go and pack, Yara asked Amin, 'What did you think of Kelvin's parents?'

'I liked them both a lot. Darius is a brilliant rebel, and he said his mining concessions in South America have clauses guaranteeing a decent food supply for the locals. The levels of protein deficiency and kwashiorkor in children there shocked him. I can collaborate with a man like that. What did you think of Layla?'

'It takes enormous love to give up being a doctor to travel with your husband. I suspect Kelvin is capable of such love, which makes me happy. They will be good to have as in-laws.'

A similar conversation had unfolded between Layla and Darius in the car on their way home.

'I like Kate's parents a lot,' Darius had said, 'and I don't have sufficient superlatives to describe Kate – a lovely woman! I did, however, wonder why another man hadn't snapped her up. And knowing Kelvin's conservative side, I can understand his reluctance to marry after only two weeks together.'

'Two continuous weeks, Darius,' Layla said, 'which is probably worth a year in interrupted contact. And Yara told me that Kate had married young, but it lasted less than six weeks. She said she had almost abandoned the idea that her daughter would form another relationship.'

'That answers my question,' Darius said nodding. 'What did you think of Yara?'

'She's probably a damned good doctor and working too hard, but that's what happens when you have children as patients.'

Kelvin had his final dinner on board with the passengers and then packed for his departure the following day.

27

ON MONDAY, KATE WENT TO WORK determined to think of work, not Kelvin. Her schedule included meeting the visiting marketing director from America, Ken Moy, at two that afternoon.

The vice president of marketing, Gertrude Lenferna, a tall woman with a chin that showed determination and dresses worn to contradict her empathic interior, had also asked her to join them for dinner that evening. Kate was sure Gertrude had chosen her for the dinner because she was single. *I must tell the VP that has changed. Otherwise, she might try to match me up with a man.*

Kate spent an hour that morning reading the American visitor's official company profile and checking articles about him on the internet.

The afternoon meeting was interesting. A recent head-hunt from another company, Ken was visiting, as he put it, 'to see what you do in Europe and learn what I can apply in the US'.

'As we are in the same group, I doubt there is much difference in our procedures. Where would you like to start?' Kate asked him as they made themselves comfortable around the table in the spacious conference room.

'The first thing of interest is a high-level one: who makes decisions, what drives change, and who manages it?' Ken asked.

'I'm new to the marketing director job,' Kate admitted. 'The best person to ask is the VP, Mrs Lenferna, when we have dinner with her tonight.'

'Then tell me from the viewpoint of your last appointment before your promotion.'

'Okay,' Kate replied, 'I'll summarise. The ideas come from all sorts of people. They may be internal staff, but they may also come from external contractors, such as those doing surveys, producing TV and newspaper or fashion magazine ads, and their distribution experts. Those ideas, we hope, will flow up the line until they have sufficient backing to force implementation, although they often don't.'

'Why not?'

Kate explained, 'Someone in the chain is too busy, not interested in developing new ideas, thinks it's a bad idea, or doesn't want to risk promoting something that may not work in case they become labelled a failure by association.'

'So what can you do about it?' Ken asked.

'Various strategies. One is I first began attending meetings of my staff where my presence was unnecessary, only to learn of any new ideas. When this led to overwork, I appointed assistants to attend the meetings, with instructions to listen for new ideas and tell me about them.'

'And another?'

'To keep repeating at every opportunity, "My door is open to anyone with a new idea, just come and tell me."'

Ken laughed. 'Don't you waste too much time listening to wacko ideas?'

'No, only the ones the person believes outstanding, but no one has listened to.'

'That's a good point. Building a culture where employees believe the top boss will listen to an idea must be difficult.'

'Ken, I'll arrange for you to spend at least the morning with the survey department. Maybe you can give them some new ideas, especially ones using digital media. I must go; I have another meeting.'

'I'll see you tonight, then.'

The dinner went well. Gertrude Lenferna's husband, a tall, spare man with a warm smile, Kate found charming, and the VP monopolised Ken, asking him to tell her all about his life in the US.

When Ken excused himself briefly to go to the toilet, Gertrude asked Kate, 'How do you find him, Kate?'

'A nice guy, and maybe he has some ideas he can share. I've just commissioned two independent surveys, so I'm sending Ken to see the survey team tomorrow.'

Gertrude looked surprised. 'I haven't seen any budget requests?'

'They're low budget. I can pay for them from the existing budget. I'll let you know about them when I have the results. It's an idea I must prove will work. I've asked Ken to talk to our survey team about how they do US surveys.'

'That's fine, Kate.'

Back at her flat after dinner, Kate prepared for bed, then climbed under the covers before she called Kelvin.

'Hello, my darling. Aren't you in bed yet?' Kelvin asked.

'I am. I've just snuggled in. I have three pillows in a row beside me, and I shall sleep with my arms and legs wrapped around them.'

'Now you've ruined my sleep; maybe I should do the same,' he chuckled. 'Why are you getting to bed so late?'

'Dinner with the VP, her husband, and a visitor from the American company. He's surprising; I've always thought

Americans were like cowboys, tall and laughing. Ken Moy is short, Chinese, and profoundly serious.'

'That's a relief. You won't be galloping into the sunset on the back of a horse with me running behind yelling.'

'No, but my storyboard for the ad shows you galloping into the sunset on a stallion with me in your arms.'

'I'd probably drop you,' Kelvin joked.

Kate laughed. 'Kelvin, you know that won't happen. What did you do today?'

'I went to the museum and met with the head librarian.'

'Explain, please?'

'The hieroglyphics can tell me no more. The problem now is old maps. If there are any, they will be on papyrus, so I asked the librarian.'

'Did you find anything?'

'As I expected, only maps of the Nile valley; you could write "Here be Dragons" on the rest of Egypt. The librarian rec-ommended I go to Alexandria. He said he'd arrange for me to see the librarian there.'

'When are you going?'

'I'll check into my hotel tomorrow. I'm staying at the Ramses, and they've upgraded me to a suite, number 2606. You can call it direct. Then I'll take a taxi to Alexandria. I've booked into the Miramar Hotel there for three nights. It's a one-kilometre walk along the corniche to the library.'

'So you'll be back at the Hilton on Friday?'

'Late Friday, for sure.'

'Call me then and tell me what you found.'

'Of course. Good night, my darling.'

'Mmmmh, mmmmh, ooooh.'

'Kate, are you okay?'

'Yes, my love. I'm just kissing my pillow-Kelvin goodnight. Bye.'

Kelvin spent five minutes with a smile on his face, imagining Kate kissing him goodnight.

On Tuesday, Ken Moy called Kate before midday. 'I'm going to lunch with the survey guys and then I'll spend the afternoon with them. We're visiting one of the contractors. Can I invite you to dinner to discuss my day's findings tonight?'

'Sure. Where?'

'I'll find out and let your secretary know after lunch. Chinese okay?'

Before she left the office, she received a short note from the survey department head: 'The US operation does nothing different from Europe, except that they have a much smaller population and lower per capita costs. We survey each country. Their surveys include the state, and they break down the results accordingly due to local TV stations. Digital data is not part of their mandate.'

That evening, at dinner at the Chinese restaurant, Ken was as charming as the night before. She learnt more about surveys in America and the questions that never appeared on the European questionnaires; one interesting one was, 'What are your three favourite television channels?'

As they finished their dinner with small bowls of refreshing jasmine tea, Kate said, 'Ken, I'm going to the south of France tomorrow to meet with a perfume producer. I've organised for you to spend the day with our TV media department here. TV ads are our major budget item. Compare our requirements and yours, and our respective costs for a TV ad – not the display costs, but the production costs. I'll see you Thursday morning.'

She took a taxi home from the restaurant.

Kelvin left the boat after back-slapping from the crew and the captain's farewell: 'I don't expect you will want to do another cruise with us before next year, but if you do, you have a job.'

By three, he was in a taxi. Because of traffic, it took far longer to reach the Miramar Hotel in Alexandria than he'd thought it would, and after dropping his bags in his room, he went for dinner at a nearby restaurant.

When Kelvin finally fell asleep that night, he dreamed of a map. He recognised the Nile, a line wandering from a narrow crescent on the Mediterranean at the top of the map to the bottom, and what had to be the Red Sea on the right. The land was green, and small rivers drained it to the Nile. Writing across it read 'Here be Dragons'.

When he woke, the map image was still fresh in his mind. He took a tourist map of Egypt from the room desk and tried to draw the rivers and streams he had seen on the map in his dream.

I must have seen that map somewhere.

After some thought, he sent a WhatsApp to his father: 'Dad. Can you find me a satellite view of southeastern Egypt, the best quality for details? Call me after you wake up if you need more info.'

Then he went for breakfast.

He had just finished when his phone pinged; his father had sent a return WhatsApp: 'Please give the point of most interest and boundaries in GPS coordinates.'

It took Kelvin half an hour to find those using Google Earth.

Four hours later, he received three map links in an email. 'The maps are the same view at dawn, midday and sunset,' Darius had written in the accompanying message. 'They are far too big to view on a screen. You must print them in A0 size or cut them into pieces to see the detail. Shadows generated at sunrise and sunset show relief running north-south, not east-west.'

Before leaving the hotel to walk to the Alexandria Library, Kelvin asked the hotel concierge where he could order A0 prints.

'Doctor Shareef, it's a pleasure to meet you. Dr Hassan has told me about you. I'm afraid you will be disappointed by your visit.'

'Dr Habib, it's a pleasure to be here, but why do you say that?'

'Our catalogue of maps shows over nine thousand. Fortunately, you can view them on a computer screen in low resolution, so you can choose which ones you want in hi-res. But it will take months to work through them all.'

'Can the views be sorted by age?'

'Of course.'

'Are there any other criteria available to use in a sort?'

'Upper or Lower Egypt, and estimated scale. What area interests you?'

'Upper Egypt from the Nile to the Red Sea.'

'That's a large area, but I can calculate an approximate scale to fit that area on a papyrus sheet, then I can sort on those criteria, with oldest first. Come with me.'

The nine thousand maps dropped to five thousand when they eliminated Lower Egypt. After calculating a scale, it fell to under a thousand.

Kelvin asked, 'If you sort by age, oldest first, what age is the number two hundred?'

Seconds later, they received a reply: 1950 BCE.

'I have two and half days. I'm sure I could look through two hundred; if necessary, I could stretch it to another day.'

'Then I'll leave it to you. Click on the entry in the list to view the map. If there's one you want, use the "Order hi-res" menu item, and the service will send a share link to your email. You can then view it or print it.'

'Thank you, Dr Habib. May I invite you to dinner at the El Shatby Casino restaurant tonight or tomorrow?'

'Tonight I'm free. What time? And why the Casino?'

'We can make it early – between six and seven? It's close to the library; the weather's good, we can eat on the terrace, and the sea view is marvellous. Although I've never dined there, I passed it this morning on my way here and thought it splendid.'

'Six thirty then, I'll come directly from the museum.'

Kelvin had managed to view seventy maps by six that evening. He had requested links for five; after a quick study, he had eliminated the others because he was sure the mapmakers had drawn from hearsay with no detail.

He returned to the hotel, showered, and met Dr Habib in the restaurant.

'Dr Shareef, can you tell me about your interest in the area?' Dr Habib asked as they seated themselves at a table under a parasol on the restaurant terrace with a 180-degree view of the Mediterranean and coastal dhows gliding in both directions. 'Dr Hassan said you hoped to find hieroglyphics mentioning ancient herbal treatments.'

'That's correct, but I'm afraid I've had little success so far. Hieroglyphic panels tell stories of events, not illnesses.'

'Have you studied the medical papyri?'

Kelvin nodded. 'Hundreds of medicines remain unidentified, some so old they are mentioned but once.'

'So, what do you hope to find in the area that interests you?'

'A legend, nothing more, that I heard in Aswan, of Nubian traders who once came from the southeast and brought medicines for sale. I've wondered if there isn't a village now lost in the dried-out sands, where the inhabitants grew medical plants, and if some ruins with hieroglyphics might still exist. It might be in Sudan or Eritrea.'

Dr Habib seemed lost in thought for a minute, then said. 'I read a tax collector's report years ago, an old papyrus. He had gone south along the Nile, and his report included a line stating that to the southeast, there might be a place where people did not pay taxes.'

'Could you find it again?'

'I doubt it, unless I can remember something more in the report to search for. The library has many tax reports. As with any government, tax is essential.' Then Dr Habib added, 'I'll sleep on it and perhaps remember something else.' Taking a sip of his wine, he changed the subject. 'So, are you married?' he asked Kelvin.

'Not yet, but I hope to be soon. I'm in love with a goddess.'

'That's not unusual,' Dr Habib smiled. 'Which one?'

'Hathor.'

Dr Habib studied Kelvin for a long moment, then said, 'Was that you and the goddess on the front page of the *Cairo Times* recently?'

'Yes, I must admit it.'

Dr Habib beamed with delight. 'Congratulations! We all dream of marrying a goddess, but few achieve it.'

28

KATE LEFT FOR THE AIRPORT at five am. The flight to Nice took two hours, and a limousine was waiting to take her to Grasse, France's – and the world's – perfume capital, a forty-minute drive.

The tanners of the region in the late 1500s had begun making leather gloves and handbags for the Renaissance Italian fashion industry. The leather had the not-terribly-pleasant odour of tannin, so, using the flowering plants growing in the region, particularly jasmine, they developed a method to perfume the gloves and bags. This evolved into the perfume industry. By the early 1800s, it had grown significantly; in the 2020s, thousands of visitors interested in perfumes came from around the world.

Kate was meeting with Gallimard, one of the oldest companies in the region, for they were developing a new perfume for one of her clients.

Kate loved visiting Grasse to join the experts, smelling different perfumes, and then lunching in the town square under the spreading plane trees, unchanged for centuries. Usually, in the true French tradition, they made the important decisions during the meal while sipping glorious wines from the region.

Sitting in the Gallimard conference room that afternoon, the executive beside her turned to her and said, 'Miss Mansoumi, I shall visit London in two weeks. Could you give me your number? I would enjoy an evening with you.'

A month ago, I would have said yes; he's handsome and was attentive all morning. 'Merci, Monsieur, but I'm engaged to be married, so I do not give my number to other men.'

Kate left after the meeting disappointed. She had found her client's representative to be a self-opinionated fool, and her day had been a waste. She would have to report the meeting to Gertrude Lenferna.

That evening, back at her flat in London, she called Kelvin.

He answered immediately. 'Hello, darling. I'm in my hotel room, thinking of you. It seems that if I think of you, you call.'

'Then, dearest, I must believe you're alone.'

'I am. My only company is a bunch of old maps.' Kelvin laughed. 'What did you do today?'

'I spent the day at Grasse, in France, at a perfume manufacturer. I love the place, and you would too. I hope you can come with me the next time I go.'

'Count on it. I'm making progress. I've some interesting ancient maps, and more are coming. Darius has sent me three satellite images of the area. I must match the ancient and the new, but it's not obvious how I can do that; it needs identifiable common features on all the maps. I hope I'll have it sorted by next week.'

Kate suddenly had another thought. 'Darling, can you tell Ahmed to ask Soraya to call my mother? Mother would like to speak to her, and if everyone agrees, she'll invite Soraya to stay with her for two weeks, as it's convenient for work.'

'And for propriety, I imagine,' Kelvin said, a smile in his voice.

He could hear the laughter in Kate's as she said, 'Damn the propriety, Kelvin! Ahmed and Soraya can meet on weekends. Now, I've had a long day, and I must read some reports for tomorrow before I get some sleep, so I must say goodbye, my love.'

'Bye, Kate, I'll dream of you.'

'Me too, darling.'

Earlier in the day, she had received a WhatsApp from Brenda: 'I have sent the survey results to your work email.' Now, she opened her laptop and looked at them. The survey results astonished her – they were outstanding for what she had paid and confirmed her idea of who bought men's perfumes.

There was a second report from her media department. It was short but exciting: 'The US does what we do, but they use film-producing companies in Puerto Rico because it's cheaper, and they dub the films into Spanish for local TV in the south and into French for Canada. They have more significant problems than we do with making ads that are gender acceptable and must refilm them with different-race actors. Their costs are similar because we film the same ad in other countries.'

It gave Kate something to think about.

Among the maps he viewed during a long day, Kelvin found another eight that interested him.

Desperate for fresh air that evening, he ran ten kilometres eastwards along the corniche and back.

On his final day, after viewing fifty more, he found only one map of interest; it seemed the focus of mapmakers had switched to mapping the Nile in detail, and it made sense as the population living beside the Nile grew.

He was about to pack up when Dr Habib brought him a document. 'Dr Shareef, I've sent you a link to this. I remembered that only seven tax reports mentioned the town of Dehmit, so it was easy to find. I hope your visit has been of assistance.'

'I value your assistance the most, Dr Habib; thank you. But as the original Dehmit is now under the Aswan High Dam, the place the tax collector referred to has probably suffered the same fate.'

'I came to the same conclusion, Doctor.'

Kate made an appointment to see her VP the following day, thanked Brenda for organising the survey, and met Ken.

'How was your day yesterday?' she asked the visiting American.

'Great, except that I had to eat dinner alone. Can I invite you to join me tonight?'

Kate wondered if it was just loneliness, but she had something to discuss with him, so she agreed, then asked, 'Did the media guys organise for you to see the other half of the media department?'

'Journals, posters and newspapers?'

'Yes.'

'They did. My first meeting is in five minutes.'

'Ken, you may find Europe, with its many languages, quite different to the States; it should be an interesting day.'

Just then, Brenda popped her head around the door and said, 'Miss Mansoumi, your meeting with the VP is in five minutes.'

Kate collected the survey reports and headed for the VP's office. 'Good morning Mrs Lenferna.'

'Hello, Kate. How was your trip to Grasse?'

'Not that successful. Our client didn't like their proposed perfume; we tried five samples.'

'What was wrong with it?'

'The client wants perfume for an eighteen-year-old girl's deodorant, a girl looking for romance, not marriage. The perfumes were too heavy.'

'That's a pity.'

'In my opinion, the client hasn't thought it through properly,' Kate continued. 'They must think of where the girls will wear the perfume – most likely in a night club, for example. So it should be light and airy but sexy, and they should check what the perfume smells like when mixed with perspiration, as dancing in a nightclub is energetic and sweaty.'

'Did you tell the client?'

Kate nodded, frowning. 'Unsuccessfully, I'm afraid. He's a macho man who wouldn't listen to a woman.'

'Shit, one of those. I'll call the client's VP; I know her well. Now, what did you want to see me about?'

'Look at these survey results, please. The question asked is on the first page.'

Gertrude scanned the surveys quickly and efficiently. 'They're excellent, Kate,' she said. 'Why did you ask these particular questions?'

'I had an idea when I was on holiday in Egypt. The male perfume market targets men, but then I wondered who bought the perfumes. The survey shows sales to women of eighty-five per cent of the male perfumes, so the ads target the wrong market.'

'Do you think you can steal that market from our competitors?'

'I don't know. I want your authority for a low-budget TV ad for test purposes. I'll make it in Egypt.'

'It's worth trying,' the VP said, nodding her approval. 'How much did your survey cost?'

Kate slid the invoice across the table to her.

'Kate, this is impossible.'

Kate laughed. 'It's not. It's an idea from my secretary, Brenda. She may be young, but she's smart, and said she could find the answer to one question more cheaply than a traditional survey. We make no use of what the world calls big data, and like most people, I don't know what the data is. I propose we sign up a consultant statistician to teach us how to use big data. I know a statistician; he's at Cambridge University.'

Gertrude looked impressed. 'Email me his details. A change of this magnitude can become a hot potato. I'll investigate and see the president. Maybe a smart girl like Brenda needs a promotion.'

'I'd be sad to lose her, but she deserves it.'

Then Gertrude gave Kate a close look and said, 'Kate, you've changed. What happened in Egypt?'

'I met a man, fell in love, and have promised to marry him.'

'Congratulations!' Gertrude said. 'I'm glad for you – but does that mean we'll lose you? Will you go to Egypt?'

'No, he's English and will return to England in a month or so.'

'Marvellous! I hope you'll be happy together.'

I hope so too. Maybe I'm throwing caution to the winds, but I can't help it.

At dinner with Ken that evening, he was once again polite and charming. He discussed the differences between the US and Europe when making TV ads. When he ended, Kate asked, 'Ken, with all your media experience, can you answer a question?'

'I can try.'

'Our ads have a message, and the message is the same, irrespective of country, creed or colour; the target is always human. We make different ads for different communities, yet the message is the same. Is it possible to make a single ad that will suit everyone?'

'I don't think so, Kate. Where did this idea come from?'

'Historically, our business grew as separate companies in each country, when jet-airline travel and worldwide media didn't exist. We consolidated the companies but have kept the segregated ads, and yet today, anyone who watches TV can recognise an igloo in the Arctic.'

'True, but can you make an ad using igloos and the Inuit to sell a perfume in Jamaica?'

Kate smiled. 'I don't know, but I'm confident we could do it if the message is clear.'

'Well, thanks for the idea. It's well worth trying. It might revolutionise our business. I'll investigate next week in the States.'

Kate nodded her thanks. 'Right, tomorrow you have a short day,' she said. 'I've arranged two meetings, one with accounting and the other with HR. I'm particularly interested in how we compare financially with your marketing department and how our personnel profile, age and qualification compare with yours.'

'That will be interesting. Then will you leave me to mope tomorrow night or join me for a last dinner?'

He's been friendly and helpful. I'm not going to my parents until Saturday.

'Okay, Ken, that'll be a pleasure.'

As during the week and at the previous dinners they had enjoyed together, Ken Moy had made no play for her, and, apart from shaking hands the first day, he had not touched her, Kate expected nothing more than their usual business talk. However, just before dessert, he asked, 'Kate, would you like to visit America?'

'As a tourist or for business?'

'Well, it could be both. I've learnt a lot this week; perhaps if you visit us in the US, you can learn something new too.'

'That's an interesting idea, Ken. I must consider it. I couldn't do so for several weeks because I've many projects on the go, but a quick visit might be possible in two or three months. There is a question I haven't asked that you might answer.'

'What's that?'

'How many men do you have in your marketing department?'

'Very few, and I'm the only senior management male.'

'So you *are* unusual. I thought so. Can you tell me why you're in the job?'

Ken had to think about it. 'It's true that women's cosmetics naturally attract many female employees, which becomes a self-fulfilling policy; women employ women. I was surprised at the offer I received to join the company, so I asked our vice president about it, and she said that she had received an instruction to employ someone with a media background as an experiment to see if a new marketing approach might result.'

'And what have you discovered so far?'

'That marketing cosmetics is quite different from what I did before, marketing motor vehicles, and I must be cautious to avoid breaking the machine. I haven't yet identified anything sig-nificant, although some minor improvements seem apparent to me.'

'Then please, if you implement any minor improvements, tell me what they are. Perhaps I can do the same.'

Ken said as they left the restaurant, 'Kate, I've enjoyed my week, especially our meetings and meals together. I hope for the chance to continue in the US. Can I invite you to my room for a nightcap?'

His bluntness, with no previous indication of any desire, shocked Kate; her only thought was an instant reaction: *Is this how Americans propose sex? Without affection, like a business deal?*

'Ken,' she said, 'I've committed to marry the man I love, and he loves me. He's a scientist and is currently in Egypt. Next week I'm flying to join him. And even if it weren't for him, I don't sleep around; sex without love is not my thing; it takes months to learn to love.' *It took me four days.*

'Kate, I felt it would be fun, so don't take it badly.'

'I won't, Ken; knowing I'm desirable is flattering. Good night.'

As she waited for the taxi, she asked herself, *When did I decide to go to Egypt and marry Kelvin? Is that new, or has it been in my mind since we parted?*

29

ON SATURDAY MORNING, Kate called Marylyn. 'Hi Em. Are we still on for dinner?'

'Yes, Kate. Can you come a bit earlier, say, at five?'

'Why?'

'I need some help – just the simple stuff. I'm doing chicken tetrazzini.'

'Em, that's complicated! Have you made it before?'

'Every night this week,' Marylyn laughed. 'My folks are sick of it, but I have it taped, except Mum says to watch out as Darryl's oven might not give the same results.'

Wow, she's determined. 'Okay, Em, I'll be there. Where's Darryl? Can't he help?'

'He's in Manchester at a maths conference and will reach his rooms at seven. I have a key.'

At least she's made some progress to have a key.

Kate rang the doorbell to Darryl's apartment at four-thirty that afternoon. She had taken the train from Kings Cross in London and would return to her parents' home after dinner.

The intercom squawked, 'Is that you?'

The door buzzed when she said, 'Me, Kate, you, Em.'

'Come up, the first floor.'

On the first floor, she found a door open and heard Marylyn call, 'Put your bag in the lounge and join me.'

She found a flushed Marylyn, hair flying in all directions and wearing an oversized apron, in the kitchen.

'There's another apron behind the door.' Her friend pointed. 'Can you tidy up?'

Kate looked around the kitchen and decided Marylyn did need help: it looked like she had used every pot and utensil available. Still, she said, 'The kitchen does need cleaning up, but any man who walked in now would find you adorable, and if you had no pants or panties on, he'd drop his immediately. You're the image I would use in a TV ad for chicken tetrazzini!'

Marylyn laughed and wiped her hand across her forehead, leaving a greasy brown streak. 'I hope to have enough time for Darryl to think I can produce a meal without disturbing a hair on my head, but thanks, Kate.'

The apron behind the door was as big as Marylyn's. 'Darryl must be a massive man.'

'No, Kate, but he's not much good at choosing clothes.'

Forty minutes later, Kate had washed everything and put it away in the cupboards that Marylyn indicated.

As she finished wiping down the table, Marylyn said, 'Kate, there's a wine fridge in the lounge, and the cupboard above has wine glasses. Can you fetch us two glasses of white wine?'

'Sure, Em.'

Kate entered the lounge. She hadn't looked around when she'd dropped her handbag on a chair there earlier but now she was seeing it properly; she thought it looked exactly like the room an absent-minded professor would occupy, with a potpourri of items on every surface, all in total disorder. A large desk beside the window had a collection of folders and papers. Kate thought Darryl had placed it strategically to shed light on the documents, but his computer screen would be in shadow.

Kate opened the cupboard, selected two wine glasses, placed them on the desk, and removed a white wine bottle from the fridge. She found the corkscrew on the desk, lying on a document. Reaching for it, Kate glanced at the paper. It didn't surprise her, for it was a scientific paper with two columns, but as she began to turn away, she saw the words 'Vatican Library' at the top.

Kate poured a glass of wine for Marylyn, took it to her, said, 'I'll fetch mine,' and then returned to the lounge. Curiosity had snuck in. *Why is a Vatican document in a mathematician's lounge?*

She looked more closely at the paper. The title, below the Vatican Library heading, was in two languages, Italian and English. 'Survey of marital status and practice in Italy with statistical analysis.'

It piqued her curiosity, so Kate went to her bag, fetched her phone, took a photo of the cover page, poured the second glass of wine, recorked the bottle, put it in the fridge, and then returned to the kitchen. *I'll study that tomorrow.*

'Em, you've drunk half your wine already! If you continue like that, you'll be on your back when Darryl arrives instead of much later!'

'I was thirsty. I'll have a glass of water so my resolve doesn't waver.'

Kate helped Marylyn move the dining table from where it obviously stood habitually in the corner of the room – the imprint of the table's feet in the carpet showed a long period without movement – and then laid the table with cutlery for three people.

Darryl arrived shortly before seven. By then, Kate and Marylyn were almost two glasses of wine ahead of him.

He kissed Marylyn thoroughly, then turned to Kate with a wide grin. 'You must be Kate, the chaperone.'

'I gave up trying to chaperone Em years ago,' Kate laughed. 'It's the secret of a long friendship: don't tell the other what to do, and even be careful with suggestions.'

While they ate – Kate thought the chicken tetrazzini was

delicious – she closely watched Darryl and Marylyn's interactions. She especially noticed the small details, such as how he helped her whenever he could, how he brushed against her at every opportunity, and his smile and tender looks at her friend. Kate decided that Darryl was deeply in love with Marylyn, and she felt Marylyn was in love with him too.

She saw another side of Darryl when she asked what statisticians did at Cambridge. After a detailed description, Kate had an idea and asked, 'Darryl, have you had anything to do with surveys?'

'The lifeblood of the statistician, Kate. That's what we are employed to analyse.'

'Do you have anything to do with data mining?'

'What do you know about that, Kate?'

'Very little, but I feel it may be the future of marketing surveys.'

'Then I shall study the possibilities.'

'When I know more, can my company employ you as a consultant?'

'A pleasure, Kate. I assume you use a questionnaire system. Can you send me twenty old questionnaires to look at?'

'If you give me your email, I will.'

On Sunday morning, Kate lay in bed at her parents' house for a few moments, thinking about her last interaction with Marylyn the previous night as the two women said goodbye to each other. 'The meal was superb, and Darryl is deeply in love with you,' Kate had told her friend. 'He's a marvellous guy.'

'Then why doesn't he ask me to marry him?'

'He has a problem. You need to find out what it is.'

Remembering the photo she had taken of the document on

227

Darryl's desk, she took out her phone and studied it. It was an abstract bearing the title and author's name. The first page was an introduction to a summary, but the summary was on pages she hadn't photographed. It did, however, stir her interest and determination to find out more, for it said, 'This report and analysis are the result of an extensive survey, conducted in multiple towns in Italy, into marital longevity. The results prove the methodology is valid, and repeated surveys annually will give a good picture of the evolution of marriage expectations. The summary below gives details of the scope and the process followed.'

She asked herself, *What would Kelvin do?*

She tried to access the Vatican Library but needed to log in. Attempting to register, she discovered she didn't have the proper credentials; the site kept repeating, 'Affiliation is a required field.'

She shrugged on a dressing gown, went downstairs, and sought out her father. 'Dad, how do I access the Vatican Library? I tried registering, but I'm not an accredited church leader or a scientist, so I can't enter an affiliation.'

'Why do you want to access their library?'

'So I can find a technical paper.'

'Okay, I'll come and log in using your computer.'

'Why are you accredited?'

'Because the library has data on the death rate of children.'

Five minutes later, Kate said, 'Thanks, Dad,' and then entered the name on the document: Marco Zeffirelli.

Marco had five papers listed; he was a researcher at Milan University. Although it was all in Italian, she recognised the one that interested her and found references to three people who had collaborated. Kate wrote down their names, then opened a new web page and tried to log in to the Milan University library. She had the same problem, and her father couldn't help her this time.

'I'm sorry, Kate, I don't have access. Is there someone at your company lab who might?'

Kate called Sofia Bertone, an Italian colleague and lab chemist. 'I'm sorry to bother you on a Sunday, Sofia, but I'm trying to access the Milan University library to find a technical paper.'

'Unless you speak Italian, you'll be disappointed,' Sofia replied. 'Most of the translated technical papers are in Rome. I've access to the Rome library, so if you give me the reference, I can download it and send it to you.'

'Sofia, that would be marvellous.'

'Give me half an hour, Kate. What email address for you should I use?'

'I'll SMS it to you with the paper's reference. Our next lunch is my shout.'

Kate went to make a coffee, and when she returned, she found the email and the attached document.

The summary chapter was relatively short. It covered why the Vatican had commissioned the survey, stated that the results were valid, and listed the contents. The first chapters covered the study; it was extensive. Kate learnt that it covered thirty-five towns, a thousand Catholic people in each, of all social classes, and only where a partner was between the ages of forty-five and forty-seven. She didn't understand the reason for the age limitation; it had to do with statistical reliability.

But Kate did tuck away in her memory something she had never considered: the survey cost might have been low, as in each town, the churches had received instructions to do the survey. She thought of finding cheaper market survey methods and decided Brenda's idea was worth developing. Perhaps data mining wasn't the only route to more affordable surveys.

Turning to the chapter that had the questionnaire, Kate thought it pretty standard: personal information, age, sex, and space for the date of marriage and date of divorce repeated three times, and age of partner at marriage, then children, with dates of birth and death – no names, only 'M' or 'F'. She did have the thought that three marriages and divorces before age forty-seven were unlikely.

Kate thought the last part of the questionnaire was unusual. One question asked, 'Did you or your partner propose marriage?' and another, 'Did you or your partner suffer from any medical/physical conditions listed below?' The extensive list mentioned limited eyesight, hearing problems, diabetes and paraplegia.

The following chapter covered the analysis. Kate read, 'The first graph, Fig 1, shows how long each marriage lasted, as dots, years along the bottom and age at the date of marriage on the vertical. No statistically valid trend existed in the raw data. However, after eliminating marriages with an age difference exceeding ten years and then six years as outliers, the graph in Fig 2 shows a statistically significant increase in marriage duration with age at marriage. Fig 2 shows that marriage at age twenty-two had a thirty-six per cent probability of lasting ten years whereas, at thirty-two, it was eighty-one per cent.'

That's me. I married at twenty, and it lasted six weeks.

The last chapter dealt with the final two questions in the survey: 'Significantly, marriages due to the female partner making the request have a ninety-seven per cent probability of lasting longer than ten years. However, these marriages are in the over-twenty-eight groups and may account for the high percentages of the groups.'

Kate stopped there and went to join her parents on the terrace for a glass of wine and lunch. She discussed what she had found, and her father said, 'Kate, send me that paper. It sounds like one I should read.'

Two hours later, Kate returned to her computer. She looked for

Marco Zeffirelli and found his blog. It was all in Italian, but she paged down the past questions to Marco and his answers. A few questions were in English.

One asked. 'To what physical cause do you attribute the effect shown in Fig 2?'

Several people had commented. Kate pasted Marco's answer into Google Translate and read the result: 'Inexperienced selection. Intolerant youth. Money.'

I was the first.

She paged down further until she saw the question, 'To what do you attribute the high success rate of marriages where the woman proposes?'

And the answer: 'Due to the skew of such marriages to the older age group, the increase is not as significant as it first appears. However, further surveys may reveal an inability of many men to take on the responsibility of a family until they mature further. The fear of marital breakup involving children deters men far more than women. Refer to a paper by AG Thomas at Baltimore.'

Kate highlighted the research paper, the Figure 2 analysis and the remark on marriages instigated by women, then addressed an email to Marylyn, attached the highlighted research paper, and then cut and pasted the two blog questions and answers into the email.

Then she added, 'Em, look at the stuff on Darryl's desk. You will find a reference to the paper. Ask him to marry you; that's what he's waiting for. You can also tell Darryl I have given his name to the VP of marketing, who may contact him to discuss consulting on data mining surveys.'

Then she emailed Darryl's details to Gertrude Lenferna.

She read a list of what she had to do the next day, then booked the EgyptAir flight to Cairo, departing at 15h00.

30

ON MONDAY MORNING, Kate arrived at the office with her suitcase and spoke to Brenda. 'I'm going to Egypt for work; I have a TV ad to produce. You must hold the fort here, but please email and call me as often as you wish if anything needs my attention.'

'When are you going?'

'Organise a taxi to take me to Paddington at twelve.'

'It'll be just as quick from here if you take the taxi to the airport, as it's not rush hour.'

'Okay, I'll check with the driver. Now, what must I look at this morning?'

'The departmental reports.'

'Print them out for me, please. I'll take them with me and read them on the flight.'

'You have a meeting at eleven and another at three. I must cancel that.'

'Don't. Write a notice for my signature, saying that I'm away and have appointed you to attend all meetings in my absence and report back to me. And please, from now on, call me Kate.'

A flabbergasted Brenda did what Kate said.

Kate reached Heathrow Airport at 12h45, where she had another surprise. Someone had flagged her name in the EgyptAir computer, and when her boarding pass was issued, it said 'First Class.'

She had the time in the first-class lounge for a delicious Egyptian lunch and a call to Kelvin. Happiness filled her as she thought of seeing him again.

With a devilish grin, she called the Ramses Hilton hotel direct line and added the suffix #2606. Then, as she waited for Kelvin to answer, she covered the phone's mouthpiece with the sleeve of her cardigan to muffle her voice.

'Kelvin Shareef.'

Speaking Arabic, Kate said in a gravelly, low-pitched tone, as if she were the receptionist, 'Dr Shareef, we have received a request to change your booking to a double. Your wife says she's coming to stay with you.'

'There must be a mistake. I'm not married or expecting anyone to join me.'

The gravelly voice replied, 'Oh dear, then I must find another room, and the hotel bookings are full.'

Kelvin felt like a lightning bolt had hit him; the voice had used an Iranian word for 'room'. Feeling thrilled, he stifled an exclamation. 'Go ahead, change the booking, and send the woman up when she comes. If I don't like her, I'll find her a room in another hotel.'

Kate removed the cardigan and said in her normal voice. 'Kelvin, you're a dog.'

'And you're a devil, my darling. Are you coming to Cairo?'

'Arriving at nine-forty tonight. I'm at Heathrow now. In that sinful city, you'll fall into trouble. I'm going to watch over you day and night.'

'I approve of the night bit.'

'I'm not surprised. Already, you're having lewd thoughts, inviting strange women to your room.'

Kelvin refused to contradict her. 'Shall I meet you at the airport?'

'No, stay there and keep the bed warm.'

'Okay. I had a dinner date with Ahmed tonight, but I'm sure he and Soraya will want to meet you, so I'll cancel for tonight and invite them to join us for dinner tomorrow instead.'

'Ahmed, is it too late to cancel dinner tonight?'

'Why, what's up?'

'Kate is arriving tonight at 9:40. Can we reschedule for tomorrow? Here at the hotel?'

'That's wonderful news. We can reschedule, but not at your hotel. You and Kate are our guests, so come to my parents' house early. I'm sure Soraya and Kate will have much to discuss. Tell Kate that Soraya's still reluctant to go to England.'

'It's a date. See you tomorrow.'

'Bye, Kelvin.'

Kelvin didn't leave his suite. He called reception and asked them to give Kate a keycard to his room when she arrived. Then he tried to concentrate on the collection of maps that decorated the lounge area, but knowing that Kate was airborne and on her way to him made it impossible; his heartbeat and adrenalin levels were too high. He called room service and ordered dinner, and once he'd eaten, he took a long hot bath, then tried to watch the news on Egyptian television. Finally, when he realised he had absorbed nothing said on the TV, he got into bed.

He lay still, feigning sleep, when the door lock clicked a bit later. Kelvin sensed Kate enter the room, so he snored. Then he heard the rustle of clothes as she stripped, and as the bed moved when she tried to sneak in, he mumbled, 'Hathor, I shall never love another.'

He heard a whisper, 'Pharaoh, I'm here.' Then her lips sealed his.

234

When he could breathe again, she whispered. 'You promised once to feel me all over. Please do so.'

They didn't leave the bed when they woke; a mutual reluctance to be the first to rise kept them there.

'Darling, flying here was worth it. Either my memory is bad, or last night topped the last time,' Kate said, snuggling contentedly in Kelvin's arms.

'For me, too.' Kelvin grinned. 'But I can tell we need lots of practice to achieve perfection.'

'Then we had better start now.'

An hour later, with plenty of 'practice' under their belts, Kelvin declared that all the exercise had made him hungry. Kate ordered food from room service, and then, for the first time, they shared the bathroom.

Kate filled the bath. 'Kelvin, if you don't keep your hands off me, we will never be ready before room service comes.'

'I can't help it, my darling. You're far too beautiful, like a statue of Venus I saw in a decorator's workshop.'

'Okay, I know when you want to tell me something. Go ahead.'

'I had to visit a workshop that made plaster decorations for houses, and there was a statue of Venus that they had to duplicate. It was on a small plinth, and it was beautiful.'

'So what about it?'

'Her backside was about the same height as yours, and her bum was shiny because the statue was of pale alabaster. I caressed her bum without thought, and the decorator said, "I can tell a man is normal when he does that."'

Kate laughed, and Kelvin reached out and caressed her bum.

She slapped his hand away gently. 'Kelvin, I'm not a statue.'

'No, you're a living, breathing Venus I cannot resist.'

'Then resist for a while longer; we must dress.'

Ten minutes later, Kelvin opened the door for room service. A man and a woman set up and laid the table by the window with a view over the Nile and left a trolley with the food.

'Kelvin,' Kate said, seating herself at the table and choosing from a beautiful platter of freshly cut fruit, 'I'm going to stop calling you "darling", except at night.'

'Why?'

'It's okay on the telephone, but I can tell that when I do so, you stop thinking of serious things.'

'What serious things?'

'You have your investigation to do, and I'm not on holiday; I have work to do.'

Surprised, Kelvin asked, 'What work?'

'Brenda, my secretary, will send me reports and requests for decisions, and I have a TV ad to produce.'

'What for?'

'A new male deodorant called "Undress me".'

'How are you going to do that?'

'First, I must find a film production unit.'

'Okay,' Kelvin said, pouring them both coffees. 'Once we've finished eating, you can open your laptop, and I'll return to my maps.'

By early evening, Kate had found six film companies and had arranged for two each day to come and fetch her from the hotel to visit their offices and studios.

The first four had been easy to uncover: Kate had looked up ad agencies on the web and called the one that claimed the most clients, and the director hadn't hesitated to name four film companies for her; he said he dealt with them all.

Kate looked them up, made appointments, and then felt something was wrong. She looked at ad agencies again, searching until she found one formed only three years ago. The manager was chatty and impressed to be talking to the marketing director of a worldwide marketing company.

Kate explained what she wanted, and he replied, 'We use two. The director of Avant Garde Films openly admits to being gay, and he's weirdly artistic. We can't use them for run-of-the-mill advertising; our clients would go elsewhere, and managing the director's crazy ideas takes skill. I think you'll be safer with Desert Motion Pictures.'

Kate called both.

Kelvin, meanwhile, had spent the day looking at maps. He had messaged his father again to ask if he had any smaller-scale maps of the target area before returning to the oldest maps from Alexandria. Finally, he found two that worried him: they gave him a feeling, one that he couldn't pin down.

'Kate, do you have a moment?'

'Of course, my darling.'

'I thought you weren't going to use "darling"?'

She smiled at him. It made his gut turn upside down. 'I've changed the rule. Only direct speech, not in a reply.'

'You're going to make my life hell, I can tell.'

'Of course. What is it?'

Kelvin explained, 'I've two maps. I want you to tell me your reaction when you look at them.'

She looked for less than a minute. 'A guy in an office who had never been there drew this one,' she said, pointing to the first, 'and a man who had been there drew the other.'

'How do you work that out?'

'The man who visited added tiny little details he had seen. Look at that rock; it's not square but a half-moon.'

'My wonderful darling, can I kiss you?'

'No,' Kate said and laughed at Kelvin's stricken expression. 'That's punishment for using "darling". Go back to work.'

Kelvin noted the name of the man who had made the map and began a web search for information about him. As the man might have been a trader, Kelvin thought his name might have been Saudi, so he included Saudi sources.

By the time he packed up, he had found the name occurred frequently in Saudi Red Sea ports and became convinced the man came from one of them. He would try to match each feature from the map with similar features on the satellite images.

He found matching them difficult when he studied the satellite images because the photos showed countless dry rivers and streams. They all seemed to lead to the Nile or the Red Sea.

He sent a WhatsApp message to his father again. 'Hi, Dad. Those satellite images show the land covered in rivers and streams, even lakes; although dry now, where did the water come from? I can't find a reference to heavy rainfall even six thousand years ago.'

Darius replied within a few moments. 'Hi, Kelvin. Refer to the African Humid Period. Desiccation was progressive and much later in Eastern Sudan. Geologically, the area has successive porous and impermeable layers due to periods of sedimentation and vulcanism. The Eritrean and Ethiopian highlands still supply Nile water. Infiltration through porous layers will have contributed to maintaining surface water flows through springs in this period.'

'Where is the water now?' Kelvin messaged back.

'Extensive underground water and aquifers exist throughout the Sahara between impermeable layers. Refer BRGM report on

Mauritania. Twenty-three million tons of mineral quality water in the Benichaab basin, at 120-180 metres depth. Ethiopia may still maintain them in the Eastern Sahara.'

31

AHMED CAME TO THE DOOR when Kelvin rang the bell. Beaming at Kate, he said, 'At last, I get to meet the goddess.'

Kelvin did the introductions: 'Ahmed, Kate; Kate, Ahmed.'

Laughing, Kate reached out to shake hands. 'Ahmed, shall I never escape that title?'

'I doubt it. In the flesh, you are even more beautiful than in the photo. Hathor would be jealous! Please, come in and meet Soraya and my parents.'

When they entered the lounge, Soraya came to meet them, and Kate thought, *She has a lovely face, and her black eyes are striking.*

Kelvin thought, *She looks like Nefertiti.*

Taking Soraya's hands, Kate said, 'You're lovely. I'm glad Kelvin didn't see you before he saw me!'

Soraya laughed. 'Kate, he would have left me the moment he saw you. The photo of you didn't lie.'

Ahmed said, 'Now, please meet my mother. She has prepared Kelvin's favourite dish, especially for him.'

Kelvin and Kate offered a formal greeting, and then Kate said, 'You remind me of my mother. Have you spoken to her?'

'I have. Your mother's a lovely warm woman and has promised to speak to Soraya's mother if Soraya wants to go to England.'

Turning to Soraya, Kate said, 'Soraya, come. Let's go into the ladies' lounge and have a chat.'

As the two young women left the room, Kelvin said to his friend, 'Ahmed, you've picked a beauty. Have you ever looked at a bust of Nefertiti?'

'I've seen photos.'

'The paintings and photos don't show the beautiful curves of her face. Soraya looks just like her.'

'Thanks, Kelvin. I hope Kate can persuade Soraya to accompany me.'

'She will, Ahmed, for apart from helping you, she has another motivation. Her mother is working too hard and needs assistance, but the only assistance she has found in England is too unskilled to take the load off her and training a new assistant would increase her workload. Then Kelvin paused for thought. 'Ahmed, start thinking about where you'll live – Guildford to Barnet is too far for Soraya to commute.'

'Okay, Kelvin, tell me what you've been up to.'

Kelvin did, and had just finished when Kate and Soraya returned, smiles on both faces.

Kate had begun by saying, 'Soraya, can we speak English?'

'Of course. I read and write English better than I speak it, but I'm okay with it.'

Kate laughed understandingly. 'Even I have a problem understanding some English people, and I went to school in England.'

Soraya laughed too. 'Okay. What do you want to know?'

'Soraya, my mother is overworked and needs help, so first, tell me: if you went to help my mother, what would you expect to do?'

'Your mother told me about some things on the telephone. Can you tell me what she does and why she's overworked?'

Kate told Soraya what it was like working in a National Health hospital from her experience of visiting her mother at Barnet, concluding, 'So, my mother, a specialist, often sees patients who should go to a junior doctor. She should only see those who need an advanced diagnosis and treatment; some, she refers to my father for surgery.'

'Kate, I don't know what problems come to your mother – they may differ from those I've experienced here – but at a rough guess, if all her patients came to me, I could and would treat about seventy per cent and the others would go to your mother. In return, I would expect your mother to teach me how to diagnose and treat the thirty per cent needing her attention. At first, I might not be that good, but it would build quickly. So I expect and hope she'll allow me to treat patients independently after the first week or two.'

Then Kate thought of where Soraya would live. Kelvin had told her that Ahmed lived in an apartment, and she thought it would be unsuitable for children. 'Are you going to have children with Ahmed?' she asked.

'Not for a couple of years. I'm still young and want to be sure I can raise my children comfortably. Ahmed lives in a flat, and I don't want that for my children. How about you and Kelvin?'

'I'm older than you, Soraya; I want kids as soon as we marry.' *At least, I hope it will be possible.*

Kate switched back to Arabic. 'Your English is excellent, Soraya, far better than that of many Londoners, so never think it's your fault if you don't understand something; ask them to repeat it. You'll love my parents, and if you want to become a surgeon, Dad can organise it. He teaches at the university hospitals. Ahmed loves you and will stand by you, so don't worry, just come. But be careful, you are beautiful, and men in England are more likely to try to take you from Ahmed than in Egypt. Turn them away immediately if you feel they are interested, and always let Ahmed know when you'll be late home and why.'

'Do you have that problem?'

'Yes, all the time, but I grew up in England and learnt to turn them off. Tell them you are married and have four kids. That's usually enough.'

Soraya laughed. 'Will you be my older sister?'

'For sure, but older sisters are often a pain. I have one, so I know! So if I act out of turn, please tell me. Now let's join the others.'

Dinner passed with much laughter and leg-pulling.

As everyone finished eating, laid down their cutlery, and relaxed, a happy Soraya said, 'Listen, everyone. I've decided that I'm going to England to work with Kate's mother. Ahmed, you asked me to marry you; I will if I can settle in England.'

The applause was unanimous, and Ahmed kissed Soraya in front of his mother, something frowned upon in traditional households. Kelvin thought, *His mother's not as formal as she seems.*

Then Soraya added, 'I'll call Kate's mother tomorrow, have my mother talk to her, and then Ahmed can book our air tickets.'

For the next three days, one film company collected Kate in the morning and took her to their studios to view their ads and meet the directors, and then after lunch, another did the same. She gave each director her script and storyboard.

After the last meeting, she returned to the hotel and found six quotations in her inbox. The first five companies all included in their quote the item 'Writing and approving script'.

She knew it was standard practice for a production company to take responsibility for writing a detailed script and obtaining the client's approval, with modifications if necessary. Then, after editing, if the client didn't like the result, they would charge extra for retakes.

Although all five quotations were twenty per cent cheaper than English equivalents, she was unhappy: they were standard run-of-the-mill ad producers, and she wanted more.

She looked at the company called Scarabads. There was no itemised script fee in the quote, which also stated, 'Unlimited retakes verbally specified and agreed by both client and Scarabads, on our premises or location using video. Final cut and sound by joint decision.'

The price was fifty per cent cheaper than the equivalent in the UK, with another clause that read, 'Two starring actors supplied by the client, all others at Scarabads' discretion.'

Kate remembered the director: his mannerisms labelled him as gay, and the ads she had viewed were brilliant.

'Kelvin, my darling?'

'Now you're doing it, Kate.'

'Doing what?'

'Calling me "darling".'

'It's after working hours.'

'That's not an excuse. Are you asking for something?'

'Yes. I've five traditional ad filmmakers and one with a gay director who doesn't need a detailed script. I want to go with him. Am I being foolish?'

'I don't know. Tell me more.'

Kate had to think carefully. 'The first thing I said to all the companies was that I wanted a generic ad. I said that nowadays, the entire world knows what an Inuit, a desert, a camel or a rhino are, and that, in my opinion, an ad had to send a message, and it didn't matter what the background was if it was universally recognised.'

'I agree, Kate. Did everyone react the same?'

'All except the last director were shocked. The last one said, "I agree. Where do you see the setting?" When I said the desert, he said, "Then the costume must be thobes and an agal. All the world has seen the Saudis; even the old silent films had sheikhs dressed like that."'

'Good for him – he's on the ball. What else?'

'He asked for the message. I said, "Directing the ad at women, it must be, if you buy this perfume for a man, it means you want to go to bed with him."'

'Wow. Kate, you should go with your hunch.'

'Then he asked me who I wanted as actors.'

'So, who?'

'I said he could recruit whomever he wanted for the scenes where a face is not visible, but I gave him our photo for the pivotal scene. And said, "Us."'

'Kate, I can't act.'

'You don't need to. Can you ride a horse?'

'Yes. Why?'

'Because then we won't need the stuntman to do the scene where you ride up to me – you can do it. I'm sitting on a rock. You lean down to look at me, dismount, and say a few words – it doesn't matter what because the sound man will dub the speech in afterwards. Then you remount the horse and ride away.'

'That's all? What do you do?'

'They'll shoot the same scene with a stuntman on the horse, and after he remounts, he'll lean down and lift me onto the horse before riding off.'

'Can't I do that?'

'You can try.'

'I'm sure I can do that, Kate. Now let's go to bed; it's practice time.'

245

An hour later, their bodies entwined around each other, feeling warm and exhausted, Kate, her head on Kelvin's chest, whispered, 'Darling?'

'Yes, dearest.'

'Did I feel a little bump where there wasn't one before?'

'I think so, although it was only a little bump.'

'Would it like some help?'

'My love, we must let it happen naturally. Don't frighten it.'

Still in each other's arms when they woke in the hotel bed, Kate was reluctant to rise. She snuggled closer and said, 'Must we get up? I could stay here all day.'

'We could, but I've made appointments I would have to cancel.'

'Who with?'

'I should have told you yesterday, but a naked goddess distracted me,' Kelvin replied with a broad grin. 'I've finished my map work, and now I must plan for a trip into the desert. The first thing is to find a vehicle. I called the Land Rover and Unimog agents, and we'll go and see them this morning.'

'Ok, I must bath, but the tub's big enough for two.'

'You do have great ideas, darling.'

The Land Rover agent gave them documentation describing the available models and extras, told them it would take three to four months to deliver a new vehicle to Kelvin's specifications, and said recent diesel models were rare, and rarer on the second-hand market.

The Unimog agent gave them a delivery time of four months

on a new model and said the agency didn't deal in second-hand Unimogs, so he couldn't suggest where to look for one. Then, seeing the disappointment on Kate's face, he added, 'But let's go to the spares department. They sell Unimog spares and can tell you who is buying them. That will give you a lead.'

The spares manager was helpful. Saying he would ask the accountant, he left the office. When he returned, he said, 'It'll take half an hour. Would you like some coffee?'

Kelvin and Kate said yes, so he sent his secretary to fetch two coffees.

It was then that fate stepped in. Kate would later swear she recognised Shai when he entered the room, but Kelvin saw an ordinary man in a workshop coat.

'Excuse me, boss. We have a problem with a spare driveshaft we supplied; it doesn't fit.'

'Okay, I'll come in a minute, Aten,' the spares manager said; then, seeing the look of curiosity on the other's face, he added, 'This is Dr Shareef. He's looking for a Unimog. Would you know of one available?'

'Not in Cairo, but one broke down in El Salloum some months back. We quoted on the spares, but when the company couldn't pay for them, we didn't deliver them. Five months ago, I called the garage asking if they still wanted the spares. The vehicle was still there. The guy said he hadn't seen the owners; if you want to know more, I can call again next week and find out if it's still there.'

Kelvin replied, 'I'll be grateful. For what was the Unimog used?'

'A travel company owned it. They were doing a tour from Morocco to Port Said with many youngsters, probably overloaded and without maintenance on the road. If it's there and still broken, it will need trucking to us here for overhaul.'

'That sounds like a plan. When should I call you to learn if it's still there?'

'Monday afternoon, about three.'

The accountant then arrived with a list, which he gave Kelvin.

The manager of the spares department showed them out, saying, 'If you call the numbers on the list, ask for the vehicle's year of manufacture, and buy nothing more than three years old. Older ones will have modifications with Chinese parts. Original parts won't fit, and finding Chinese parts is impossible, leading to more modifications.'

32

'KELVIN, THIS VIEW IS SUPERB. It must be romantic at night.'

At Kelvin's suggestion, they had gone for lunch at Crimson, a rooftop restaurant with a view over the Nile.

Before Kelvin could respond, Kate's phone pinged, and she had to look for it in her bag. After at least a minute of scrabbling in her purse, she produced it, exclaiming, 'Ha! Caught you.'

Kelvin laughed. 'Why did you say "caught you"?'

'Hasn't at least one of your many girlfriends explained about mobile phones and women's handbags?'

Kelvin grinned. 'No. Tell me.'

'My bag is well organised, and everything in it is necessary for my wellbeing, and repairs and maintenance as the day passes. Before *men* invented the mobile phone, bags stayed that way, but since the phone arrived, it's changed. Good bags have a little pocket inside at the top for a phone. If I make a mistake and put it in the main bag – something women do when distracted by a handsome and sexy man – the phone comes to life and burrows down to hide. It's telling me not to bother with a phone when there's a sexy man around.'

'Nothing else?'

'Oh, yes. Sometimes, when I try to find the phone and the man is extremely sexy, it keeps trying to escape me. I feel and find it's not there on one side, then I go to the other side, and the phone slips back to where I've already searched. It's the number-one indicator of a man's sexiness: the longer it takes to catch the phone, the sexier he is.'

Kate could see Kelvin was trying hard not to burst into laughter as he asked, 'So, how do I rate?'

'You're the world record holder.'

'So, when you take ages to find your phone, I should sit patiently counting my sexy points instead of becoming annoyed?'

Kate nodded and grinned. 'You're not just a pretty face!'

It was too much for Kelvin. Shaking with mirth, he said, 'Okay, so now you've trapped your phone, shouldn't you look to see who called?'

'It's a WhatsApp from Marylyn. She says, "Call me."'

'Well, put your phone on the table, and put a plate on it so it can't escape. Let's order, and then you can call Marylyn.'

A few moments later, they ordered, a lamb shawarma for Kelvin and an oven-roasted chicken shawarma for Kate; and both chose koshary, Egypt's longtime favourite, a mixture of rice, lentils, chickpeas and pasta cooked individually, then tossed together and topped with cumin-scented tomato sauce and crunchy fried onions.

Kate called Marylyn. Putting it on speakerphone and turning down the volume so it wouldn't disturb the other diners, she and Kelvin, heads together with the phone between them on the table, listened.

'Hello, Kate. Where are you?'

'With Kelvin at a rooftop restaurant in Cairo for lunch. Where are you?'

'I've just left the bedroom. I'm about to make breakfast.'

'A wild night, Marylyn?'

'No, a wild morning. I'm with Darryl.'

'So you've broken your resolution.'

'No, Kate. That's what I want to tell you. I came to his rooms early because he said he would take me out for the day, but when I arrived, I remembered what you said, so I told him I love him and want to marry him and spend my life in his arms, and that if he didn't say yes, I was going straight to a convent to become a nun.'

'Did he say yes?'

'We're going to the registry office first thing on Monday!'

'Marylyn, that's wonderful! Don't let him escape.'

'I won't,' her friend laughed. 'I brought enough food for the weekend, and I'll keep him here until we have the marriage licence.'

'When's the marriage?'

'We'll discuss that on Monday. I have stacks of bed-time to catch up this weekend, but I had to tell you. Bye, Kate, and thank you.'

'Bye, Marylyn.'

As Kate ended the call, Kelvin said, 'First Soraya and Ahmed, now Marylyn and Darryl. You are a red-hot marriage broker. Who's next?'

'Us,' she said.

The waiter arrived with their food, and they waited in silence while he set down the plates.

As they began eating, Kate said, 'Kelvin, now tell me what you've discovered from your maps. Where is Isis's wadi?'

'I don't know exactly, Kate, but I've found three possible sites. And that's why we must go and look. And I may be wrong about all three.'

'How did you find them? Did you invoke the genie of the maps?'

'There's no magic in what I've done. The only two things we know about the wadi are that a man sometimes walks or rides a camel to Dehmit or Aswan from it, and that water was there thousands of years ago. Today it might be only a well.'

'So what did the maps tell you?'

'A likely route people took when crossing from the Red Sea

coast to the Nile. I hope that if such a route existed thousands of years ago, the man who visits Aswan would use it today.'

'Okay. But that's a long route. Where do we look for the wadi?'

'The satellite map shows the remaining effect of water on the land: dry rivers and eroded valleys. The wadi won't be in a river valley. But there are three places I've spotted along that supposed trade route. They appear to have once been the source of a small tributary. Maybe they once had a lake. The satellite map shows them filled with sand. I don't know if we will find anything, but it will be fun riding around looking.'

'I still don't understand, Kelvin. How did you decide on the trade route?'

'Back then, the magnetic compass was unknown, but the ancients did understand how to use the sun's shadow for navigation: a stick in the ground was the original sun compass. Eratosthenes, in Alexandria, used this method to measure the earth's diameter in 350 BCE.

'If a trader travelled to Aswan from the Red Sea and drew a map, he would have used this method to fix the physical objects on either side of his track. He would also have mapped things far away, like distant mountains. However, sun compass errors grow with distance, so while close features would be accurate, those farther away would be inaccurate.

'I used the first Nile cataract, Wadi Halfa, and a fishing port as three known base points, then stretched and overlaid the five ancient maps on the satellite map so these points matched. I found the five maps had a close correspondence with each other along a squiggly line I labelled as the trade route, and then I visually searched along it on each side.'

'Okay, so it's more than guesswork?'

'Yes. I reckon we must drive three hundred kilometres across the unmarked desert and the same to return, and I've allowed three hundred kilometres for searching. That's roughly fifty hours of driving – say, six days. We'll have several stops for on-foot searches, so I've allowed twelve days. We'll take food and water for fifteen days, just in case, and twenty litres of kerosene for cooking. There's no wood in the desert.'

'We must find the vehicle first,' Kate pointed out.

Kelvin nodded. 'If I can't find a Unimog, I must look for an all-wheel-drive truck. One of those may be easier to find.'

'Change of subject, my darling. Can I have an ice cream?'

'Of course. And what would you like to do tomorrow?'

'I'm visiting the film director now that we've decided. I'll probably be with him for five days.'

'If I didn't know he was gay, I would come with you,' Kelvin laughed. 'Okay, so while you're busy with your ad, I'll try to find the items we need, starting with a satphone.'

On the first day she spent with the director, Tenis Hussein, Kate knew she had made the right choice. He had a list of items to work through, and she was pleased with his attention to detail.

'What is the height and weight of our principal actor, and what size clothing does he wear?' was his first question.

Although Kate had an excellent idea of Kelvin's bodily proportions, she didn't know them in detail, so she called and asked him. 'How tall are you, and what do you weigh?'

'Why, Kate?'

'Because we must make you a thobe.'

'Can't I buy one?'

'No. The stuntman will wear it as well.'

'I'm one metre ninety, and I weigh eighty-four kilograms.'

'Thanks, darling.'

She gave her height and weight to Tenis as well.

The next item was the deodorant bottle: Kate's script called for a 'phallic symbol or clothed male' bottle.

'We must decide on the deodorant bottle and how the actor will manipulate it,' Tenis said, placing a dildo on the table. It had testicles at the base. 'We can work from this. If made in glass, the testicles will only be a suggestion, but a tall narrow bottle needs wider support.'

'It's too straight. It needs a curve.'

'I agree. It's also too long. It needs to be no longer than necessary, say a palm width, plus a spray head with a cap. I suggest a spray with a side button that a thumb can press and the spray coming out the top. What about the cap?'

Kate replied, 'Make it look like a roll-on deodorant, one of the rounded top ones. Hinged or pull-off?'

He replied, 'Pull-off. It might be a bad idea, but what about a thick white string from the top of the cap? The actor can raise the deodorant to his mouth, grip the string between his teeth and pull the cap off that way.'

Kate thought about it. 'In production, we could drop the string or include it loose with a hole in the cap. The bottle could be on the shelf, with the string hanging invisible behind until the actor takes the bottle and sprays it under his arms. But how will you film that sequence without seeing the man's face?'

'We'll steam up the mirror before him, so his reflection is blurred, and shoot over his shoulder from behind.'

'That should work,' Kate said. 'Where will you source the perfume bottle?'

'We have a hundred glassblowers in Cairo. I'll have one here after lunch. A final question before lunch: I know your man has no beard. Can I ask make-up to add a small spade or pointed beard on his chin?'

'Why?'

'Two reasons. The first is that it's a facial feature that will tie the stuntman to your actor. Second, a pointed beard is common among thobe-wearing men. Like the agal, it makes for authenticity.'

Kate smiled at the thought of Kelvin with a goatee. 'Then I agree. What colour for the agal?'

Tenis answered, 'I told the wardrobe mistress I wanted to make the man look rich, so I think it should be black and gold. Then, on Tuesday and Wednesday, we have stuntmen coming and will do videos of the scene in the tent, no makeup or clothing, to choose the stuntman. On Thursday, we'll take you into the desert to choose a site and meet the horse.'

33

KELVIN WENT SHOPPING. The first item on his list was a satphone, which proved challenging to find. He tracked down two satellite companies. The agents were in tiny one-person offices and only met him after a phone call. They said he could sign a contract and buy airtime, but they didn't sell handsets. Both gave him the names and contact details of possible suppliers in Cairo.

The first three handset suppliers, also housed in tiny rooms, said they didn't stock satphones, but they could order one for Kelvin, delivered by air.

The fourth supplier was a hive of activity in the middle of a souq, selling new and used cellphone handsets, doing repairs at a table to one side of the alcove, and selling airtime for various mobile-phone networks.

A young woman with lively eyes introduced herself to him. 'I'm Bennu. I come from Abu Minqar, where they use satphones, and I know all about them. May I offer you a coffee while you tell me why you need a satphone?'

The coffee arrived quickly – a young boy had fetched it from a coffee shop in the souq – and Bennu pulled two stools from under a shelf. They sat before a cupboard in one corner with at least twenty phones.

'We don't sell new phones. These are second-hand,' Bennu said, indicating the cupboard's contents. 'The owners bring them to us when they don't need them or they break down. Now tell me, why do you need a phone?'

'I'm researching ancient Egyptian history. Many years ago,

there was a trading route from the Red Sea to Aswan. I want to travel the length of the route, looking for any signs or relics that show the route. I shall start from Aswan. I may be out in the desert for two or three weeks at a time, and although I'll have a colleague with me, I'll need the phone to call for help if something goes wrong.'

Bennu smiled at him. 'I hope the colleague is lovely.'

'What makes you think it is a woman?'

'The desert is a good place to go as a couple. It is alive and has moods. It can create an unbreakable relationship or break one forever. Sometimes it does both. Are you going in a vehicle, on a camel or on foot?'

'We shall drive and walk on excursions on either side of our track. Why do you ask?'

'Charging, battery life, and the weight to carry.'

Kelvin nodded. 'So, you have something in mind?'

'I do. I have two. One is only five months old and never used. The owner bought it for a cancelled trip. The other is two years old. Never repaired, but I'll change the battery if you take that one. Both are Iridium.'

She opened the cupboard and took a box from it. 'This is the unused one. You will also need a belt pouch and a dashboard holder. It is okay for SMS and speech. If you want to email, I can sell you a small satellite dish and a terminal to fit into the vehicle.'

'I don't need email. It's for an emergency only.'

'Well, you know where to buy the equipment if you change your mind. Will you take the unused one? You must sign a contract with the network agent.'

'Yes. How long does the battery last?'

'If you leave it off and switch it on only when you want to make a call, it will last a week or two. If you need to leave it on to receive a call, then about twelve hours is safe. A small solar panel charger will keep it alive for ages if you leave it plugged in during the day.'

'Then I'll take the phone, holder, belt pouch and solar panel.'

'Great, I'll show you how to use it. The battery should have enough power to make a satellite connection.'

By lunchtime, Kelvin was back at the hotel with instructions to try the phone the next day, when the network had activated his registration.

He called Ahmed.

'Hello, Kelvin. I'm glad you called. I was going to call you later.'

'What's up, Ahmed?'

'I wanted to tell you that I shall leave with Soraya on Wednesday for England. It's all arranged with Kate's parents. They'll give her a three-week trial to decide if she wants to stay and they want to keep her; then I must find a house.'

'That's wonderful! Have you fixed a wedding date?'

'Soraya has agreed to marry me at Kate's house if she decides to stay, and then we will return here once we have set up the house and have an Egyptian wedding.'

'That's fantastic, Ahmed. Well done.'

Then Ahmed asked, 'How's your goddess?'

'She's making a TV ad, then in two weeks, if I can organise it, we're taking a trip across the desert from Aswan to the Red Sea. I guess you'll see us in England in a month.'

'Then keep in touch, Kelvin. If you can make it, we'd love to have you at our wedding in England and again in Cairo. How about yours?'

'It's coming, Ahmed. No date fixed yet.'

'Don't give up, Kelvin. Thanks for calling.'

'Bye, Ahmed. Good luck.'

Kelvin could tell that Kate was happy when she returned to the hotel. She kissed him passionately.

He asked, 'My darling, something must have stirred you up. What was it?'

'I've fallen in love with you all over again.'

'You have? Why?'

'Well, the director said you had to have a goatee beard, and when I imagined you in a thobe and agal with a goatee beard, it gave me the hots.'

Kelvin asked, 'Does that mean you don't want to go to Crimson for a romantic dinner?'

'Did you book?'

'Yes, for eight thirty.'

Kate knew what she wanted. 'Then we have enough time for some practice first. Come.'

Nearly an hour later, Kate felt she was flying again to the grass beside the pool and waterfall, and minutes later, her back arched in ecstasy.

When the hotel room swam back into focus, Kate asked, 'Darling, have you ever seen a place with a milky-blue pool, a waterfall and emerald-green grass?'

'Not before the first time we went there together, dearest.'

Puzzled, she asked, 'But how can we see the same place?'

Kelvin didn't know; he could only guess. 'Perhaps it's a genetic memory. Have you never felt you had seen a place years ago yet were sure you had never been there?'

'Yes, two or three times.'

'I can only make a wild guess, but maybe feeling like that gave rise to the belief in reincarnation. Scientifically, an old memory that deteriorates with time can have sufficient matching points to what you see to give that feeling. But perhaps our genetic ancestors saw that pool, and when we lose ourselves in love, it rises from the past. During the fifteen thousand generations that have come and gone since the first *Homo sapiens*, if reincarnation does happen, we might have reincarnated many times!'

On Monday, after a morning's shopping, Kelvin called the Unimog agency at three pm as arranged and asked for Aten.

'Hello, Doctor Shareef. I called El Salloum, and you're in luck. The garage says the vehicle is still there. Can I give you their number?'

'Please. And how much, approximately, will you quote to fix it?'

'I can't give you a firm quote until we've done a full inspection. I can give you an updated price for what we quoted, add a full service, new tyres and rubber belts, and suggest new wheel bearings and universal joints. The vehicle is now two years old but has been standing for a year.'

'That would be excellent. All I need now is a basis for negotiation for the purchase price: the cost of a two-year-old Unimog in good condition, the estimate to fix it, and the cost to truck it to Cairo.'

'I can do that for you, Doctor. I'll ask sales for a price, and we have a breakdown-trucking company; I'll ask them for an estimate.'

Kelvin rang off, then called the number Aten had given him. 'Good afternoon, I'm Dr Shareef, and I'm calling about the Unimog at your premises.'

'Yes, Doctor Shareef. Aten told me you would call. Have you an email so I can send you photos?'

'Yes,' Kelvin said and spelt it out. Then he asked, 'Who is the owner of the vehicle?'

'It's a bank in Alexandria. They seized it when the company failed to pay back a loan. I'll include the bank details and the contact person in the email.'

'Thank you very much. Is there anything you know about the vehicle that I should know?'

'I don't know much about it except that the tyres and the two spare wheels are flat. Oh, and I'm afraid you can't take it away until I receive payment for storage.'

'Naturally. Please include the amount in the email.'

'With pleasure.'

'When can I come to inspect the vehicle?'

'On Saturday. Call me, and I'll come and open for you.'

'Thank you. Saturday will be perfect. I'll confirm.'

Kate returned to the hotel, where Kelvin was at his desk. He stood up as she arrived and dropped her bag on a chair.

'Hi, Kate. How did your day go?'

She stepped up to him, and he put his arms around her and kissed her.

Kate kissed him back, then said, 'Fantastic, Kelvin. We chose the right director. Guess what I did today.'

'You said you were meeting the wardrobe mistress.'

'I did, and she's great. We spent some time choosing the underwear to throw from the tent and how it should look lying on the ground. The horse will stand outside the tent and toss its head as each piece of clothing flies out, then there'll be a pause, then a dove will take off from above the tent, a falcon will dive on it and screech, and the horse will rear and scream.'

'Kate, that sounds great!'

'And we've got the perfume bottle. A glassblower made it especially.'

'That's unexpected. I thought you would use an existing one.'

'So did I, but the director wanted a unique bottle, and there are so many glassblowers that getting one cost little. Here, I have a picture.' Kate removed her phone from her bag, found the photo and said, 'Look.'

'My God, Kate. Will TV broadcasters allow that?'

'I don't know, but I'm making this video as an ad to prove a point in a demo, not to broadcast it – although, with a few minor mods, it could be broadcast.'

'When are we supposed to do our scene?'

'Tuesday, and you will look dashing. I agreed to you having the goatee beard.'

'What the devil for?'

'If imagining you with a goatee gives me the hots, think what it will do for the viewers!'

'Okay, Kate. Can I wear it back to the hotel?'

'That might be fun. The hotel staff will believe I'm taking a sheikh to our room.'

'Then I'm not going to.'

'Spoilsport.' Kate laughed. 'What have you done today?'

'I found a Unimog. Tomorrow I'll negotiate with the bank that owns it, and if all goes well, by Friday, we'll go to Marsa Matruh for the night, go and see the Unimog on Saturday, and return on Sunday.'

'I'm filming on Sunday, Kelvin. Can we return on Saturday?'

'For you, my darling, anything is possible. I'll work out the alternatives. Would you like to see the photos? It has a closed truck bed with windows.'

Kate flicked through the pictures. 'Those bench seats in the back look worn out,' she observed.

'We'll throw them away. But look at the back seat – it's on a water tank, so we don't need to get one fitted.'

'I don't like the colour.'

Kelvin grinned. 'Typical female,' he said, rolling his eyes. 'It's a truck, not a house.'

'My concern is that blue is visible in aerial photographs. If a satellite or aircraft sees it, we might have the Egyptian army arrive to find out if we are terrorists. Can you have it painted a desert yellow?'

'I'm sure I can, darling. Do you want the interior padded in pink?'

'If you weren't so big, I'd slap you,' Kate said, giving Kelvin a mock cross lock. 'You've just earned two nights without cuddling. And you're stepping on dangerous ground with your "darlings".'

Kelvin grinned. 'I can't help it, my sweet. So, what are you filming on Sunday?'

'The scene where the stuntman sprays on the deodorant.'

'Alexandria Commercial Bank. Good morning.'

'Good morning, I'm Dr Shareef. Can I speak to Mr Abbas, please?'

'Certainly, sir. I'll transfer your call.'

'Abbas. Good morning.'

'Good morning, sir. I'm Dr Shareef, Egyptology research. A garage in El Salloum has told me that your bank owns a Unimog they have in their yard. I wish to purchase it.'

'Are you prepared to make a written offer?'

'I am, sir, conditional on a visit I will make on Saturday to inspect the vehicle.'

'Then please do so. I shall fetch the file and await your offer. Do you have my email address?'

'Yes, sir, the garage gave it to me. How long before I know if my offer is acceptable?'

'If I approve it, I'll email you confirmation today and tell the garage you will visit the vehicle. Final approval will take another day.'

Before the bank closed, Kelvin received the confirmation.

34

EXCITED BY HIS SUCCESS, Kelvin was boisterous when Kate returned from the film studio office to the hotel. 'Darling, we have the Unimog, subject to our visit and final approval.'

'That's marvellous, my darling! So we're going on Friday?'

'Yes. It's two hours to El Alamein, where we'll stop for lunch, then two hours to Marsa Matruh, where we'll be for the night. We'll leave early the next morning for the two-hour drive to El Salloum, inspect the Unimog, then drive back.'

'That will be great – I've never been to that coastline. But have you asked yourself if we need to go?'

'What do you mean?'

'Ask the garage to start the engine, and if it runs, isn't that about all you don't know? We won't see more than the pictures show.'

'I've never bought a car without seeing it first.'

Kate grinned. 'Typical male: more excited by a bit of machinery than a sexy body.' Then, becoming serious, she said, 'It's our only option; there isn't another. Buy it.'

'Kate, you've just earned yourself two nights without cuddles.'

'We can still visit El Alamein on Friday and return on Saturday morning. Isn't that worth a cuddle?'

'I must think about that. What did you do today?'

'Interviewed two actors and filmed them spraying themselves with perfume. We repeated the video twice for each.'

'And?'

'The second one was rather good, but we have two more tomorrow. I'm hungry. Where are we having dinner?'

'Right here in the hotel, Kate.'

'Then it's bath time – double bath time.'

Kelvin called the garage at nine, and the manager called back an hour later. 'The engine runs, Doctor Shareef. We've also pumped the tyres. The transmission is faulty. It won't drive, but the steering pump is okay. It's towable with a driver in it.'

'Thank you. I'll call the bank. I don't need the seats in the back. If there's someone who wants them, you can remove them.'

Kelvin called the bank. 'Mr Abbas, Doctor Shareef here. Do you have approval for the Unimog sale?'

'I do, Doctor. When you transfer the quoted amount, I'll send you the papers by courier.'

By five o'clock, Kelvin had arranged the transport, paid the bank and the garage for storage, and asked Aten at the Unimog agents to arrange a quick repaint to a desert yellow. Aten also agreed to store any equipment Kelvin sent them until he collected the vehicle.

'Have you selected an actor, Kate?'

'Yes, the first one today. He matches you perfectly.'

She's going to tease me, I can tell.

'He's so like you; I must be careful not to think he's you. I might kiss him by mistake.' Kate gave Kelvin a coy look, and they both laughed. 'He's coming on Sunday for the dress rehearsal of the tent scene, and if that goes well, then the filming. Monday is riding on the dune. Then, on Tuesday, it's your turn.'

'Is that the end of it?'

'No, Kelvin. They have the final scene with the clothing thrown from the tent, the dove, the falcon and the neighing horse. I must approve the bottle and the label; then they'll photograph that and overlay the text "Undress Me: the perfume that works".'

'I hope the falcon doesn't kill the dove.'

'Tenis films separate steps: the falcon will dive for a dead chicken on the tent, and the dove will escape,' Kate reassured him. 'Then they'll send me the complete video for approval before editing, and they must fit a soundtrack. I've so much confidence in Tenis that I'll let him choose, although I'll have the final say. Then we can disappear into the desert on Thursday.'

'It'll be more like Saturday, Kate. I must test-drive the Unimog; then we must buy food; I want dehydrated packets we can carry if we walk. The rest we can buy on the way to Aswan.'

Kate said, 'Okay, and I must buy desert boots.'

'Darling, shall I book a hotel at El Alamein?'

'Yes, please. What's it like there?'

'It's an odd mixture. The tourist cities like Hurghada and Charm El Cheikh went from desert villages to tourist resorts in one step. El Alamein developed slowly, so a new part exists: a luxury tourist resort, and then there are other, progressively older, areas.'

'Can you book somewhere we won't feel swamped by tourists?'

'I can try the hotel I stayed at last time, the Hotelux la Playa. Shall we go early?'

'That would give us a full day on the beach to unwind, Kelvin. Yes, let's do that.'

'This beach is lovely, and the sea is warm. We can spend all day here.'

'If we do, we'll end up having skin grafts!' Kelvin said. 'We'll go for lunch at twelve-thirty and make it last three hours before returning to the beach.'

'How will we do that?' Then Kate saw the lascivious grin on Kelvin's face. 'Ah, I see. Yes, siesta is a great idea.'

When the sun became too hot on the beach, they returned to their room and changed from swimwear to clothing acceptable in the restaurant, then, after a light lunch of salads with an ice cream desert, Kelvin announced. 'Siesta time!'

Lying naked on the hotel bed in Kelvin's arms, Kate asked, 'Darling, do you believe we'll find the wadi in the desert?'

'I do, dearest. I've no doubt we will.'

'How can you be so certain?'

'Come here, and I'll show you.'

It took an hour of slow, languorous kisses and caresses before the sound of wings that Kate now welcomed accompanied her final moments of ecstasy.

When Kate descended from the ecstatic flight back to the hotel bed, still wrapped in Kelvin's arms, she said, 'I believe it too. We have only to trust in Isis and Hathor.'

Then they slept.

After a five-kilometre run along the golden beach that afternoon, and another swim in the warm Mediterranean, they drank a cocktail under the palm trees beside the pool while the light faded. Then the lights switched on, and they seemed to be in a fairyland.

Dinner by the pool was delicious, and when the orchestra began to play Western ballroom music, Kate said, 'Darling, this has been my favourite music since I gave up techno. Dance with me.'

She drifted around the dance floor in Kelvin's arms and felt they were in heaven. 'Pharaoh, I love you. Take me to bed.'

Another hour of kissing and caressing seemed to bring them both to even greater heights of pleasure, but there was a difference. After Kate finally got her breath back, she said, 'Darling, that bump has grown some more.'

Kelvin lifted the sheet and looked down. 'Are you sure?'

'Yes, the end is not touching your tummy.'

'Then, Kate, we're getting there.'

When they reached Cairo on Saturday morning, they visited the garage to see the Unimog. It was on jacks, without wheels or transmission, but Kelvin could check what extra equipment came with it.

On their return to the Hilton, he began a search for companies that took tourists into the desert for a night or two, and soon found one that would help him buy the needed equipment. Meanwhile, Kate checked on her filming programme for the next two days.

By Monday night, they had both progressed, and Kate said, 'Kelvin, tomorrow morning, at six, the film guys will collect us from the hotel and take us into the desert for you to do your scene. You'll meet your horse, we'll do a practice run, then makeup and wardrobe will step in, and we'll film it.'

'I've never done this before. Are you prepared for a catastrophe?'

'Darling, just be yourself. You'll be fine. It's not a blockbuster movie; it's just an ad.'

'Can I lift you onto the horse?'

'You can try,' Kate said. 'How would you do it?'

'Just reach your right arm up to me, and I'll grasp it as far up from your wrist as possible. Then you hold my arm, and I'll lift you.'

The car stopped, and they walked over a low sandy ridge into a small valley. A tribe of goats grazed at the bottom.

A man was pushing small pegs into the sand, tracing a path down the opposite slope that turned at the bottom to continue to a desert-coloured rock on a slight rise. Kelvin wondered if the boulder was natural. Several people were setting up tripods and cameras.

When a man giving orders saw them, he came over, and Kate introduced Kelvin. 'Tenis, this is my star actor, Kelvin Shareef.'

Kelvin shook hands, thinking. *Tenis doesn't look gay.* Then he said, 'Tenis is an unusual name. I've never heard it before.'

'It's a nickname. When I was a toddler, my dad told my mother that I was like a tennis ball, bouncing around the room, and he called me Tennis. I used it with a single en when I went to art school. Most of my friends think it suits me.'

Kelvin laughed. 'From what Kate has told me, it does.'

Tenis said, 'We mustn't waste time; the sun will be too high by eleven. Kelvin, there is your horse.' He pointed to a spectacular white stallion being led towards them by a man. 'Please mount it and ride it in a circle. Its handler, Ahmed, will help you.'

Kate and Tenis watched Kelvin join the handler, then smoothly mount the horse and, holding the reins in his left hand, walk it around in a circle before increasing his speed to a slow triple.

Kate thought, *He's terrific and looks like he was born on a horse.*

Kelvin rode over and asked, 'Now, what do I do next?'

Tenis replied, 'Ride around us, then to the pole up the slope. Avoid riding across the film set. Then follow the pegs with the white tops and stop next to the rock where Kate will be sitting. You say, "Woman, where is your father? He has stolen my goats." She'll not answer or look up. You then dismount, step up to her, and, with one hand, push up her chin so you look into each other's eyes. She'll say, "He has gone to market to sell your goats." Then she'll look down, and you say, "Then I'll take your goats." She'll then look at your face and say, "Take me instead." You look at her for five seconds, turn, mount your horse, and ride away up the slope. In the finished film, we'll cut to the scene where you reach down your right hand and say, "Come," then lift her onto the horse before riding off. We'll film the stuntman doing that.'

Everyone took their places. Kelvin saw the signals from three cameras, and then Tenis said, 'Okay, go.'

With a lean forward and a hiss, Kelvin urged the stallion up the slope and around to the pole, then followed the pegs at a triple to the rock. The scene played out as Tenis had directed, without a hitch, and then, when Kelvin remounted, he leaned down, stretched out his hand and said, 'Come.' Just as they'd discussed, Kelvin gripped Kate's arm, and she grabbed his, and he lifted her effortlessly onto the horse. She wrapped her arms around him and looked up at his face. He smiled down at her, then the horse reared and began to run.

'Darling, you can turn back now.'

'I won't. I'm going to gallop to our bedroom.'

Kate laughed. 'What about the film crew?'

'If you insist, Kate, I'll go back. I can take you to our bedroom after the costumed take.'

Tenis was in raptures. 'You were both fantastic! Now do that again, in costume this time. That bit at the end, when Kate was on the horse and looked up at you, is superb, and the horse rearing as it takes off was great.'

Forty minutes later, while filming the scene in costume, when

271

Kate looked up to say, 'Take me instead,' she didn't need to remember to take a deep breath and push her breasts forward; it happened without thought, for she thought, *Please!*

As the crew was packing everything back into the van, Tenis said, 'It has been a privilege to film with you both. If I had to film *Anthony and Cleopatra*, I would do so only if you accepted the roles. In ten days, you can come to see the finished advert.'

'We're going into the desert south of Aswan this weekend,' Kate said, 'and I don't know if we will be back in two weeks, but I'll email you the address to send your bill, and I'll pay it before we leave.'

The loaded Unimog ran smoothly at ninety kph. Kelvin didn't try to go faster. With stops for meals and a night at Asyut in the Nile Goddess Hotel, it took two days.

The welcome at the Cataract Hotel was overwhelming: Three baggage handlers came to the Unimog, and a car valet took it away for cleaning. The hotel manager showed them to the Presidential suite, with a murmured instruction to hand their clothes for washing to the room attendants. Champagne in an enormous bucket of ice stood on the lounge table, along with a selection of eastern delights to nibble.

They bathed in a huge bath big enough for three or four, splashing each other and laughing, but finally managed to don bathrobes and sit on the terrace to sip the champagne.

'Darling,' Kate said with a sigh, 'there's something to be said about the life of a celebrity.'

'This is the best bit, my darling. The worst bit would be a horde of reporters pestering us. Fortunately, the hotel won't allow that.'

When they went for dinner that night, they dressed as they had the previous time, to the great delight of the staff and the other diners. The maitre d' had made every effort to impress; he had a complete Takht music ensemble to accompany the diners.

For them both, it was an evening they would never forget – and, as they made their way back to their room, Kelvin snuggled Kate's neck and whispered, 'There's more to come, dearest.'

'I know. I can't wait.'

Kate felt the wings come much sooner and stay longer – and there was another difference. 'Kelvin, the bump is bigger.'

'I think so too, Kate. I'm getting there.'

'Oh, Hathor... I am too!'

35

THEY HAD TWO DAYS DRIVING at twenty-five kph and two nights in the desert, following a route plotted on the GPS.

On the second night, as they set up their camp, Kelvin said, 'The first possible wadi has an entrance about five kilometres ahead. Tomorrow we may have to walk.'

The following morning, they left early, anticipating success. Kelvin turned into a wide sand-filled valley. 'It should become narrower as we go down the valley. The wadi shown on the map is at the end.'

He engaged the low range, and the Unimog crept across the sand on its balloon tyres. The valley narrowed and became shallower. 'It seems this narrow end has filled with sand,' Kelvin observed. 'If the wadi was here, the sand has buried it.'

Four kilometres on, the valley walls had disappeared, and they found themselves in flat desert. 'That's it, Kate. It's not here. We must turn back.'

'There are two more, Kelvin. Don't lose heart.'

That evening, they discussed where the next wadi might be located. 'It's about another five kilometres on; it's the same formation but a different valley,' Kelvin explained. 'About halfway along, there's a side entrance to another valley. We'll try the main one first.'

The second day's searching was only slightly different; at the end of the valley, the sand rose sharply, and the Unimog couldn't climb it. They had to walk.

After eating lunch, they climbed the dune to find the same

endless expanse of sand as the first time. They walked back down the dune, and Kelvin said, 'Let's camp here, Kate.'

'Kelvin, are you giving up?'

'No, Kate, but maybe I got something wrong, and I must return to my maps.'

'Well, we have one more to search for. Drive back to the entrance to the third; we can camp there.'

After ninety minutes of driving, Kelvin said, 'This is it, Kate, according to the GPS, but I see no entrance.'

'It's too dark, Kelvin. We're in the shadow of the walls. Tomorrow, the sun will be on the other side at dawn, and then we will see it.'

That evening, lying on their camping mattress, Kate understood Kelvin's disappointment and decided he needed comfort. 'Darling, please cuddle me,' she said.

The wings came, and Kate felt them carry her and Kelvin again to the valley, and when the final explosion came, she felt different. She wanted to stay.

In the morning, Kate woke before dawn. She was sure they would find the wadi that day.

They sat waiting for the sun's rays to shine on the valley wall two hundred metres away. As the rays touched the top of the wall, they scanned along them.

'There, Kate. Could that be the entrance?'

'I'm not sure. Let's wait until the sunshine reaches the bottom; it may be a shallow break in the top.'

They watched as the sun rose enough to see the top half of the wall, and in a voice of desperation, Kelvin said, 'It's not the entrance, Kate. It doesn't go all the way down.'

'That's okay. I think it's just behind us. There's a dark shadow as if the entrance hides behind the rock on one side. Wait.'

When the sunshine lit the wall from the foot, the shadow was still there, but fifteen minutes later, as the sun rose further, the shadow narrowed, and then the wall seemed one continuous rock.

'Darling, that may not be a hidden wadi, but it's a hidden entrance. You can only see it for a few minutes at dawn.'

'Okay, let's drive to it. I don't know if we can drive into it; it may be too narrow.' He started the engine and turned the Unimog.

At the front of the entrance, Kelvin observed, 'It's wide enough, but it turns after about fifty metres. Let's walk in and see what's around that corner.'

The narrow passage between the rock walls turned and then spread apart into a wider path with a sand cover. 'Kate, let's go back. I'll drive the Unimog. You walk in front to signal if I'm getting too close to a wall.'

Once through, Kate said, 'Darling, let's have breakfast – a good one. We can't go exploring on empty stomachs.'

An hour later, fortified, they began the drive along the passage, which widened further into a narrow valley. The sand was soft, and the Unimog struggled to do more than two kph.

Five kilometres on, they reached the end of the valley. A massive dune blocked it.

'Well, that seems like the end, Kate.'

'Let's climb that dune and see what's on the other side of it.'

'Okay, but I'm thirsty. Let's have some tea first.'

While Kelvin lit the kerosene stove and put water on to boil, Kate decided to walk along the dune's edge, where it rose steeply. The silence was total: there was no wind, and nothing stirred, so it was easy for her to call from seventy metres away. 'Kellllviiin!'

He looked up. Kate was waving at him. He switched off the stove and made his way to her. 'What's up, Kate?'

'What's a smooth round rock doing here, on top of all this sand?'

'Maybe it's a walking rock.'

'Is this another story?'

'No, Kate, moving rocks exist. Let me turn this one over and see if it's smooth on the other side.' He dug the sand away from one side, then pulled it up and over.

Kate exclaimed, 'It's a bowl!'

'It's man-made,' Kelvin confirmed. 'It's an ancient grinding stone for grain. People once passed here and left this behind. It's heavy, and that may be why they left it.'

'What kind of grain?'

'Probably sorghum. The plant spread from this area some six thousand years ago.'

'Now we have no choice,' Kate said. 'We absolutely must climb this dune and see what's on the other side.'

Returning to the Unimog, they had their tea, and then Kelvin filled a backpack with what they might need for a trip on foot that might take a few hours, including bottles of water, toilet paper and the satphone. 'Wear a hat and sunglasses,' he reminded Kate.

They set off, trudging through the soft sand as the sun rose into the sky above them.

About halfway up the giant dune, Kate said, 'Kelvin, I must rest. I'm exhausted. For every three steps up, I slide back two.'

'I should have thought of this and brought desert slippers.'

'What are they?'

'Slippers made from sheep or goatskin, with the wool underneath to insulate the foot from the hot desert sand, and inside a thick hide plate that spreads your weight. Desert dwellers in the Sahara wear them. Let's rest, and then we'll begin climbing again; it'll be easier if I climb about two metres, then anchor myself in the sand while I help you up and past me, and then you do the same for me.'

Employing this tactic, they reached the top.

'Kate, I think we've found it!' Kelvin gasped as he looked down over the edge of the cliff ahead.

The wadi stretched before them like a hole in the earth with vertical side walls. From the near-vertical clifftop on which they stood, it was like looking down a canyon that stretched ahead and disappeared into gathering gloom as the sun descended to the horizon.

'It's beautiful, Kelvin. But how do we get down into it?'

'I don't know, but that grinding stone tells us that people must have come this way, so there must be a way down. You go to the right; I'll go to the left and look. Careful of the edge; the sand is loose, and you could slide over. The dune is like a barchan, sloping on one side and near-vertical on the other, except this vertical is rock all the way down.'

Making his way carefully a metre or so from the edge, Kelvin stopped every thirty steps and looked back at Kate, plodding away in the other direction. As he approached the valley side wall, he turned around to look again and saw Kate gesticulating. At first, he didn't understand, then thought, *She wants me to walk further.*

He walked ten metres on, looked back, and saw Kate repeat the gesture, so he walked another ten and then another. Then he saw her raise her arm straight up. Kelvin lay down, anchored his toes in the sand, and eased forward. Looking carefully over the edge, he saw a narrow shelf that rose and met the clifftop a metre to his left.

Kate joined him ten minutes later. On his knees, Kelvin was scraping sand from the cliff top and making a shallow channel to the edge.

'It's a trail down, Kate, and at the top here, under the sand, it's worn into a shallow U-shaped channel. People and animals must have walked here for thousands of years. How did you see it?'

'Like this morning, the setting sun briefly showed a squiggly black shadow line on the cliff. I could see it from where I was, but you couldn't.'

'Okay, Kate. The sun is setting; we don't have the time to descend into the wadi. Let's sit on our bums and surf down to our truck.'

The two thrilled explorers reached the Unimog in a tenth of the time it had taken them to climb the dune.

'Darling, I'm starving! Dinner.'

An hour later, lying on their backs, staring at the stars, Kate asked, 'Sweetheart, do you feel a kind of pervading peace?'

'Yes,' Kelvin said, reaching out and taking her hand. 'The stars are beautiful, and the only sound is your breathing and perhaps your heart beating. With you beside me, I could stay here forever.'

'That's it exactly,' Kate said, with a satisfied sigh. Then she added, 'But how can we descend into the wadi?'

'Once we go down that path, we must stay for at least two days. We can take food and water for five.'

'But how do we haul it up to the top? I couldn't climb it with a rucksack.'

'I've been thinking about that. I've five long ropes, and two or three tied together will reach the top. If I take the camp tabletop and connect it to a rope, we could tie everything onto it and then haul it up once we are on top. It'll be about a hundred kilos, all told.'

'Can you pull up that much?'

'It depends on how easily it slides. If necessary, we can do two hauls.'

Kate nodded her understanding. 'And then how do we take it down on the other side?'

'Like a stretcher on a mountain. It'll slide down the cliff-face trail you found. I'll walk behind, letting it slide a step at a time. You can walk ahead and guide it if it wants to go over the edge. It'll take us all tomorrow to go up and down. We'll camp there, then take a rucksack in the morning and explore. We can take just two days of water each and return to the camp to fetch more if necessary.'

'We won't need to. There's a waterfall there. Let's pray to Isis and Hathor, then you will know.'

'The pool with the waterfall?'

'Yes.'

'You do have some great ideas, my love. Let's pray. Come.'

Kate, naked, came from her camp bed to his, into his arms. Relaxed but thrilled by their success in finding the wadi, it seemed the heights they reached while caressing each other were even more incredible.

'Now, do you believe, darling?'

'Yes, Kate. Let's sleep.'

'Is that everything, Kate?'

'All I can think of. I've included the packet of Anit.'

'Why did you do that?'

'If we find any plants, we can compare the leaves.'

'I didn't think of that,' Kelvin said, 'but I've included water test strips to check the water drinkability if the waterfall is there. We must move the Unimog tight against the cliff to keep it out of satellite view.

Kate had an idea. 'If you plug the solar panel into the fridge box, do you think it will stay cool?'

'I don't know. I'll place the solar panel facing the opposite wall's top. It might give enough power,' was Kelvin's reply.

'Kate, I'll go up with the rope. I'll attach a tail rope to the tabletop. I'll pull it up ten metres, then rest while you climb up using the tail rope. Then you can stop while I pull the table top up further.'

Three hours later, they were at the top. 'Kelvin, finish your water bottle and refill it. I'll do the same, and we'll rest an hour before going down.'

It took two hours of careful manoeuvring, but they made it, working with the ropes as they had discussed. They stood at the bottom of the rock trail, looking towards the far end of the wadi.

Kelvin kissed her. 'Welcome to Isis's wadi, Kate.'

She kissed him back. 'Kelvin, I feel welcome here. But once the sun has gone, we have no light, so fetch one of the dehydrated packets and add water, and I'll make some tea.'

As they lay on their mattress roll, Kate said, 'Kelvin, we're both exhausted. Let's sleep.'

Kate dreamed.

36

IN THE MORNING, once they'd had tea and eaten some food, Kelvin asked, 'Which way shall we go?'

'Along the cliff on the other side.'

'Why there?'

'Isis told me in my dream. And that's the sunny side.'

They packed two backpacks and set off.

Walking on the soft red sand near the base of the cliff, Kelvin said, 'Thousands of years of spalling has made this sand.'

'What's spalling?'

'The sun heats the cliff, and the nights cool it, and eventually, small grains that expand and contract come loose and fall. With no wind to disturb them, they have built up into this soft sand.'

It was slow going, and checking every metre of the cliff for a fissure or a cave made it slower, but after four hours, Kelvin stopped. 'Kate, this is different.'

'Why?'

'Feel the sand.' Kelvin stamped a foot. 'It's harder, and a low rivulet of sand is coming from the cliff. Water used to flow here.'

They walked to the cliff, and Kate said, her voice tight, 'Look, Kelvin, there's a crack in the cliff. I think we can squeeze through.'

The crack turned right, and left, then widened but became darker, although there was light ahead. A few more metres and they came out into a small amphitheatre; it was at the bottom of a fifteen-metre-diameter chimney open to the sky above the desert surrounding the wadi. 'Kelvin, there's no grass, only sand, but it's our pool! And look, there's still a small trickle of water from the rock above.'

Kelvin, looking around in awe, said, 'The wings of Isis must have shown us this place aeons ago, when grass covered the sand. Let's take a break.'

They leant on their backpacks against the wall for about an hour, resting their weary feet.

Then Kate pointed out, 'Kelvin, we won't find a better place to spend the night. Try the water; let's see if we can make tea.'

Using his strips to assess the water, Kelvin told her, 'The pool water has a high pH that resembles the water in stalactite caves. I'll check the waterfall.' And a few moments later, he called out, 'This is okay to drink, Kate. Bring the pot.'

'Why's the pool different?'

'I don't know. It must have accumulated over centuries. Perhaps the waterfall water doesn't mix and flows out from the top. Fresh water floats on heavier, salt-laden water.'

While Kelvin unrolled the bedroll, Kate made tea, and as the light faded, they undressed, lay down naked, side by side, and slept. Kate didn't dream; she felt enveloped in warmth.

They woke as the first rays of sunlight hit the top edge of the chimney above them. 'I haven't slept like that since I was a baby,' Kate said, indulging in a luxurious stretch.

'The same for me, Kate. It must be this place.' Kelvin stood, put on his pants and socks, and picked up his boots. He was putting on the first one when he exclaimed, '*Shit!*' and pulled it back off.

Kate saw something small and black fall from the boot, then scuttle across the sand and bury itself by the wall. 'Did it get you?'

'I think so.' Kelvin pulled off his sock, and Kate had a look.

'Yes, there's a red mark on the big toe. It didn't look like a scorpion.'

'No,' Kelvin agreed. 'Whatever it was, I hope its bite or sting isn't venomous.'

After giving them a good shake, Kelvin put on his boots, and Kate did the same.

They hadn't gone far when Kelvin said, 'Kate, my foot is swelling. The boot is getting tight. We'll have to go back.'

Before they reached the pool, Kelvin was leaning on Kate and limping.

She was worried. She helped Kelvin sit on the unrolled bedroll, then removed his boots. She saw his swollen foot and a thin red line running up his leg.

Within a few minutes, he was sweating and beginning to thrash, so she removed his shirt, fetched a cloth, wet it in the waterfall, and sponged him down. She searched his backpack for medicines, finding nothing except paracetamol. Then she remembered the Anit. In her head, she heard, 'A quarter of a leaf for good health, a half to cure, a whole leaf to bring back life, three for eternity.'

The small coffee pot, with water from the fall, was soon boiling, and she carefully broke half a leaf and crumpled it into the water. She watched as the water turned a dark brown, and then she set it to cool at the side of the pool.

Twenty minutes later, she murmured a prayer: 'Isis, goddess of healing, this man has dedicated his life to healing; he's yours. Please save him from the evil that has wounded him. I promise to help with whatever tasks you have for us.' She then lifted Kelvin's head and fed the Anit tea to him, a sip at a time, until it was gone.

Half an hour later, he seemed calmer, and after another half hour, he slept.

Kate undressed and lay beside him, holding him in her arms,

and slept too. She didn't notice the shadow at the entrance to the pool.

Much later, the shadow moved, and in the starlight, a small man with a shiny bald head ghosted towards them. He had no facial hair at all. He stood for a moment, looking down at them. Then he turned, lifted the coffee pot and raised it to his nose. He looked again at Kate and Kelvin, entwined around each other, smiled happily, and disappeared soundlessly, leaving no tracks.

Kate woke when the sun lit up the western edge of the amphitheatre. She first looked at Kelvin's foot: the swelling was down, and the red line had gone.

He was still sleeping soundly, so she wrapped her arms around him and slept again.

Two shadows appeared in the narrow entrance. In the morning light, the bald man was wearing a desert-coloured gallabiyah, and his desert slippers made no sound on his feet. Behind him was a young boy carrying a tray with an oval pottery bowl, two round ones, and two fired pottery cups. The boy's gallabiyah, an identical colour, had a hood that hid his face.

The man took the bowls from the tray and placed them carefully on the sand at the feet of the sleeping couple. The boy vanished. The man bowed reverently, backed away, turned, and seemed to disappear too, as he went back through the entrance.

A few minutes later, Kate woke. She had an odd feeling that she and Kelvin weren't alone, so she raised herself on her elbows and saw the bowls on the sand at their feet, then looked around and saw no one. 'Kelvin, wake up,' she whispered.

Kelvin mumbled, 'What is it, my darling?'

'We are not alone.'

Kelvin came awake rapidly and sat up. 'Where are they?'

'They've gone, but they left us something to eat.'

'Where?'

'In those bowls.'

Kelvin, who had eaten nothing since breakfast the day before, simply said, 'Then let's eat it.' He reached down, took a bowl, and looked in it. 'It's porridge, Kate. Fetch the spoons.'

They ate ravenously.

'This porridge tastes good, darling. What is it?' Kate asked, spooning the mixture into her mouth with evident delight.

'It's sorghum, probably the ancient variety, dating back four thousand years,' Kelvin said as he pulled the oval bowl between them. 'Look, this is different. I think it may be dried goat's meat and some vegetables I don't recognise.'

They ate the whole bowl between them, then Kate reached for a cup, tasted it, and said, 'This is herb tea. It has a perfume that reminds me of something. Look – the bowls and cups have decorations. Do you recognise the designs?'

Kelvin lifted a bowl and turned it around to look. 'Without access to historical records, I can't say, but four thousand years ago, the people in this area developed a culture we named the Butana Group. It originated in the Neolithic, but they made pottery and decorated it. If I remember correctly, the decorations were like this – just lines and the whorls resemble fingerprints. Whoever brought this food may not speak Arabic.'

'How's your foot?'

Gingerly, Kelvin got to his feet and put weight on the injured one. 'It's tender, my sweet, and I don't think I can walk far, but it's getting better. Last night you gave me something for it. What was it?'

'Half a leaf of Anit.'

'Why?'

'I found nothing else that would have helped except para-cetamol, and I thought Anit could not do any harm.'

'Why half a leaf?'

'Isis told me. It had to be her; I heard a voice in my head say, "A quarter of a leaf for good health, a half to cure, and a whole leaf to bring back life." Before I gave it to you, I told her you were a doctor and begged her to save you.'

Kelvin, overwhelmed with emotion, could only say, 'Kiss me, Kate.'

She did and said, 'We're staying here today. We can cuddle.'

They moved the bedding into the shade close to one wall when the sun and the temperature rose. Kate made tea; they ate another biscuit.

'That sorghum must be a whole food, like wholewheat bread. I don't feel hungry.'

The heat made them sleepy, and they dozed.

Later, when the light began to fade, Kate woke and saw the morning's bowls had gone, and another set had replaced them. 'Kelvin, more food has come.' She looked around. 'Darling, it's magic. There are no footprints, and I heard no one.'

'Not footprints, Kate, but the sand has a brushed look,' Kelvin said, pointing. 'Whoever brought the food must have worn desert slippers. Perhaps they will show themselves tomorrow.' Tasting the food in the bowl, Kelvin said, 'It's sorghum again, but it tastes different.'

'The tea too.'

In between bites and sips, Kelvin asked, 'What do you suggest we do tomorrow?'

'Darling, I don't know. Doesn't it depend on whether the people here come to us or we go to find them?'

'I suppose so, Kate. I want to know more about the sorghum; maybe they can give me some seeds.'

'And I would like to know what herbs they use in the food; they are delicious. Some seeds of those herbs would be worth having.'

'Darling, now that we have food and water, I've stopped thinking about when we must return.'

'Me too, but we can't stay too long, otherwise, people will start looking for us.'

'Yes, that's a problem. Anyway, we can think about it tomorrow or the next day. I'm feeling sleepy now; maybe the tea is soporific. I'm going to strip.'

'There are people who come and see us, Kelvin.'

'They've seen everything already, Kate. It's warm, and I like sleeping naked with you.'

Kate stripped too. 'I'll take the wall side, Kelvin.'

'Okay.'

Kate opened her eyes when the almost full moon was high enough to shine into the chimney above the pool. The light had woken her.

Kate was facing the wall, lying on her side, with Kelvin behind her. In front of her, the wall was ablaze with a pale blue light. For a moment, she wondered where the light came from, and then she noticed the shadow of an obelisk on the wall. *Where did an obelisk come from?*

She turned onto her back and saw the moon, then, beyond her feet, the pool, glowing blue in the moonlight. *Where's the obelisk?*

She turned further, then saw what had caused the shadow: Kelvin, lying on his back, had an erection that stood proud.

A rush of desire shook her very being; she felt weak and thought, *Thank you, Isis, you have my promise to help your wadi.*

She pushed herself up with her hands, stepped across Kelvin, sank to her knees, and then, with a light touch to guide him, she dropped slowly down as she felt the entire length and exultation fill her. *Hathor, give us strength.* She began to move, a languid belly-dancer's rhythm.

Kelvin was dreaming a wonderful dream. Hathor had come to him. He recognised her immediately. She had taken him by the hand and led him to a small pool with soft grass beside it that he had seen before. There she had laid him down on the grass and, with a soft, delicate touch, had caressed him until he felt alive, every nerve tingling, and then she touched his manhood. It sprang up under her touch, bigger than it had ever been, and then she straddled him, swallowing him between her thighs, and she began to move.

Then the dream became confusing: he heard noises, gasps, panting breath, and what seemed a groan. Then a blue light shone through his eyelids, and a voice whispered, 'Hathor, help me.'

He understood that, so he seized Hathor's hips, helped, and felt himself grow further with every thrust. His orgasm came, an agony that made him cry out, and he woke at that moment, feeling Hathor's pulsing contractions and his own.

Kate felt his reaction, and then the ecstasy took over. Her back stiffened as lightning pulses shot up her spine from thigh to brain, and when they died, she relaxed and fell forward onto Kelvin. Her last thought was, *Thank you, Hathor.*

Kelvin opened his eyes. The moon was directly overhead, and in the light, he could see Kate's hair and feel her lying on him. *It wasn't a dream.*

He whispered, 'Kate, is it you?'

There was a long pause before she replied, 'Yes.'

'Kate, did I have an erection?'

The pause was shorter; it seemed her voice had a warm tone he hadn't heard before. 'Yes, my darling and it was incredible.'

'So we made love? I ejaculated?'

'Yes, and I'll prove it. I'm still full of you.'

She began small movements again.

'Dearest, I can feel you.'

'I think you're growing again.'

The movements grew.

The thought that burst into his consciousness, *Isis has cured me!*, brought a fantastic feeling as a rush of blood filled his member, and he felt Kate's intimate interior.

Kate sat up again and cried, 'Oh, Hathor!' Her movements changed from controlled to abandoned.

Kelvin gripped her hips, stopped thinking, and lost himself in waves of pleasure until the finale.

37

KELVIN WOKE IN THE SUNLIGHT, with Kate lying on top of him. He caressed her back gently, from shoulders to buttocks. Then he kissed the top of her head.

'I can move higher, and you can kiss my lips.'

'Please.'

'We did, didn't we?'

'Yes, my darling, your erectile dysfunction is over.'

'Then will you marry me?'

'We're married already, Pharaoh. I'm your queen. Isis and Hathor have blessed us. Anything else is just paperwork.'

Kelvin kissed her again. 'Why do you call me Pharaoh?'

'Because that's what you are. Isis brought us here to help your people.'

'How do you know?'

'I felt it and gave Isis my promise to help if she cured you.'

'We must find out what help the people need.'

'Water, Kelvin. Remember the legend? Geb gave this wadi to Isis to grow her medical plants. It must have been beautiful then, so the sand by the pool was green grass. There is probably little water left. It may have dwindled for centuries as the land dried.'

'If that's the case, I shall do something to bring back water.'

'We must meet the people first.'

'Let's dress, eat, then go to find them.'

'I must use some precious water for a sponge bath.'

'Me too.'

Half an hour later, as they donned their gallabiyahs, Kate

looked up and said, 'We don't need to find them, darling. They're here.'

Kelvin turned to look at the entrance and saw two men, followed by two boys bearing trays.

The elder man approached Kelvin and Kate, then bowed and spoke in a tongue Kelvin didn't understand.

Kate replied.

The man smiled as he spoke back to her, and the boys placed the food on the sand.

'Darling, what did you say?'

'It's an ancient greeting. It has existed in Farsi since a time before Muhammed. If you know how to pronounce the words of the hieroglyphs, try that. His name is Shekti.'

It was easier for Kelvin to try Hieratic, so he thought of the script that would say, 'We thank you for the food,' then spoke.

The old man's smile was one of pleasure, and Kelvin understood the reply in Hieratic, accompanied by a bow: 'Pharaoh, your pleasure is our gift.'

'Kate, it won't be easy, but I'm sure I can understand.'

'I won't be able to, Kelvin; I don't know how to speak ancient Egyptian.'

When, much later, Kate met a woman, she found it didn't matter; in Arabic, the woman told her that all the women spoke Arabic, and that some of their husbands, especially the young ones, knew many words. Kate decided to find out why.

They agreed to split their investigations. 'You concentrate on the women, the life they lead, their customs and morals,' Kelvin suggested. 'I'll talk to the men and learn about the history, religion and the water.'

For three days, they left each morning to visit the wadi to meet people, although at first, they saw only a few gallabiyah-clad hooded figures with dark-skinned faces. If they saw faces, they were much like Shekti.

In the evenings, they drank tea and compared notes beside the pool.

Kate told Kelvin, 'From what I've been able to glean so far, they have only one religion, the old gods, Geb and Nut, and their children, but it must have evolved a bit because they believe in pharaohs. The only clothes I've seen are desert-coloured gallabiyahs with hoods. They live in caves. I only went into the entrance of one, but it looked old, and they have excavated deep into the rock over centuries.'

'Kate, I think they wear the desert-coloured gallabiyahs to remain invisible. You might find the women dress differently in their home caves; remember the story we heard about the Nubians buying silk and cotton?'

'Oddly,' Kate said, 'I've seen boys and young men but no girls.'

'I haven't either. I'll try to find out where the young girls hide.'

At the end of the second day, with a ceramic cup of tea in his hand, Kelvin asked, 'Darling, what did you learn today?'

Kate pondered for a moment, then said, 'Although the women are friendly, there's a sort of reverence in the way they treat me. If they believe I'm their queen, that would explain it.' Kelvin nodded, and she continued, 'They don't use wood. They burn goat dung to cook on in tiny earthenware stoves. There are little cracks up and down the wadi sides inside which plants grow, and the goats go to feed. There's no running water, but the ground is damp.'

'That chimes with what I've learnt,' Kelvin said. 'The only running water is the waterfall into this pool – Isis's pool. It's also the guardian of the portal to the underworld. Shekti is their religious leader and has said he'll show us before we leave.'

'It's behind the waterfall. I've seen a horizontal crack when the sun is exactly right.'

'Well, I'll wait until they show us; we don't want to trespass. Did you find the girls?'

'No, there are none, by a decree of Isis.'

'They kill girl babies?' Kelvin was aghast.

'No, no,' Kate reassured him. 'It's just that none are born. Everyone here seems healthy and intelligent, and there's no sign of inbreeding – these people aren't doing as the pharaohs did and marrying their sisters or mothers. But Isis decreed that women could conceive only boys. When the boys grow up, they leave the wadi to avoid overpopulation; some return and bring wives; that's why the women speak Arabic, and it ensures genetic mixing.'

Kelvin looked relieved.

'And everyone here also drinks Anit at religious ceremonies,' Kate continued. 'Shekti is a hundred and fifteen years old.'

Kelvin told her, 'They have two deep wells that provide water. They have deepened them for millennia and cannot dig any further, for they have hit a rock layer. It must be basalt. I asked for the depth and then measured the length of the rope with the bucket. I estimated it at 175 metres.

'Then I asked them about the construction. Not only did they dig down, but as the sand collected in the bottom of the wadi, they had to build the wall around the well higher. One of the boys rode down in the bucket to measure how deep the rock walls go; it's twenty-five metres.'

Kate said, 'They grow the sorghum, Anit and other herbs in

caves where water drips from the walls, but the sunlight has reduced as they have had to move further back for centuries.'

'Kate, the wadi will die like the others and fill with sand unless I can find a reliable water supply.'

As the sun approached the horizon on the third day, Shekti said, 'Come, we shall pray to the gods.'

He walked ahead towards Isis's pool, with Kelvin between two others behind. They collected Kate from a cave, where she was sitting at the entrance with two other women.

At the waterfall, the men kneeled and prostrated themselves facing it. Kate and Kelvin, although surprised, followed suit.

Shekti intoned, 'Isis, goddess of life, we who guard your wadi, as you guard the health of those who serve you, beg for your protection so we may enter the underworld portal with the Pharaoh and his Queen you have brought us. We also beg for the protection of Hathor, who has joined them in love, so they may choose their place of rest under your protection before their reincarnation.'

Kelvin didn't know if he felt a feeling of welcome, but Shekti must have done, for he stood and said, 'Come.'

Kelvin whispered his translation of the prayer to Kate.

The sunlight, shining through the trickling waterfall, lit up the low horizontal crack in the cliff. They had to crawl along the damp rock for the first several metres.

Kelvin heard Shekti blowing, saw a red glow, and then a light that grew from a small oil lamp. The other men each had one that they lit from the first and held up.

The crack was not high enough to stand in without a bowed head. For Kelvin, it was more like a crouch.

They walked forward and down some steps – Kelvin counted a hundred – and the crack grew into a cavern as they did so. Within another hundred paces, the light reflected on white walls, and Kelvin whispered to Kate, 'Calcite.'

The cave was enormous. Stalactites hung from its roof, with matching stalagmites below, and they could hear the slow, irregular tac-tac of drops of water.

They stopped, and Kelvin saw the path continue, descending into darkness.

'The path to the underworld is long,' Shekti said. 'Since Geb gave the wadi to Isis, we have carried our pharaohs and their queens into its depths after Anubis calls them. After treating their bodies with Anit, we lay them where Isis embalms them until she decides on reincarnation. We have carried here many hundreds of pharaohs. Here is the resting place of the last.'

He raised his lamp high, and so did the other two.

In front of them was a narrow rock platform covered in a gleaming white calcite deposit; the back of the shelf was a wall of similar calcite. But the calcite was thin because, like looking through a sheet of milky glass, Kate and Kelvin could see the form of a naked man and woman entwined together.

'The water that makes the stalactites has dripped on these two for centuries and encased them in calcite,' Kelvin whispered to Kate.

Overcome with emotion, Kate said, 'They are beautiful. It's the ultimate gift of Hathor, to sleep in each other's arms for eternity.'

'Come,' Shekti said. 'We must not overstay our welcome.'

'Kate, have you packed up?'

'Yes,' Kate said. 'I asked the women if they could offer a few sorghum and herb seeds as a parting gift to Pharaoh, and those I've safely stowed in my backpack. I also have the Anit we came with, and the extra six leaves we promised Dr Makeen. You have the water bottles, maps, satphone and the kerosene stove, and we each have our clothes and boots.'

Kelvin said, 'I'll roll up our bedroll tomorrow morning. We'll collect the short rope to join us when we climb the path, and we can leave the long ones and the tabletop.' He added, 'We'll say goodbye and leave after breakfast tomorrow. I asked for two pairs of desert slippers. With those on our feet, it will take two hours to reach the cliff trail, then, I guess, about three to walk up the cliff face to the dune, and then a bum surf down to the Unimog.'

'It's a full moon tonight. Can we make love by our pool in the moonlight?'

'You're clairvoyant, dearest. I had the same thought.'

They lay side by side, waiting for the moon, discussing their plans.

'Kelvin, what will we do with the Unimog?'

'We promised to take six leaves of Anit to Dr Makeen, so I shall ask him to find a lock-up to store the Unimog.'

'Darling, the Unimog will pass unseen in Aswan, but it will stand out at Dr Makeen's. I think it will upset him if we go there with it. We should go to Aswan and take a taxi to see him.'

'Then we'll stay at the Cataract Hotel until we've sorted that, and then fly to Cairo. What do you need to do?'

'View the film, and if I'm happy, that's all. We can take it with us.'

'Kate, can you get five or six bottles of the perfume?'

'I can ask for the bottles, but the perfume will be the one we had. That will change if a perfume producer decides to market it, but why?'

'So you can give one as a present to each person you might have to persuade to give you the contract to market men's deodorants and perfumes.'

Kate nodded her agreement. 'Then I must get them boxed.'

Then the moon peeped over the edge of the rock wall around the pool, and they forgot about everything but each other.

38

THE DEPARTURE WAS FORMAL. Shekti and two young men accompanied them to the path up the rock face, where they prayed, thanking Isis for their Pharaoh and asking for her protection for their Pharaoh and Queen until they returned.

Then they and two others climbed, with one of the young men ahead and one behind, carrying long goatskin sausages with skin ropes for smoothing the sand to wipe out their tracks. At the top, the young men left two goatskin smoothers with them.

Kate and Kelvin reached the bottom five hours later, leaving a virgin slope above them. But Kate said, casting a close eye over the traces they'd left, 'From close up, I can still see the sand looks different.'

'It will be fine, Kate,' Kelvin assured her. 'You can't see it from a distance, and the sand will smooth out from the sun and wind.'

'There's only a slight breeze. Where does it come from?'

'The air in the wadi heats up during the day and rises, causing a local wind. Over centuries it has brought grains of sand along this valley and built the dune. But the first sandstorm will destroy all traces, including the Unimog's tracks.'

Back at the vehicle, Kate looked in the cooler box. 'It worked – the food is still cool. Let's cook up a feast.'

Some hours later, in the vehicle, a hundred kilometres down along the outward track, Kelvin looked in the rearview mirror and said, 'Kate, we must stop and phone the Cataract Hotel and my father. Otherwise, we'll lose reception.'

'Why?'

'To book for tomorrow night, and to tell him we're okay, he can tell your parents.'

'Yes, but why now?'

'Look behind us. I believe Isis has brought a sandstorm to hide our tracks.'

Turning to look out the back, Kate said, 'You do believe in Isis, don't you?'

'And in Hathor,' Kelvin said. 'We have seen the evidence and felt their presence.'

'Especially Hathor.'

They smiled at each other.

They drove on after a stop for tea and the two phone calls. Kelvin kept glancing in the mirror. 'The sandstorm seems to be catching us,' he said worriedly.

Kate turned and watched for a few minutes. 'I don't think it's catching us, Kelvin. It's just keeping up with us.'

A hundred kilometres further on, Kelvin stopped in a sheltered canyon. 'We'll camp here, and if the sandstorm catches us, we'll sleep in the Unimog.'

Two hours later, sitting beside the sheltered canyon entrance, Kate said, 'I can see the sand moving across the surface, but the storm has died. By tomorrow our tracks will have gone.'

'There are things we'll never understand, Kate, but I want to thank Isis again.'

'And I want to thank Hathor.' She grinned at him. 'Let's pray – both kinds.'

Kelvin bowed his head in silent prayer; then he heard Kate say, 'Hathor, I thank you for the gift of my Pharaoh and his love. I shall be your servant and his until Anubis calls.'

Then Kelvin said, 'Isis, I shall bring water to your wadi as you have commanded. And I thank Hathor for the gift of Kate's love.'

'Now, Kelvin, the second kind of prayer.'

And the wings came.

The Cataract Hotel welcomed them and took their suitcases to their suite. Kate and Kelvin soon joined their luggage, where they bathed together and changed.

They went for lunch on the terrace overlooking the Nile. They sat silently, looking at the view, until Kate said, 'This scene has remained unchanged for centuries.'

'No, Kate, the river and the feluccas perhaps, but it has changed. It no longer floods. As late as 1960, it flooded annually, rising up to ten metres, so everything on the sides of the river is recent history. I wonder what the gods think of what we have done to it.'

Kate replied, 'I wish I knew, but they haven't done much to stop the change.'

'Our fate is in our own hands, Kate.'

The young woman was not in the room when they entered. Her place on the chair by the inner door was occupied by a young boy, who spoke through the doorway and gestured as the girl had done.

Dr Makeen welcomed them as he had done the first time.

'As-Salaam-Alaikum.'

'Wa-Salaam-As-Alaikum.'

'As-Salaam-Alaikum, aljadu al'akbar.'

301

'Welcome back. I knew you would come. I can see you are well. Have you been successful in your research?'

'We have. And we've come to bring your present and ask for a favour.'

'Then ask.'

'We have a Unimog in Aswan. We have work to do in Europe and will return, I hope, in less than two years. Is there someone you know who can store the Unimog safely for us in our absence?'

Dr Makeen looked at them shrewdly. 'So you have been into the desert?'

Kelvin erred on the side of a small white lie, to ensure the secret of the wadi remained safe. 'Yes, and we will try to discover what we seek when we return.'

'I have a son in Aswan. I shall tell him to contact you tonight at the Cataract Hotel.'

'Thank you.' Kelvin passed over a small packet. 'These leaves are old, but they are still viable. I bought them from a herb seller in El Balyana when I found a second mention of Anit at Abydos.'

'So there are two hieroglyphs?'

'Yes. The second reads, "Pharaoh was anointed with Anit, invoking the protection of Isis, before the embalmers carried him away."'

Dr Makeen nodded his head but said nothing.

Kate asked, 'Is your great granddaughter well? She's not here today.'

'Like all young women, she has found a husband. I shall not see her again, for he's a desert man, and she has gone south with him.'

Kelvin murmured, 'Isis and Hathor decide. You may be proud they have blessed her.'

Dr Makeen smiled and nodded again. 'If the gods wish, you may meet her when you return to the desert. If so, tell her of my pride.'

Kate replied, 'We shall remember to do so.'

The flight to Cairo had Kelvin and Kate on board two days later. They had left behind the Unimog, stripped of everything perishable, and stored on jacks in a safe building in Aswan with Dr Makeen's son.

They moved into the same suite in the Hilton in the Egyptian capital city. There, Kelvin called his father again.

'Dad, when are you going to Africa?'

'In two weeks, Kelvin, why?'

'I need some help. I want to drill some wells in the desert, over two hundred metres deep, where the sand depth is twenty-five metres. I don't want to stir up any public interest, so having you look for the right equipment is safer.'

'Such equipment exists, but how will you get it there without piquing the interest of journalists?'

'A low-altitude parachute-drop at night from a cargo plane.'

'I'll think about it, Kelvin. Maybe I'll stay home longer to help; it could be a fun project.'

They both went to see the finished film ad, and Kate declared it excellent and whispered to Kelvin, 'I don't know why, but that ending gave me a thrill.'

'The stallion's scream?'

'Maybe.'

They left with the film and five black and gold boxes containing the perfume. Kate called her office, spoke to Gertrude Lenferna, and left instructions with Brenda.

Muammar collected them from Heathrow and drove to Kate's home first. Their welcome was relief and happiness, kisses and hugs, and when Kate said, 'We must tell you, we've married, but we want a registry office wedding as soon as possible.'

A delighted Yara replied, 'Then talk to Ahmed. He's organised his marriage for Saturday week.'

Kelvin's reply was a huge smile. 'I'll call him. Muammar must take me home now, but Kate, would you like to stay with your parents for three days and then join me with your parents on Saturday? They can stay the night.'

'That's great. I'll have time to pack the things I want to bring. I'll allow you the three days, my love.'

Back home, Kelvin's welcome was equally overwhelming, and when Layla heard Kate and her parents were coming for the weekend, she rushed off, visibly excited.

Darius said, when she left, 'You've made us both happy, Kelvin. What will you do now?'

'I've some plants to negotiate rights for, Dad, and then drilling wells to organise.'

'I've made a couple of enquiries. Do you want me to front the first part, the specifications for what you want, and the purchase? What can you tell me?'

Kelvin thought about this. *I want to tell Dad, but I can't. The slightest slip of the tongue could ruin Isis's project. I'll have to get his approval without explaining fully.* He said, 'Dad, I don't want to be associated with the project until the last minute, and I will remain the only person who knows where I will drill. I will be on-site with Kate when the aircraft makes the drop, and the pilot will not know where to drop until I call him with a satphone en route to the drop. So I must know how to operate the equipment. If no one knows I'm associated with drilling or drilling in Egypt, no one will try to find out where.'

'Then we must do a trial run in the western Sahara. The project may take two years to set up.'

'It's worth it, Dad. But I can't explain why I must do it.'

'I understand, Kelvin. You're like me. I'm keeping quiet about my kwashiorkor project. Once others get involved, greed almost always ruins the results.'

'Hello, Grandad.'

'Greetings, Pharaoh,' said the old man sitting in his wheelchair on the terrace in the late summer sunshine when Kelvin came to see him. 'Where's Hathor?'

'She'll be here on Saturday.'

'I'm looking forward to that. I first met Hathor seventy years ago.'

'I didn't know that, Grandad.'

'I never told you. Hathor was beautiful, and I've never forgotten her. I last saw her when your grandma died. You're a lucky man to have met her.'

'Good morning, Brenda.'

'Kate! Welcome back.' Brenda looked at her closely. 'You've changed. You look different.'

'I'm married.'

'My gosh! My congratulations. When do we meet him?'

'When I can bring him. Have you arranged the meetings and the equipment?'

'Yes, Kate. Mrs Lenferna will meet you at nine, and a car is taking you to the client you proposed at eleven.'

'Kate, you look lovely. Have you married?' Gertrude asked her as their meeting began.

'Yes, in Egypt, but we will have a registry office marriage here.'

'That accounts for it. Congratulations! Will you give me a rundown on what you want to discuss with the client?'

'That's why I'm here. I gave you survey data previously, and the client has a problem with male deodorant sales. I told you they aim their ads at the wrong market.'

'You did, and I'm learning a lot about big data. I've commissioned a survey to see how it compares with one we did nine months ago. The results are due in ten days.'

'That's wonderful. I want to say that we do all our advertising in the most expensive way possible.'

'Really?' Gertrude didn't look pleased. 'You must explain that to me.'

'We started this business before the internet, pay TV, and worldwide TV in every hotel room, bar and restaurant. We remake our ads in each country using actors with local characteristics. I'm sure that's unnecessary now. Worldwide, people recognise an igloo, a kayak, a camel in the desert, and other stereotypes. With language dubbing, we can make one ad that will suit everywhere.'

'And the same perfume?'

'No, but the cost is minimal to add or deduct a little something.'

'Is this what you will tell the client?'

'Yes – and with proof. Come into the boardroom and see the ad I made.'

Watching the ad with her mouth half-open in shock, Gertrude blurted, 'My god, Kate, is that you?'

Kate laughed. 'Yes.'

'I almost didn't recognise you. And what did this cost?'

Kate handed her the invoice, adding, 'And the man is my husband. So there are two actor fees to add to that for a fair comparison.'

Stupefied, the VP looked at the invoice. 'Where did you get the perfume bottle?'

'A Cairo glassblower made the bottles, and a perfumery filled them. The price is on the invoice.'

'Run that ad again.'

When the screen faded to the view of the perfume, Gertrude said, 'It'll work in most countries. There might be some mods for local censors, but they're minimal. Where can I get a bottle of that perfume?'

'Here. It's for you.' Kate had come armed. *Kelvin was right. I need gifts.*

'Kate, don't tell the client how little that ad cost!'

'I won't,' Kate replied. 'What I will do, however, is ask for a signed memorandum of agreement today, or else we go to their competitor.'

Gertrude frowned. 'That's skating on thin ice.'

'He's a man, Gertrude. He'll remember that his mother and later his wife bought his deodorants for years.'

Gertrude laughed. 'Okay, go for it. I'll meet you downstairs at twenty to eleven.'

After Kate left, Gertrude took out the perfume, sprayed it on her wrist, smelled it, and smiled.

39

KATE HAD NEVER MET Christian de Beauvoir but knew all about him: tall, spare, with a full head of silver hair and no moustache, he had known and dealt with Gertrude for years.

Kate liked his smile when he greeted Gertrude and then her, adding, 'My, you are a beauty. I hope you use our perfumes.'

After a few minutes of polite chat, he asked, 'Well, Gertrude, apart from your people setting up a big display screen in our boardroom, I've no idea what this is about.'

'This is all Kate's idea and project, so I'm going to hand over to her,' Gertrude said.

Kate repeated what she'd told Gertrude earlier, and when she handed over the stats on his male perfume sales, Christian said, 'Yes, those numbers are not new. We've discussed this for months, although I didn't know they were this bad. Where did you get them?'

'We did a survey, Mr De Beauvoir,' Kate said and summed up their findings.

The survey results on who bought male perfumes brought another reaction. Christian frowned. 'That's new. Was this a separate survey?'

'Yes.'

'Okay, continue.'

When Kate said they needed only one ad worldwide, he protested. 'Do you believe that?'

'I do. Come and see an ad in the boardroom.'

There was a long silence when the video finished. Christian sat with his chin in his hand for several moments, then said, 'You paid for two surveys and filmed an ad to convince me you should manage our male line. What's it going to cost me?'

Kate's reply shocked him. 'You get the ad, the copyright on the bottle, and the perfume for free. Your current marketing costs are twenty-two per cent of the gross on any new perfume, which breaks even after two years.'

'Yes, I know, but what will you cost me?'

'Seven per cent of the gross for two years and four per cent after that. Any minor tweaks to the ad because of censors are at our cost. Any changes in the perfume for local markets are yours.'

'*Mon Dieu*, Kate, you surprise me. Your proposal will take much thought.'

'I'll surprise you more, sir. Sign this memorandum of agreement before the close of business today, or we go to your competitor tomorrow.'

Christian smiled coolly. 'I like you, Kate, but aren't you being just a bit pushy?'

'No sir. We have a product that will sell in millions, and you are in trouble in this market. You must take the chance, not me, and I'm being completely fair. We want you as our client for the next hundred years.' Then she added, 'And I'm sure you can remember who's been buying your deodorants and aftershaves since you were eighteen.'

Christian laughed. 'I can, and you are right. I'll send my people in, show them the ad, read your MA, and talk to them at two. If I sign, I'll send it over before five. Now, ladies, can I take you to lunch?'

'You can,' Kate replied. Then, handing him a wrapped bottle of deodorant, she added, 'Please remember, a woman gave you this deodorant.'

The signed MA arrived at four. Kate had much to do before the weekend.

Kelvin had spent the time investigating who he could deal with for the sorghum and herb seeds. Initially, he was looking for significant seed suppliers for agriculture, but he changed his mind when they asked for chemical analyses of the plants for sales promotions. With only the few leaves he had brought from the wadi, it wasn't possible. Then, remembering his discussions with Kate about marketing, he switched to looking for small experimental farms that might plant his seeds and grow the first plants. Then a lab could analyse the herbs and sorghum so he could tell the major seed suppliers what the plants contained.

He realised it would take a long time to get results, but he had the time and would collaborate with his father on well drilling.

Kate and her parents arrived on Saturday at eleven, and after Kate had endured half an hour of hugs and congratulations, Kelvin took her to meet his grandfather.

'He hasn't lost his mind, Kate, although he'll tell the same story several days apart. He told me the last time he met Hathor was seventy years ago. I'm unsure, but I think that may have been Grandma.'

'He's your grandad, Kelvin. That's enough for me.'

Lateef was in his wheelchair on the terrace, and when Kelvin and Kate approached, he heard them and spun the chair, silently watching them come.

Kate saw an aged man, but one with bright grey eyes.

'Grandad, I've brought my goddess.'

'I can see that. I would recognise Hathor in my grave. Come here and let me see you.'

Kate bent down and kissed him on the cheek. 'I can tell you are Kelvin's grandad. He looks like you.'

'And you look like Hathor when I met her, although she dressed differently.'

'Tell me about her.'

For the next twenty minutes, Kelvin and Kate could sense Lateef's enjoyment while talking to a beautiful woman from his past.

'Kate, thanks, that made him very happy,' Kelvin said once the caregiver had come to fetch Lateef.

'Me too, Kelvin. He's a lovely man. I will talk with him more. I want to learn more about his youth.'

Kelvin then took Kate upstairs to have a look at his suite.

'It's lovely, Kelvin. Can I redecorate it?' Kate said, wandering around the lounge, the study, the bedroom and bathroom, and the terrace-sized balcony that comprised Kelvin's living quarters.

'If you live here, Kate, even if only for a short while, you can do whatever you wish.'

'What's next door?'

'There's an unused room on each side, one for a valet and the other for a lady's assistant. There hasn't been an occupant for years.'

'Can you show me a plan?'

'I'm sure there's one in the library. I'll find it.'

'Thanks, darling,' Kate said, pulling Kelvin into her arms and warmly embracing him. 'The next thing on our agenda is to visit the registry office on Monday.'

'Are you in a hurry, Kate?'

'No, but I don't want to delay too long; otherwise, our wedding photos will show me in a loose dress.'

Kelvin didn't get it at first, then he took her in his arms, 'My darling, are you saying you're pregnant?'

'Since the night Hathor anointed us, my sweet.'

He kissed her, picked her up in his arms and carried her into the bedroom.

Later, lying with Kate in his arms, Kelvin asked, 'When do we tell our parents?'

'Our mothers are doctors, darling. They'll guess in a month. We'll ask the registry office how soon we can book our wedding.'

'That's perfect.' Kelvin bent and kissed her, and said, 'I hope you want a boy.'

'We conceived our baby in the wadi. What else can we expect?'

'Darling, I've been thinking about that. If one of the herbs we brought back suppresses the conception of girls, I must destroy it.'

'I suspect it's the Anit, my love. We both drank it, so our baby will be a boy. That's why the secret is so well guarded. If the world learnt of it, the boy-girl birth ratio would change drastically; remember the Chinese one-child policy. If we ever revisit Abydos, I'll bet both hieroglyphs have changed.'

The president of Kate's company summoned her to his office two weeks after the meeting with Christian de Beauvoir.

Ian Stewart was a short, compact, somewhat overweight man with faded red hair; he had the reputation of a bulldog. Kate knew he had worked his way up from a door-to-door salesperson in the company, and, like many other chief executives who came through the ranks, he worked too hard, wasn't in great physical shape, and once a year showed the effects of too much sun on pale skin. Nevertheless, she admired him.

'Kate, you look fabulous. Gertrude says you've recently married. It suits you.'

'Thank you, sir.'

'I asked you to come because I must tell you something and ask you for something else. First, I know you said your secretary, Brenda, originally came up with the survey idea, and you ran with it, but I'm taking it away from you. I'm appointing Gertrude as VP of a new department to implement this new method of obtaining survey data throughout our company. It will stir up many feelings – change always does – but she has the experience to deal with it. I realise that losing Brenda may make your life more difficult, but I've agreed Gertrude can have Brenda, who we will promote to a managerial position.'

If Gertrude will be VP of a new department, who will he put in her place?

Ian continued, 'Now, I also know what you have done to revolutionise our advertising and get the new account for male deodorants and perfumes. I've decided you are the ideal person to make sure it happens, so how do you feel about stepping into Gertrude's shoes?'

I'll hold the record for the youngest VP in the company! Kate thought. 'I'd be delighted,' she said, then added, 'but as a newly married woman, I hope to have at least one child. Have you considered that?'

'Yes, Kate. I discussed it with Gertrude. She said you had successfully run your department from Egypt, and she was sure you could do so from home.'

'Then I accept, sir. I'm also glad for Brenda – she deserves it.'

'That's great, Kate. Oh, and one minor thing: the VPs call me Ian.'

40

TWENTY-TWO MONTHS AFTER their return to England, Kate and Kelvin, with their son Namer Seb Shareef, collected the Unimog from the garage in Aswan and drove into the desert. This time they had desert slippers.

A week later, a cargo aircraft refuelled at Aswan Airport and took off for Aden. Shortly after takeoff, the transponder failed after dark on a moonless night, and the plane disappeared from radar and satellite surveillance.

At scarcely more than three hundred metres above the ground en route, the captain received a satphone message with coordinates; an adjustment to the autopilot ensured the aircraft overflew that point in the darkness below, and at that precise point, three palettes of equipment rolled to the open cargo door. Black parachutes pulled them into the void. The aircraft began a slow climb.

The captain reported the transponder problem to Aswan and had it repaired in Aden, where the empty plane loaded cargo for Dubai.

In the small, untidy, overheated room with two guitars hanging on one wall and garishly coloured posters of street art and rock bands covering the rest, a young man wearing boxers lay on a bed against one wall, reading a comic book.

Opposite him in the tiny home sound-analysis studio, a young woman in underwear sat before a wide plank on trestles that carried four computer monitors displaying wavy lines and numbers, a pictorial display of recorded sound. The pictures changed as she moved a mouse to connect different recorded sounds or alter the volume. Above the monitors and fixed to the wall, a TV screen showed the unmoving image of a tent in a desert, a falcon swooping down to it, and a stallion beside it, rearing, with nostrils flared.

'Joe, this is art. Real art.'

'What is?'

'This TV ad. It's been going for two years and has won the prize for the best TV ad in the world two years running.'

'Whadda ya mean, "art"?'

'Like when you see a painting, and in your gut you feel the artist is great.'

'So what about the ad?'

'It gives me a feeling low in my gut. I've figgered out why, and it explains the ad's success.'

''Kay, tell me why it tickles y' pussy.'

'I joined the screams of the falcon and the stallion, and the sound analysis pattern matches a woman screaming a word.'

'Howdja know?'

'I screamed.'

'Wotsa word?'

'Hathor.'

'C'mere, en you can scream it again.'

She did, and her underwear landed on the bare desert-coloured floor tiles in the same positions as the underwear on the desert outside the tent on the TV screen.

Although the TV was silent, ten minutes later, a scream filled the room...

'Haaaaathhhooooor!'

Epilogue

SEVENTY-EIGHT YEARS LATER, a sprightly Namer Shareef and his wife Nephthys disappeared into the desert on a month's touring holiday. They drove an unusual vehicle adapted to the environment. In the back seat, Kelvin and Kate, their ancient and fragile bones protected by soft cushions, looked out the windows and remembered.

Pharaoh Namer and his Queen returned from that desert trip.

Kelvin and Kate never did.

When Kate knew Kelvin's last day had dawned, a young woman aide brewed six Anit leaves, then poured the tea into two small flasks.

Holding Kelvin in her arms on the green grass beside the blue pool, where the waterfall fell strongly, Kate fed him the cup of liquid, kissed him, and only she heard his last words: 'My darling, my love for you will never die.'

Three days of mourning later, a procession entered the mausoleum, and the bearers laid the pharaoh on the stone shelf he had chosen on his second visit. They left Kate alone with Kelvin's body.

She undressed him carefully, then herself, and, naked; she climbed onto the shelf. She held a small flask in her hands. She lay down, drank the flask's contents, then turned and took Kelvin in her arms in an intimate embrace.

The next day four men in a relay carried buckets of the calcium-loaded pool water into the mausoleum. They carefully poured it over the enlaced bodies until a thin layer of translucent calcium had sealed them together safely.

There, Kate and Kelvin slept for eternity in each other's arms.